RISE OF
THE TITANS

Also by Kate O'Hearn

The Flame of Olympus

Olympus at War

The New Olympians

Origins of Olympus

RISE OF
THE TITANS

KATE O'HEARN

Aladdin
New York   London   Toronto   Sydney   New Delhi

ALADDIN

An imprint of Simon & Schuster Children's Publishing Division
1230 Avenue of the Americas, New York, NY 10020
First Aladdin hardcover edition December 2015
Text copyright © 2015 by Kate O'Hearn
Jacket illustration copyright © 2015 by Jason Chan
First published in Great Britain in 2014 by Hodder Children's Books
All rights reserved, including the right of reproduction in whole or in part in any form.
ALADDIN is a trademark of Simon & Schuster, Inc., and related logo
is a registered trademark of Simon & Schuster, Inc.
For information about special discounts for bulk purchases, please contact
Simon & Schuster Special Sales at 1-866-506-1949 or business@simonandschuster.com.
The Simon & Schuster Speakers Bureau can bring authors to your live event.
For more information or to book an event contact the Simon & Schuster Speakers Bureau
at 1-866-248-3049 or visit our website at www.simonspeakers.com.
Jacket designed by Karin Paprocki
Interior designed by Mike Rosamilia
The text of this book was set in Adobe Garamond.
Manufactured in the United States of America 0116 FFG
2 4 6 8 10 9 7 5 3
Library of Congress Cataloging-in-Publication Data
O'Hearn, Kate.
Rise of the Titans / by Kate O'Hearn—First Aladdin hardcover edition.
pages cm.—(Pegasus; book 5)
Summary: Caught in the middle of this ancient power struggle, Emily and Pegasus must head to Diamond Head volcano in Hawaii to track down the one thing that can save Olympus—before the Titans get there first.
[1. Pegasus (Greek mythology)—Fiction. 2. Titans (Mythology)—Fiction.
3. Mythology, Greek—Fiction. 4. Fantasy.] I. Title.
PZ7.O4137Ri 2015
[Fic]—dc23
2014046976
ISBN 978-1-4814-4714-0 (hc)
ISBN 978-1-4814-4716-4 (eBook)

For Toulouse

Who always says: "I don't write the books,

I just make them better . . ."

Thanks, Tou . . .

Love you

RISE OF
THE TITANS

In the Long-distant Past

THE WAR BETWEEN THE OLYMPIANS AND the Titans had been fought and won. Jupiter, leader of Olympus, along with his two brothers, Neptune and Pluto—plus Chiron the Centaur and the three giant Hundred-handers—gathered in the remnants of the throne room, facing the most vicious Titan warriors.

The final battle had played out on Olympus. The landscape around them was scorched and destroyed. The beauty of the world, fouled. But from the ashes of battle, Olympus would rise again. It would be greater and more breathtaking than could ever be imagined.

Standing before Jupiter, Neptune, and Pluto—also known as the Big Three—was Saturn, their father and leader of the Titans. His manacled hands shook with rage as he glared at his sons. Locked in chains beside him were his brothers and most powerful followers, defeated but still utterly defiant.

"You expect me to kneel before you?" Saturn sneered. "Beg my children's forgiveness for their challenge to my power?"

Jupiter looked at his two brothers and shook his head sadly. "No, Father, we do not seek your apology. Nor would we believe its sincerity if you did apologize. Your words mean nothing to us."

"Then what?" Saturn demanded. "What can you do to me? You cannot destroy me or any Titan; we are too powerful."

"You are correct, Father. We cannot destroy you. It grieves us that you would even suggest such a thing. We are still your children."

"My children?" Saturn spat at the ground. "You should never have escaped Tartarus. Ungrateful orphans—that is what you are. You are no children of mine!"

Neptune sighed. "Your words and actions reveal the depth of your hatred for us. All you know is lust for power. You are a sickness that must be cut from our lives before you can spread your infection further."

Saturn laughed with contempt. "I will ask again: What can you do to me? You are nothing more than shadows of my greatness!"

"No, Father, we are not shadows," Neptune said. "It is you who fought with shadows."

"You tortured innocent beings in order to create your army of Shadow Titans," Pluto agreed. "But even they could not defeat us. They are gone and we are still here."

"It was your secret weapon that destroyed my Shadow Titans, not you. You have hidden the girl from me, but that is only a temporary setback. I will find her, and when I do, my Shadow Titans will rise again and I shall finally rule the worlds of Olympus, Titus, and Earth, as is my destiny."

"Emily is beyond your reach!" Jupiter shouted. "The war is over. You were defeated!"

"Calm down, brother," Neptune said. "He is trying to bait you."

Jupiter took a deep, calming breath. "Peace has returned to the worlds, and in time Olympus, Titus, and Earth will heal. Your dark presence will be erased, and you will be forgotten."

Jupiter rose to his feet to give his sentence: "Saturn of Titus, you have been found guilty of crimes against Olympus. We condemn you to the same fate you set for us. You will be taken from here and imprisoned in the depths of Tartarus, never to experience freedom again."

"Tartarus will never confine me!" Saturn shouted. "Surrender now and I will be merciful."

Jupiter shook his head. "You do not know the meaning of the word 'mercy.' No, Father, this ends now. You and your people will be taken to Tartarus and locked in the bowels of the prison. You will never see the light of day again."

"You will yearn for death, Father," Pluto said darkly. "But I will not grant it. You will exist, and you will suffer as we did for so long."

Saturn raised his arms. The heavy metal manacles began to rattle. As his fury exploded, flames and powerful lightning bolts burst from his hands toward his sons.

Instinctively, Jupiter, Neptune, and Pluto raised

their hands together to create a shield to deflect the shots. Flames bounced wildly around the throne room, melting rubble and turning stone to glass. Olympians ran for cover and crouched behind columns, but thankfully the Big Three's defenses protected them from any harm.

"Father, stop!" Jupiter boomed. "You cannot win!"

"Then I will destroy us all!"

Saturn's flames and lightning surged even higher, until he began to tire and the blasts weakened, then tapered off completely. Saturn stood before his sons, covered in a film of sweat and panting to catch his breath. "This changes nothing."

Jupiter shook his head in disgust. "It changes everything." He nodded to the Hundred-handers. "Take them away, far from our sight."

The three loyal giants, each with fifty heads, nodded and bowed awkwardly. Using their one hundred arms, they caught hold of the protesting prisoners and dragged them away.

OLYMPUS AT NIGHT WAS AS BEAUTIFUL AS IT was by day. The air was clean and fresh, and a sense of peace prevailed. The temperature dropped, but only by a fraction. Flowers that bloomed only after dark unfurled their delicate petals and released their fragrant perfume into the air.

This was the time when the night dwellers emerged from their homes. Their pale, thin skin almost glowed in the starlight. Their voices were hushed. Night-dweller children never raised their voices, even while they played. And, like all Olympians, the night dwellers bowed in respect as Emily, Flame of Olympus, strolled past.

Emily walked through the gardens at the back

of Jupiter's palace with her dog, Mike, leaping playfully at her side. Mike was her newest family member, brought back from Athens on her last trip to the Human World. It seemed like a lifetime ago, even though it hadn't been that long.

Approaching the river, Emily saw the glow of torches and heard the sound of laughter. She smiled as she recognized the yelps of her friends Joel and Paelen, and she sped up so that she could join in the fun.

Just ahead she spotted Pegasus. The winged stallion's head was held majestically high, his wings immaculately groomed as he glowed brightly with health and joy. The sight of him still stole Emily's breath away.

She stopped to appreciate the beauty of the stallion and remind herself just how much he meant to her. Her entire life had changed the moment they'd met, and they'd been through so much together. He was such a part of her now that she couldn't imagine a day without him.

Pegasus was with his twin brother, the winged boar Chrysaor, who looked much less groomed. His coarse brown feathers stood at odd angles, and he looked as though he'd recently been rolling in mud.

Three young night dwellers were with them. A girl in her early teens with long white hair and a voice as soft as a gentle breeze turned and greeted Emily with a formal bow as she approached. "Flame, it is an honor to see you this night."

"Hi," Emily said back. "Please, you don't have to bow to me. Just call me Emily."

The night dweller gasped. "But you are the Flame of Olympus! I cannot call you anything else. It is said you have powers greater than those of Jupiter himself! You must be respected at all times."

Emily chuckled. She still wasn't used to this elevated status. It was true that she fed the Flame of Olympus—the source of Olympus's power. And there was even a temple dedicated to her. But most of the time she just felt like Emily Jacobs, a girl from New York City who happened to have a winged stallion as her best friend.

She smiled at the night dweller. "I may be the Flame, and yes, I do have powers, but I'm still just a girl like you. Please, as a favor, would you call me Emily?"

An odd color rose in the girl's ghostly pale complexion, and she nodded. "I am Fawn. This is my brother, Dax, and our little sister, Sapphire." Fawn smiled extra wide, displaying her small, sharply pointed teeth.

The boy was a bit older than his sister, and seemed even shyer. There was a calm beauty about them both as they stood there with Pegasus. Emily was certain that if they held their hands up to a bright light, the light would shine right through them.

Their young sister looked about five or six. She was bright and bubbly, and seemed more interested in petting Chrysaor's wings than in meeting Emily.

"I see you've met Pegasus," Emily said, trying to draw Dax out. She stepped up to the winged stallion. "Hiya, Pegs—isn't it beautiful out?"

Pegasus nickered and pressed his head close to her.

"You are magnificent," Fawn said to Pegasus as she stroked the stallion's muzzle. "I have seen you around Olympus all my life, but this is the first time we have had the opportunity to meet." She looked wistfully into his eyes. "It must be wonderful to have wings and fly." She turned back to Emily. "You are so fortunate to be friends."

"I know," Emily agreed. "I'd be lost without Pegasus."

Emily watched Pegasus blush from the compliments. Then he neighed and pawed the ground lightly.

Fawn's dark eyes sparkled. "May we?"

"What did he say?" Emily asked. Even though she had lived on Olympus for a very long time, she was still unable to understand the stallion's words.

Fawn was practically jumping out of her skin. "He said that one evening we can all go flying together. He will let me ride on his back."

"That's a great idea," Emily agreed. "There's nothing better than flying with him—especially at night."

The stallion's head bobbed up and down and he nickered softly to Fawn. She dropped her head shyly. "Thank you, Pegasus."

Emily had no idea what he had said, but from the expression on Fawn's face, it had made the young night dweller very happy.

Mike was barking, desperate for someone to play with him. Dax leaned over to pat him, and before he knew it, the large dog had jumped up and wrestled him to the ground. The boy's soft laughter rang out as they rolled on the grass together.

"We're going for a swim," Emily offered. "Do you want to join us?"

"Thank you, Flame—I mean, Emily," Fawn said. "But we must go to work."

"What do you do?"

"We work in the nectar-tree orchards," Dax explained as he wrestled with Mike. "It is our job to draw nectar from the flowers. This can only be done when the sun is down and the stars are shining, which opens the flowers."

"I carry water," Sapphire said. "It is a big job."

"I'm sure it is," Emily agreed, completely enchanted by the young night dweller.

Dax released Mike and rose to his feet. He caught his little sister by the arm. "I am sorry, but we must be going." He smiled shyly at Emily, and she noticed how strangely attractive he was. His eyes were elliptical, like a snake's, and even though they were as black as night, they still sparkled and shone. His features were sharp, but not unpleasant. It was then that Emily noticed that his ears were pointed, like elves' ears. Fawn's and Sapphire's ears were mostly hidden by their long white hair, but Emily could now see their pointy tops sticking out.

"Of course," Emily said. She focused on Fawn. "Just let me know when you have a free evening and we can go for that flight."

Fawn's eyes sparkled with excitement as her brother led them away.

"Pegs," Emily asked, watching them leave, "back when Jupiter allowed visits to Earth, did any night dwellers go?"

The stallion nickered and bobbed his head.

"I've heard that they never go out in daylight because it hurts their eyes and burns their thin skin. Is that true?"

Again Pegasus nodded.

"Hmmm," Emily mused as she studied the other night dwellers in the area. "I wonder if they're the origin of the vampire myth on Earth. They have large, dark eyes and pale skin that burns in sunlight, just like vampires. I know the dwellers don't drink blood, but their teeth are pointy and the nectar they collect is red—maybe that's it."

Pegasus nickered and Chrysaor squealed, but the meaning of their words remained a mystery to Emily.

As Emily and Mike walked over to the river, the sounds of shouts and laughter grew louder. Mike ran ahead, and when he saw Joel in the water, he leaped in.

Joel laughed as the dog paddled over to him. Then he looked up at Paelen, who was standing on a diving board. "C'mon, Paelen, just like I showed you—jump!"

It had taken some effort for Joel to convince Jupiter that they needed a diving board. But once it was built, many of the Olympians enjoyed using it, and there was talk of making another, taller board for where the river was deeper.

Emily watched Paelen bouncing on the end of the board, wearing his silken Olympian water trunks. They weren't too different from baggy shorts, but were solid white and had tiny, neatly folded pleats. His body was smooth and thin, but it didn't reveal the great strength or unique ability it held to stretch out and manipulate its shape to fit any space or reach almost any distance. Emily had met Paelen back when he had used these talents to be a great thief, but with those days behind him, Paelen was now one of Emily's closest friends.

Emily's father, Steve, stood at the side of the river, giving Paelen diving instructions, but they weren't helping. As Paelen sprang on the board, he soared high into the air and over the water. But instead of putting out his arms and angling his body to dive, he crashed into the surface on his stomach.

"Ouch!" Emily's father cried.

Paelen resurfaced, coughing and spewing out water. "I will never learn."

"Sure you will," Joel laughed. "It just takes practice."

Joel's laughter made Emily's heart flutter and caused a smile to rise to her lips. Like her, he had come to Olympus from New York City. And even though he was human, Joel looked right at home. The only thing that set him apart was his silver right arm. He had lost his real one during a fight with the Gorgons, and Vulcan had made this powerful replacement.

Three water nymphs surfaced behind Joel. Their pale eyes sparkled as they stroked Joel's artificial arm. In the torchlight, the metal looked like blazing gold.

Both Joel and Paelen blushed at the beautiful nymphs as they started to sing.

Paelen swam closer to them. "Yes, Joel has a silver arm, but look what I can do." He lifted his arm out of the water and used his powers to stretch the bones and muscles out. He wiggled the fingers on his hand. "Is this not as amazing as a silver arm?"

The three water nymphs weren't impressed. They turned from Paelen and smiled again at Joel, giggling softly. Then they disappeared beneath the water's surface.

"Wait. Do not leave!" Paelen cried in disappointment. "Come back!"

"Let 'em go," Joel said. "You've still got to learn to dive." When his eyes landed on Emily on the shore, he grinned. "Hey, Em, would you please show Paelen how to dive?"

Any traces of jealousy Emily might have felt toward the beautiful water nymphs vanished now that she was the focus of Joel's bright smile. She handed her towel to her father and climbed up onto the diving board. Then she bounced twice and leaped gracefully into the air, performing a perfect dive.

Joel splashed water at Paelen. "See, that's how you do it!"

"That is exactly what *I* did," Paelen said. "I just looked a little different."

Joel burst out laughing. "What are you talking about? You belly-flopped!"

"Same thing," Paelen said as Pegasus entered the water, followed by Chrysaor. As Emily swam over to the stallion, she noticed Paelen and Joel staring at something. Emily followed their gaze to see Diana, the great Huntress, striding toward the river.

She was wearing a golden swimsuit, and her long black hair was out of its usual tight braids and flowed across her shoulders and down her back. She always looked beautiful, but they rarely saw Diana look relaxed like this. Diana's face lit up with a smile as Emily's father turned to greet her.

Emily laughed at her two friends with their eyes glued on Diana. She splashed water into their faces.

"Hey, why'd you do that?" Joel demanded.

"You both look like you need cooling down," Emily teased.

Emily's father kissed Diana on the cheek. They

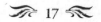

entered the water and started swimming together down the river.

"Are you okay with that?" Joel asked. "I mean, with your mother and all . . ."

She nodded. "I know my dad really loved my mom. But she's been dead a long time, and he's still young. I wouldn't want him to be alone. And I know Diana really likes him."

Pegasus swam up behind her and gave her a gentle nudge. He nickered softly.

"Diana has been alone too long," Paelen told her. "Pegasus says he is happy that she is spending time with your father—they are a good match, as your father is unafraid of her temper."

Emily stroked the stallion's white face. "I thought it would be weird seeing him with someone else, but Diana is different. She's already like family to me." Emily turned her attention away and her father and Diana swam to shore. She climbed back up on the diving board to try to teach Paelen how to dive.

Later that night Pegasus escorted Emily back to the apartment they shared with her father, Joel, and

Paelen. Even though the stallion had his own suite, most nights he kept watch over Emily. She insisted she didn't need protection, but she welcomed the presence of her dearest friend.

Pegasus dozed near the door while Emily lounged on her bed and shuffled through the pages of an old diary. It had been written by Agent B of the Central Research Unit. He had fought beside her when she had time-traveled back to the war with the Titans. At first an enemy, by the end of the war Agent B had become a very close friend.

It was still hard to believe that she could ever call an agent of the CRU anything other than an enemy. Almost from the first day she had met Pegasus, the CRU had been a dark shadow hanging over them. They had hunted down the Olympians and created clones from their blood. They had tortured her and her friends for information. The CRU was the cause of most of their troubles. Yet somehow Agent B had proved to be a loyal and trusted friend.

She had read the fading pages of his diary so many times that she'd practically memorized each entry. But still she kept coming back to it. That book, her own diary, and the silver Pegasus pendant she always wore were almost the only pieces of evidence left from their journey deep into the past.

Of course, Mike was still with her. The abandoned street dog was snoring softly beside her. Occasionally he would growl and kick out his legs as he ran in his dreams. Emily wondered if he was fighting Shadow Titans again.

But apart from the dog and a few of the Original Olympians who had experienced everything with her, no one remembered the events of the past. All the suffering they had endured, all the losses and finally the triumph, had been erased from the memories of those who had traveled through time with her.

It was exactly as Agent B said it would be. After Emily had used her powers to destroy the Titans' weapon, a cosmic reset button had been activated. Everything returned to normal—as though finding the weapon in modern Greece had never happened.

Not even Pegasus remembered their journey. That was the hardest thing of all—not being able to talk to the winged stallion about it because, for him, it was part of a different time line, and not one he'd experienced. Often she would look at the healthy young winged stallion and suddenly recall the ancient Pegasus who had died in her arms.

Because Pegasus *had* died in her arms—whether he remembered or not.

Emily stopped at a diary entry she had read so many times before that she could recite it by heart.

Emily and Joel have grown so much closer. After the death of Paelen and now Pegasus, something has changed between them. They are inseparable—and it worries me. If anything should happen to Joel, I don't think anyone could contain Emily's rage. I'm convinced she'll lose control of her powers. They'll overwhelm her and none of us will survive it.

I know Emily—talking to her won't work. All I can do is be there for her and offer whatever guidance or support I can. I'm also going to keep a particularly careful eye on Joel. I've spoken with Jupiter and the others about it and we all agree. Nothing must happen to Joel. For Emily's sake— and our own.

"He was frightened of me," Emily mused aloud as she looked down on Mike. "He was scared I might go ballistic and lose control of my powers and destroy everything." Emily knew that would not have happened.

But then Joel's handsome face flashed before her eyes and she thought again. Maybe Agent B was right. What if something *had* happened to Joel—what would she have done? She might well have lost control.

Emily flipped through the pages of the diary and found a sketch Agent B had drawn. It showed Emily and Joel sitting close together, roasting Olympian apples over a campfire. They were laughing as ancient Pegasus rested beside her.

She remembered many nights like that. Time spent with Joel—not always speaking, but saying everything. Knowing each day could have been their last made every moment together that much more precious.

Emily tilted her head to the side. The sketch was good. Agent B had captured Joel so well. Looking at the picture made her heart skip a beat. She felt her face flushing as she recalled their special kiss.

He loves you, you know, Riza said softly within her mind.

Emily smiled. The voice of the ancient Xan living within her had scared her at first, but now Riza was like a twin sister to her and she couldn't imagine her life without her.

"Yes, I know," Emily responded.

And you love him.

Emily blushed brighter. "Yes."

So what are you going to do about it? Riza teased.

Emily shrugged. "I don't know. Joel doesn't remember telling me."

You can't fool me, Emily. Riza chuckled. *The problem isn't Joel not remembering; it's you. You are too frightened to tell him everything that happened back then. You should let him read Agent B's diary.*

"I'm not frightened," Emily said in a voice that didn't even convince herself. "It's just that . . ." She paused.

Yes . . . ?

A strange sound from outside her window spared Emily from having to answer. Peering out, she caught a movement that was too quick to follow. Instantly on her guard, she called the winged stallion to the window.

"Pegs, there's something strange happening outside."

Emily pointed when he reached her side. "I heard it first, and just as I got to the window, I saw something moving very quickly toward the back of the palace."

Pegasus nickered softly, then sniffed the air. His head bobbed up and down. He peered at Emily and then dropped his wing to invite her onto his back. Without hesitation, Emily climbed up and hung on to his mane. Pegasus leaped gracefully out the window and started to fly.

The journey was short as the stallion beat his large wings and took them toward the back gardens of Jupiter's palace. In the starlight, Emily saw they were heading right for the large green hedge maze.

Pegasus touched down at the entrance of the maze and bobbed his head again.

"In there?" Emily asked. She climbed down and, with Pegasus at her side, walked into the maze. She had no sense of danger, just a curiosity that couldn't be ignored.

Pegasus sniffed the air again and started to trot. As they neared the center of the maze, Emily heard gentle sobs.

Rounding a final bend, she saw what looked like a lion but with a human upper torso and large, eagle-like wings. It was crouched down in the corner of the path, weeping quietly.

"Alexis?" she called softly.

The Sphinx of Olympus had her head resting on her paws. Her large eagle wings were drooping to the ground. When Alexis looked up, Emily saw that her lovely green eyes were puffy and red.

"What is it?" she called, racing to the Sphinx's side. "Has something happened?"

Alexis sat up and tried her best to wipe her eyes with her large paws. She sniffed back her sobs. "It—it is nothing."

"This isn't 'nothing.'" Emily reached out and gently wiped away the Sphinx's tears. "Please tell us what's wrong?"

Alexis sniffed again. "It is Juno. She has commanded me to return to the palace. She feels I have been neglecting my duties here. She just does not understand how it is for me, with the life I have chosen for myself."

"With Tom, you mean," Emily said. "You don't want to leave him."

Alexis nodded as her tears continued.

Emily sat back on her heels. Tom, once known as Agent T, had been a dangerous agent within the Central Research Unit. It was his job to hunt down and capture the Olympians to exploit their powers. Then Cupid enchanted him and the lethal agent changed. But that change wasn't complete until Tom met Alexis and traveled with Emily and Joel to Las Vegas.

When Agent T had met the equally deadly Alexis, it was love at first sight. But then Tom was critically wounded and paralyzed. The only way Jupiter could save him was to turn him into a willow tree. From the moment he arrived in Olympus, he and the Sphinx had become inseparable.

Alexis sniffed. "Tom is my life. I cannot bear to be away from him for a moment. But when I asked Jupiter to move him here, he said that Tom would not survive the transfer. At Juno's command, we are to be parted."

Emily knew how deeply the Sphinx cared for Agent T and how much he loved her.

"She just does not understand," Alexis said. "To leave Tom is like ripping out my claws, one at a time. But still she insists I must return to the palace."

Alexis looked miserable as she turned to Emily. "Tell me, what am I to do? How do I make her understand? I must not defy Juno, but I cannot stay."

"I could talk to her if you want?"

Alexis shook her head. "That will not work. She is adamant. Unless we find a safe way to move Tom here, I will lose him." Alexis lowered her head to her paws again. "It is hopeless . . . ," she wept. "Just hopeless . . ."

Emily, there is a way. Riza spoke softly in Emily's head. *I should have thought of it before. Leave Alexis here—I have an idea. But we'll need Pegasus.*

Emily patted the Sphinx's shoulder. "Don't give up, Alexis. We'll find a way for you and Tom to stay together. I promise. Just stay here for a moment. I'll be right back."

Getting to her feet, Emily directed Pegasus out of the maze.

"So what do we do?" she asked Riza.

Let's get to Tom. This might just work.

"Pegs, would you take us to Tom? Riza has an idea."

The stallion lowered his wing and Emily climbed up onto his back. In moments they were in the air. With starlight to guide them, they left the lush green grounds of the palace area and crossed over a barren, sandy desert toward the home of the Sphinx.

Pegasus touched down before a tall and leafy green willow tree. Emily looked up and saw what looked like a large tree house built into the branches of the tree. It had a large, flat platform and one wall. The rest was open for easy flight in and out.

"Tom?" Emily called.

"Emily!" the tree responded with its high, leafy voice. "And Pegasus. How wonderful of you to visit. But if you're looking for Alexis, I'm afraid she isn't here."

"I know," Emily said. She stepped up to the tree and patted the thick trunk in greeting. "We just left her in Jupiter's maze. She was crying."

The leaves on the tree started to shake. "Is she all right? Has something happened?"

Emily shook her head. "No, she's fine. She just misses you. Juno has commanded her to return to the palace, but she doesn't want to."

"I don't want her to go either," Tom said sadly. "The days and nights will be endless for me. But it is her duty. If Alexis understands anything, it is duty."

"Tom, do you remember Riza?"

"Of course I do. Hello, Riza."

"Hello, Tom," Riza said through Emily. *"I've had an idea that could help you both stay together. But we need your consent."*

"Really?" Tom said, sounding more hopeful now. "Tell me, please."

"Well," Riza began. *"For many millennia, my people knew how to manipulate matter. Not unlike what Jupiter did with you. But he was unable to repair your human body, so he did the best he could and made you as you are now."*

"And I am grateful to him," Tom said. "I wasn't much of a human, if I'm perfectly honest."

"You were fine," Emily said, taking over.

"And you're a terrible liar, Emily Jacobs." Tom chuckled. When he laughed, his long leaves rustled gently, with a pleasant brushing sound. "Emily, you know as well as I do that I'm better now as a tree than I ever was as a man."

"But you've changed," Emily argued.

"I'd like to think so."

"*Tom,*" Riza said seriously. *"Jupiter didn't have the power to restore your wrecked body. We do. But only if you want it."*

"You can really do that when Jupiter couldn't?"

"*Yes,*" Riza said.

"You mean it?"

"*Yes.*"

There was a long pause. Finally the willow tree asked hesitantly, "If you have the power to restore me, could you turn me into something else instead?"

"*That depends on what you want,*" Riza responded.

"You want to be a Sphinx," Emily guessed.

"Yes," Tom agreed. "So I can be just like my Alexis."

"*It will be so,*" Riza said

"Are you sure we can do this?" Emily asked.

"*Yes,*" Riza said aloud. *"But we need something from Alexis. Something that will help us replicate her pattern with Tom."*

"You mean like her DNA?"

"Exactly," Riza said.

"Like hair?" Tom offered. "Her hairbrush is here on her platform."

"Perfect!"

Emily climbed up the small ladder leading to the platform that Alexis called her home. Overstuffed satin pillows were scattered in one corner, forming a lounging area. On the other side of the platform was what looked like a dressing table, with a mirror above it. Laid out in a neat row were different-sized combs and brushes, which Alexis used to groom herself.

Emily frowned. "How does she use these with her big paws?"

"It's not easy," Tom answered. "It takes her ages, but Alexis is very determined."

Emily lifted one of the brushes and pulled out strands of long, dark hair. "Will this do?"

"Absolutely," Riza said. *"We'll also need a handful of new leaves from Tom."*

Emily looked up and saw some opening buds. "Is it okay for me to take some of these?" she asked Tom.

"Take as many as you need." He sounded excited. "I can't believe this. You're sure you can do it?"

"We are," Riza said.

"You are, you mean," Emily corrected. "I'd have never thought to try."

Riza chuckled softly. *"That's because you still don't understand the depth of our powers."*

Emily climbed down the ladder and stepped away from the tree. With Pegasus at her side, she looked up at the tall willow. "So what do we do now?"

"Emily," Riza said seriously. *"You must let me take full control of us. This will take a lot of concentration—we can't risk a mistake. Will you give me your full coopera-tion?"*

Emily didn't hesitate. "Of course, but how do I do that?"

"As I rise to the surface, I want you to relax. Don't speak, and try not to think. Just imagine yourself floating in a peaceful lake. . . ."

Emily felt Riza growing stronger within her. The Xan's calm presence was lulling her into a gentle, peaceful state of mind. Emily felt no fear as Riza took full control of her body and mind.

Through foggy, dreamlike eyes, Emily watched Riza lift "her" hands. She could feel immense powers course through her, almost like a kind of static electricity from rubbing shoes on a carpet. She felt that if she was to touch anything, there would be a big spark.

Riza merged their powers together and then used them to intertwine the strands of hair and the willow leaves.

"Don't be afraid," Riza called to Tom. *"You will be safe."*

Energy coursed through Emily as she'd never felt it before. Every nerve was electrified as Riza used their combined power to command the tree's physical matter to change.

As Riza drew more and more power, Emily started to feel peculiar. At first it was just an odd, tingling sensation. Not painful, but strange. Her calm feeling was fading away. . . .

"Riza . . . ?" Emily knew she shouldn't speak, but she had to warn the Xan. Something was going wrong. Pain started, deep in her mind. It was bad— very, very bad. "Riza, stop!"

Emily's tiny voice was lost in the crackling sounds of energy being drawn from their core. The Flame was there, as were all her other powers. But as the moments ticked by, something was starting to fracture and split apart. Their very center would not hold much longer.

"You're using too much power. Please stop!"

Emily tried everything to make Riza hear. She pounded on the walls of her mind. She screamed louder than she ever had in her life. But nothing was reaching the Xan.

More power surged.

Emily was spinning uncontrolled in the tight confines of her mind. She could no longer see or hear anything. But still she felt the draw of power increasing. As she started to fade into darkness, she felt, more than heard, a great tearing deep within her. Unable to cry out, Emily fainted.

"EMILY?" A DEEP, CONCERNED VOICE CALLED. "Emily, are you all right?"

Emily's head pounded as she struggled back to consciousness. A wet tongue licked her cheek, and she didn't need to open her eyes to know it was Pegasus. The stallion was whinnying and nudging her to wake up.

"Emily, please," the man's voice repeated.

Her eyes fluttered open. At first she saw the stars shining above her. Then Pegasus's face, but that was soon replaced by the face of someone she hadn't seen since Area 51.

"Agent T?"

Tom's eyes sparkled as he leaned closer to her.

"My name is Tom, remember? You know me as Tom. Agent T is gone."

"Wha—what happened?"

"A miracle," he announced. "You and Riza have made me the happiest man alive!"

"Riza . . . ? RIZA!" Emily cried. She sat up quickly and checked herself over. Arms, legs—she was still all there. "I remember. She was drawing too much power." Emily closed her eyes and reached inside. "Riza—are you there? Talk to me!"

She called again, but Riza didn't answer. Emily recalled how much power the ancient Xan had drawn from them to restore Tom. The last time they had used too much power, Riza had gone silent too. But she'd come back. Emily prayed she would come back this time as well.

"Are you all right?" Tom asked. "Even in this poor light, you look really pale. How are you feeling?"

Emily frowned and rubbed her temples. "Really weak, and I've got a killer headache. I might throw up."

"It's no wonder," Tom said gratefully. "Not after what you two just did for me."

Emily's head cleared and her gaze rested on the

ex–CRU agent. She inhaled sharply. His face hadn't changed at all! The same angular features and pale blue eyes, framed with long, dark hair. But aside from that, everything was different. His chest was bare and ended in a full, powerful lion's belly where his lower torso would have been. Instead of arms, Tom had lion's paws with sharp, tearing claws. On his back was a large set of wings.

"It worked!" Emily cried. "Tom, you're a Sphinx!"

"I know!" Tom's rough paws pulled Emily up into a powerful embrace. "I thought I was content to remain a tree, but now I can see again! I can smell the sweet fresh air and feel the wind on my face. I can taste salt on my lips and I can touch you! You have given me more than I ever deserved. Thank you!"

Emily laughed as she hugged him back.

"Just look at my wings! Can I really fly? I always dreamed of flying when I was a kid. But now, is it really possible?"

"I don't know." Emily chuckled. She had never seen him behave like this. Tom was right. Agent T of the CRU was long gone. This was a man who finally understood happiness. "You'll have to ask Alexis."

"Alexis!" Tom rose and started to hop around the area like an overexcited dog. His four large lion's legs and paws were gangly and unruly as he tried to learn how to use them together. "Get up! We must find Alexis!"

Alexis was still alone in the maze when Pegasus flew over it. Emily pointed down. "There she is—she hasn't moved."

Tom's large paws were wrapped tightly around Emily's waist as he sat like a dog, behind her on the stallion's rump. His wings were open and causing a drag behind them. He'd nearly fallen off twice on the way to Jupiter's palace. Yet despite that, his spirits were higher than she'd ever seen them as he whooped and laughed all the way back.

"Don't say anything," Tom whispered to Emily. "Let me surprise her."

Pegasus touched down on the ground beside the giant maze. Tom leaped off and crashed to the ground in an awkward heap. He laughed in embarrassment. "I think Alexis has a lot to teach me. I never realized how difficult it is to walk with four legs."

When he righted himself, he said, "Will you wait here for us? I know Alexis will want to thank you."

Emily nodded. She closed her sore eyes and rubbed her aching shoulders. She still felt nauseated, as if she might be sick at any moment.

Each beat of her heart seemed to cause her head to pound harder. "I need some aspirin," she said softly to Pegasus. She closed her eyes, leaned forward, and lay down on the stallion's neck to wait for Tom.

Emily woke and rolled onto her back. A gentle breeze was blowing her bedroom curtains, and the bright sunshine of an Olympian day greeted her.

She sat up and yawned.

Pegasus was standing by the window. He turned, nickered excitedly, and trotted over to her bed.

Emily rubbed her tired eyes. "You won't believe the dream I just had. Alexis was in it. She was miserable because she was separated from Tom. So you and I went to Tom and, with Riza's help, we turned him into a Sphinx. But something went wrong and I got sick. . . ."

Pausing, Emily became aware of the dull, throbbing

pain in the center of her head. It wasn't as bad as the one from her dream, but it was there. "Actually, I really do have a headache. I guess that's what started the dream."

Emily climbed out of bed and reached for her clothes. She frowned. "The funny thing is, I don't remember going to bed. We were swimming and then . . ."

The stallion walked to her side and nodded his head. His eyes sparkled, and she could feel his excitement. She had barely tied her braided gold belt around her waist when he leaned down, caught her hand in his teeth, and drew her toward the door.

"What's got you so excited this morning?"

Pegasus led her into the main living area of the apartment. Her father was in the kitchen, preparing breakfast. He was wearing his Olympian tunic, but he had a very Earth-like apron tied around his waist.

"You're up!" he cried. He put down the dish he was carrying and greeted her with a hug. "I am so proud of you. That was the kindest thing you could have done for those two. Everyone is thrilled."

Emily frowned. "What are you talking about? Thrilled about what?"

Her father stopped and stared at her. "Don't you remember?"

"Remember what?" Emily looked at Pegasus, puzzled. "Dad, why do you and Pegasus look so excited? What's going on?"

"Tom and Alexis," he said. "Last night? Emily, you and Riza turned Tom into a Sphinx."

Emily was stunned. "That was real? It wasn't a dream?"

"That was no dream. Alexis woke everyone in the palace with her shrieks the moment she saw him." His grin pulled in the dimples in his cheeks. "I have never seen her so excited. I thought she was terrifying when she was angry. You should see her happy—it's even worse!"

Emily laughed. "Tom was jumping around like an electrocuted cat. He doesn't know how to walk on four legs."

"I'm sure Alexis will teach him." Her father went back to preparing breakfast. "How you managed to sleep through the racket is beyond me. I'm sure they could be heard on Earth."

"Was it you who put me to bed?"

He nodded. "Me and Diana. We found you sleeping on Pegasus and brought you back here." He turned to her. "Really, Em, I am so proud of you. You have made those two very happy."

"It wasn't me," Emily admitted. "It was Riza."

Emily started to help her father prepare breakfast when an urgent banging on their door stopped her. Pegasus sniffed the air and then nickered softly.

"We'll get it," Emily called to her father.

The moment she turned the doorknob, the door sprang open and Alexis leaped at Emily, who was knocked to the ground as the powerful Sphinx pinned her down and started to kiss her all over.

"Thank you, thank you, thank you . . . !" Alexis cried. Her eyes were wild and her hair a tousled mess. But Emily had never seen the Sphinx looking so radiant.

"Alexis, please, let the poor girl breathe!"

Tom was helping Emily sit up just as Alexis pounced on her again. She threw her paws around Emily and held her tight. "How can I ever thank you for this? Tell me, what can I do? I will be your slave forever."

Emily laughed as Alexis offered a list of things she would do for her. "Please, just let me up!"

She climbed to her feet and was able to get a full look at the two Sphinxes together. Tom was taller than Alexis, and his wings were much larger. But they made a handsome couple.

"Go on, tell her," Tom said, nudging Alexis.

Alexis blushed. "We can never thank you enough for the joy you have brought us. Juno has just given Tom and me larger quarters here, near the palace. We can stay together and still serve Juno and Jupiter. And in time, Juno said, she and Jupiter will preside over our Union Ceremony."

"Union Ceremony?" Emily asked.

Tom grinned. "It's kind of like a wedding. Alexis and I are engaged." He focused his blue eyes on Emily. "And you made this possible for us."

Pegasus whinnied in celebration as Emily embraced Alexis again. "I'm just so glad Riza and I could help."

By the time Joel and Paelen joined them for breakfast, the Sphinxes had left so that Alexis could start to teach Tom how to fly.

Joel sat down beside Emily and elbowed her lightly. "I never knew you were such a romantic."

Emily blushed. "I'm not. I just hated to see Alexis and Tom apart."

"Yeah, right, I believe you. Millions wouldn't, but I do."

Emily grinned and shoved him back. Her headache was still with her, a reminder of what had happened the previous night. She realized that ever since she had first entered the Temple of the Flame and stepped up onto the plinth to relight the Flame, she hadn't been sick at all.

The pounding in her head stayed with her throughout the long day and into the evening. Normally, she would stay up late with Pegasus and take a night flight over Olympus. She was still exploring new areas of this wondrous world, and the winged stallion was her favorite guide.

But tonight she excused herself early and retired to her bedroom. She couldn't stop yawning as she dressed for bed. The moment she put her head down, Emily slipped into a deep, restful sleep.

DRIPPING WATER. SHOUTS AND CRIES . . .
arguments. It was like a tidal wave of sounds assault-
ing her ears. Damp and musty odors mixed in with
the foul stench of the unwashed.

Eyes opened slowly. It was dim, with only the
flickering of torches casting their shadows on the
stone walls. Movement—someone was drawing near.

"Can it be true? Are you waking, after all this
time?"

A voice. Close. Familiar. Excited.

"Lorin? Wake up, child."

"M- M-Mother?"

"No, not Mother. It is me, Phoebe—do you remember me? I have been caring for you."

Lorin turned slowly toward the face drawing near. Her eyes tried to focus, but they were dry and sore, and in the dim light she could not make out details. Phoebe. A spark of memory. Phoebe was the name of her mother's best friend.

She attempted to rise, but couldn't. Nothing worked as it should.

"Do not try to move," Phoebe said. "You have slept a very, very long time and your muscles are unused to movement."

Lorin looked past the pale, drawn face of Phoebe. A dark stone wall rose behind her and all around. She weakly lifted her head and saw thick bars blocking the only way out of the small room.

She frowned. "Where . . . ?"

"We are in Tartarus."

"Not home?"

"No, my child. We are not on Titus. We were imprisoned here after the war. I do not know how long we have been here, but it feels like an eternity. It no longer matters, though, now that you are back with me."

Flashes of memories came to Lorin. Sunshine, a

happy home with her parents. Her baby brother and her friends. Her pet owl and her dog. She licked her parched, dry lips.

"Here, drink this—it will make you stronger."

A cup was pressed to her lips and she tasted the sweet flavor of nectar. With the first swallow, she felt better. She looked past Phoebe again and frowned. "Where are Mother and Father?"

"They are gone."

"Where?"

"I am so sorry, my precious. They are not here. They have gone ahead. . . ."

Lorin didn't understand. "They—left—me?"

"It was not their choice."

Lorin raised her arm and inspected a hand she did not recognize. It was different from what she remembered. Lifting her head, she looked down the length of her body. Two thick plaits of long blond hair lay on her chest. Fear rose from the center of her being. This wasn't her body—it was too big, and her hair wasn't long and it was never put in plaits. Her voice was different too. It was much deeper—everything about her was different.

Panic started to take over. "I do not understand," she cried. "I want Mother and Father! Please, let me see them."

Phoebe sat on the edge of the bed and took Lorin's hands. "Calm down. You are still too weak."

"But I need them."

"I know you do, my sweet. But it is impossible."

"Why . . . ?" Her voice became a small, weak whine. Tears rose in her eyes.

Phoebe gently stroked her cheek. "If I could give them back to you, I would. But they are long gone."

"No, Mother was just with me. She sang our special song and rubbed my back until I was asleep. She kissed me right here." Lorin pointed to the spot on her forehead where her mother kissed her each night.

"That was a very long time ago."

Lorin frowned. "No, it was last night."

Phoebe sighed heavily. "This will be hard for you to understand. But you must try. A very, very long time ago, a bright flame flashed across the night sky. We thought it was just a fragment from a dying star, a meteor passing close to Titus. It continued to burn brightly until it fell from the sky and crashed into your home. You and your family were sleeping when it struck. Everyone and everything in the area was destroyed. We believed we had lost you too, until somehow you were pulled from the wreckage—alive and unharmed."

Lorin shook her head. "Stop lying to me!"

"I wish I were lying. That cursed meteor changed everything for all of us."

It had to be a lie, thought Lorin. Her family couldn't be gone. They were just with her.

As though reading her mind, Phoebe stroked her head again. "We were all so grateful when you were pulled from the devastation. But you were in a very deep sleep. Nothing could rouse you, no matter what we tried. Then the war started and I kept you safe in the hope that one day you would wake."

Phoebe smiled, but with sadness. "And now, at last, you have. But you have changed so much. You are not the little girl I used to cradle on my lap. Over the ages of your sleep you have grown into a beautiful young woman. I have cared for you every minute since the disaster and loved you like my own daughter."

More memories returned to Lorin. She remembered Phoebe. She was like a second mother to her. But as she gazed up into Phoebe's face, Lorin noticed that she looked different. Her eyes were drawn and tired. Her skin was pale and sallow, as though it had never been kissed by the sun. Her hair was still light, but it had lost its luster and was unkempt. Her clothes looked like rags and her skin was filthy.

When she had the strength to sit up, Lorin looked around her. She wasn't in a bedroom; it was a small stone prison cell with two narrow beds and no windows. Outside the bars, she could see the cell opposite and hear the occupants talking. She could sense many other people all around her, locked in their own cells. As she focused, she could sense even more on the many levels above and below them.

"This is Tartarus?" She remembered that name. Her parents used to speak of it. Saying it was a bad place for very bad people, and not somewhere they would want to go.

Phoebe nodded.

"Why are we here? Did I do something bad?"

Phoebe smiled and the smile lit her face. "No, my

child, you could never do anything bad. It was the war. We were defeated. They gathered together everyone who fought for Saturn and locked us down here. They feed us and give us what we need to survive. But we will never be free. Titus is gone for us. Now there is only Tartarus and an eternity in prison."

"I do not understand. What is war?"

Phoebe tried her best to explain it in simple terms for Lorin's young, undeveloped mind. Lorin frowned.

"Who put us down here?"

Phoebe's expression darkened. "That traitor Jupiter and his Olympians!"

EMILY WAS CONFUSED. SHE WAS SEEING THINGS
*that seemed so much more real than a dream. Hearing
through ears not her own. All around were the sounds
of screaming, arguing, and crying. She could feel things,
but didn't recognize what they were.*

*Then there was a woman's voice—soft, welcoming, and
joyful. Was someone touching her hand? Her face? She
couldn't be certain.*

*"Riza?" Emily called. But within her dream state, the
Xan was not with her.*

*She could hear dripping water hiding behind the louder
sounds, as though she were deep underground. . . .*

"Em?" Her father's voice called into the shadows. It
was louder than the distant voices. She tried to block

him out. She needed to hear the others. Somehow she knew it was important. But the more she struggled to listen, the farther away the sounds drifted, until they faded away completely.

"Em, honey, please, you've got to wake up."

Even before she opened her eyes, Emily felt the nagging headache—a deep, ceaseless pounding in the center of her skull. She opened her eyes and squinted. The light in her room was too bright and hurt her eyes.

"Dad?"

"Em, what's wrong?" he asked. "You've slept for almost two days. We're really starting to worry. Vesta said you needed rest after what you did for Tom, but this isn't right."

"What? Two days?" Emily frowned. "I couldn't have. The last thing I remember was Tom and Alexis telling us about their engagement. . . ."

"That was yesterday morning." He hovered close and pressed his hand to her forehead. "You're still very pale and have a temperature."

Emily rubbed her temples. "It's this headache. I can't shake it. I think Riza overdid it a bit when she turned Tom into a Sphinx." She swung her legs over the side of the bed and rose. Waves of dizziness overwhelmed her and she leaned into her father for support.

"I—I'm all right now," she said, steadying herself. "I might have picked up a bug or something."

"From whom?" her father asked. "No one here in Olympus ever gets sick. Especially not you."

Emily nodded. "I know. But don't worry; I'm sure it will pass."

The headache didn't pass. In fact, there were times when it became excruciating. Emily soon linked the pain to her powers. If she tried to use them, the pounding in her head worsened to the point where she cried out. The only time she wasn't in pain was when she slept. And she seemed to be doing a lot more of that lately.

Pegasus could feel her pain and hovered close. He would press his muzzle into her and lick her cheek.

"Really, Pegs, I'm okay," Emily said, stroking his muzzle. "It's not so bad when I don't use my powers. I figure it's like a pulled muscle. Riza used a lot of energy to change Tom. I'm sure it will take time for my head to get back to normal. Then maybe I'll hear her again."

Between the headaches and the tiredness, Emily stayed close to home and kept her activities to a minimum. Her friends started to notice the change in her and pressed her for answers, but Emily had none to offer.

Her teacher, Vesta, started to visit daily. When Emily told her how she felt, Vesta would suggest she needed more time and plenty of rest. But there was something in her expression that worried Emily. Did Vesta know something *she* didn't?

A week later and Emily was still feeling weak. She was so tired that she had to turn down an invitation to a concert being given by the Muses. Joel offered to stay at home with her, but Emily insisted he go with the others, saying she planned to retire early.

After a bit of arguing, Joel reluctantly left for the concert.

With Pegasus at her side, Emily headed to her bedroom. She was just about to change into her bedclothes when she noticed activity outside her window. A crowd of night dwellers were approaching the palace.

"Pegs, look down there. . . ."

The winged stallion joined her at the window. As they looked down, the crowd grew bigger.

"Do you know what's going on?"

Pegasus whinnied and nodded his head.

Once again Emily regretted not being able to understand him. As she looked at the approaching crowds, her eyes picked out the three night dwellers she'd met several nights ago. Fawn, her brother, Dax, and their sister, Sapphire, were approaching the palace and walking around the side toward the back gardens.

Emily's curiosity soon overcame her exhaustion. She reached for her tunic. "I promised Dad I'd go right to bed, but let's see what's happening first. I'm sure we won't be long."

Pegasus carried Emily into the gardens. Earlier in the day, she'd noticed more activity around the palace as large bouquets, banquet tables, and chairs were assembled and a podium was being erected.

As there were always celebrations of one kind or another going on in Olympus, Emily hadn't paid much attention. But when they arrived, she saw tables laden with food and drink and heard musicians playing merry tunes.

Emily gazed around from the height of the stallion's back and was sure that most, if not all, of the night dwellers were gathered together in some kind of celebration.

"Excuse me," Emily asked a middle-aged night dweller as he walked close to them.

His black eyes settled on her and his grin showed off his sharp, pointed teeth. He bowed his head in respect and spoke softly. "Flame, it is a great honor to see you here this night. How may I be of service?"

"Would you please tell me what's happening?"

"Of course," he said. "We have just held our selection for the next Rotation and are here to celebrate the chosen before they go. I hope you will stay and join us. Jupiter is going to give his speech; then there will be a banquet, and later we will all dance."

Emily was about to ask more when she spied Fawn standing alone at a remove from the gathering. She was staring down at the ground and looked like she'd been crying.

Emily leaned forward on the stallion's neck but couldn't see Dax or Sapphire anywhere near Fawn. "Thank you, but I can't stay. I hope you enjoy your party."

The night dweller beamed as he bowed again, then walked away. Emily slid down from the stallion's back and walked over to Fawn.

"Fawn, what is it? What's wrong?" Emily asked.

"It is nothing," Fawn said, wiping her eyes. "I am just being foolish. Please do not concern yourself with me. You have more important things to consider."

"Don't be silly," Emily said. She took Fawn's hand and led her from the crowd. "Now tell me, what's wrong?"

"I cannot. It is silly."

Emily turned to Pegasus. "Would you please tell her that she has no reason to feel silly talking to me?"

Pegasus nickered softly, and Fawn's eyes lit up. "Really? Tonight?"

The night dweller focused on Emily. "Pegasus has invited me to take that flight. But I am sure you must be tired. I heard that you have not been well."

Emily actually felt exhausted, but instead she nodded. "I'm fine. It's been a while since Pegasus and I have taken one of our flights. Please join us. We have this amazing spot by a calm lake that we like to visit. You'll love it."

LORIN PACED THE TIGHT CONFINES OF THE small cell she shared with Phoebe. Since waking, her mind was developing, as was her speech. She learned to walk again and had explored every inch of the cell. In five short steps, she could cross from one side wall to the other. In four steps she could move from the back to the wall of bars at the front. There were no windows, and the only light came from torches in the corridor outside the cell.

There was no privacy—life was lived in the open behind the bars. The prison keepers could peer in at any time to see what the occupants were doing.

What Lorin still couldn't grasp was why they were there. She had been a small child when the meteor crashed into her house. Since then, she had been unconscious. She had done nothing wrong and had committed no crime. Neither had Phoebe—all she was guilty of was caring for Lorin while she slept. So why had Jupiter locked them away in this place of horror?

As she leaned against the bars of her cell, she could hear the other prisoners around them talking, fighting, and in some cases crying—all trying to live what small lives they could.

She turned back to her guardian, sitting on her small bed. "How long have we been here?"

"I do not know," Phoebe admitted. "We have no means to know. Though I am sure it has been a very long time." She patted the bed. "Come, sit beside me. I am so joyous that you have finally awoken. I cannot tell you how lonely I have been, tending to you while you slept. But all that ended the moment you opened your eyes."

Lorin took a seat. "How long must we stay here?"

"I do not think Jupiter ever intends to release us. He won the war. It is his right to keep us here as long as he desires."

"Who started it?"

"The war?" Phoebe shrugged. "I do not know. I was too busy caring for you after the disaster. But it was not long after the meteor struck your home that the violence started. Saturn did his best to protect us, but then Jupiter and his brothers attacked. Before long, Titus was at war with Olympus and we were forced into hiding while Saturn fought for our freedom."

"Saturn cares for us?"

Phoebe nodded. "So much so, he created an army of Shadow Titans so we would not have to fight. These Shadow Titans were a powerful, fierce army and completely loyal to Saturn. Unfortunately, they were defeated by Jupiter's secret weapon. None of us could stand against it."

"What was the weapon?"

Phoebe looked as though she wanted to say, but then held back. "It does not matter now. They defeated us, and Jupiter sent us here."

"I hate Jupiter," Lorin said.

"As do I, my child. But let us not talk of the war. We have much to celebrate, with you waking."

Lorin nodded. "I dreamed while I slept."

"You did? Of your family and the fun you had playing with your friends? Your best friend was a satyr called Dyn. Did you dream of him?"

Lorin shook her head. "No, I do not remember Dyn. I dreamed about a place so different from here. I do not have the words to describe it. But it was filled with gentle people who were very tall. They had no hair and moved like they were floating. They never raised their voices or cried. There were strange, large animals there too, which the people protected."

"It sounds rather frightening," Phoebe said, taking her hand.

"Oh, no, it was not. It was peaceful. The people cared about everything—not just their world, but all the other worlds. They especially cared for the animals they brought to their world for protection. They called it Sanctuary." Lorin dropped her head. "But they grew tired of their endless existence, so one day they gathered together to release themselves into the stars. But one of their kind did not make it to the gathering in time and was left behind. She tried to follow the others, but failed. She was left alone, lost and scattered across the heavens. It was so sad."

Phoebe smiled gently. "I understand the meaning of your dream."

"You do?"

She nodded. "You dreamed of your own life, before the disaster. The Titans were a very peaceful, gentle people, and Titus was a paradise—filled with all manner of life. But then the star fragment arrived and struck your home. Somehow, even though you were unconscious, you must have known your family had been killed and you wanted to follow them. But you could not. As in the dream, you were left behind. But you are not alone, my love. I am here with you and always will be."

Lorin nodded. But Phoebe's explanation didn't feel right. There was more to the dream; she was sure of it. She just couldn't remember enough of it to piece it all together.

"I dreamed of something else too—there was a girl."

Phoebe smiled. "What girl?"

Lorin looked into the deep, sunken eyes of her

guardian. "I cannot remember much—only that it is important that I find her, because she has taken something from me."

"And who is this thief who has taken something from my precious girl?"

"Her name is Emily."

EMILY SAT BEHIND FAWN AS PEGASUS CARRIED
them over the buildings and palaces of Olympus. The
night dwellers' celebration was in full swing back at
Jupiter's palace, and it looked like it might continue
through to dawn.

With her arms around Fawn's slight waist, Emily
could feel the night dweller trembling every time
Pegasus turned.

"It's all right," Emily called, giving Fawn a light
squeeze. "Pegasus won't drop us. I promise you that
you're perfectly safe."

"I do not fear he will drop us," Fawn called
back. "But I have never been this high before, and
it scares me."

Hearing her words, Pegasus dipped lower in the sky. "Is that better?"

Fawn nodded. "I never imagined flying would feel like this. It is both terrifying and exhilarating."

Emily smiled. No matter how long she had been with him, soaring on the back of Pegasus still excited her more than anything. It actually managed to drive the headache back a bit.

Before long they were gliding over their silver beach. Pegasus tilted his wings and lightly touched down in the sand. Emily was the first to slide off his back, and she helped Fawn climb down.

"How was that?"

In the starlight, Fawn's face was flushed. But instead of pink, she had turned a darker shade of gray.

Fawn stepped up to the stallion's head. "Thank you, Pegasus. You have made me feel so much better."

Emily touched Fawn's arm. "Now will you tell us what's wrong?"

Fawn dropped her head. "It is time for the Tartarus Rotation, and Dax has been selected to go. Sapphire and I will be left all alone."

Emily shivered at the mention of the ancient prison.

She knew what it was like to be imprisoned there by Saturn, the malevolent leader of the Titans—in Tartarus she had been locked in an Energy Void and then almost killed in a violent confrontation with the Titans. But she had never heard of the Tartarus Rotation.

"I don't understand. What is the Rotation?"

"It is when all the guards posted at the prison return home and a new set of guards are sent in. They ensure the prisoners are fed and cared for. Each Rotation lasts two full cycles."

The Olympians had no formal means of measuring time. Being immortal, it hardly seemed necessary. But Emily had discovered that a full cycle was almost like a very long year.

"Two cycles," she said. "That's too long for him to be away!"

"It is a great honor to be selected for the Rotation, and Dax is very excited about it. But we wanted to go together. We asked if his Rotation could be postponed until Sapphire and I were old enough to go with him, but they said no. We will each be eligible in our own time."

This was the first Emily had heard of the Rotation. She knew Tartarus was still a prison, but she hadn't thought about the Olympians who would be sent there to guard the prisoners.

"What about your parents? Can't they do anything?"

Fawn lowered her head. "They entered the Solar Stream when I was very young. Something bad happened to them and they were lost. Now it is only us. When Dax goes, Sapphire and I will be all alone."

There was silence as Emily searched for words to comfort the young night dweller. "Maybe I can speak with Jupiter," she offered, "and see if I can get Dax excused from Rotation until you are all old enough to go together."

Pegasus nickered and shook his head.

"You're right, Pegasus." Fawn's voice trembled. "My brother must go. All the night dwellers are eligible for Rotation, but very few are selected. It is how it has always been."

"Just the night dwellers go? That doesn't sound fair."

"We are chosen because of what we are. Night

dwellers can stand living in the dimness of the prison. We do not need daylight, and rarely venture to the surface. It does not hurt us to work there, but day walkers really suffer."

Pegasus nickered again, and Fawn nodded. "That is true also."

She looked at Emily and explained. "Night dwellers cannot be influenced by those prisoners who have the power to manipulate minds. That is our power—that and our ability to communicate with family members over great distances. When Dax is gone, we will still be able to hear and speak with each other. But it is not enough. Sapphire is still very young. She needs both Dax and me."

Emily recalled just how dark and miserable Tartarus was. They had gone there during the day, but it could have been night. It would be a horrible place to have to stay for any length of time. "It still doesn't seem fair."

"The prisoners must be guarded and fed. It is our obligation to them. Dax and I knew he would be eligible for Rotation this year; we just hoped he would be chosen when we were all old enough to go together."

"I am so sorry," Emily said. "When does he have to leave?"

"In two days."

"What will happen to you and your sister?"

Fawn shrugged. "I do not know. We will still work in the nectar orchards. But . . ."

"You'll be alone," Emily finished for her.

Fawn fell silent and they spent the night walking together around the silver lake. Pegasus had said there was no altering the Rotation, but it didn't seem fair. Fawn and her sister were too young to be left on their own. What fate awaited them? Emily knew she had to do something. She just wasn't sure what.

In the distance, the sky was slowly lightening to predawn gray. "The sun will soon rise—we must go," Fawn said. "I cannot be caught in the sunlight."

Emily helped Fawn climb back onto Pegasus and then settled in behind her. "What happens if the sun touches you?"

"My skin will blister and burn. I will become weaker and finally, if I am out in the sun too long, I will burst into flame and it will kill me."

"But Olympians can't die. Ambrosia and nectar heal their wounds and make them immortal."

"Yes, but if we burn completely, there is nothing left to heal. Ambrosia does not work on ashes."

Just like vampires, Emily mused. "We won't let that happen, will we, Pegs?"

The stallion whinnied and put on more speed as he winged his way toward central Olympus. As they drew near, Fawn called instructions to Pegasus to help guide him to her home.

"Yes, over there." She pointed. "To those mountains on the other side of the Temple of the Flame. We live in the caves beneath them."

"You live in caves?" Emily asked.

Fawn nodded. "That way there is no chance of the sun touching us. They are very nice, and we have plenty of room."

Up ahead, the Flame that burned on the plinth at the top of the temple was glowing in the gray skies. This was Emily's Flame. It came from her, was fed by her, and powered the Olympians.

Beyond the Temple of the Flame rose a series of flat-topped mountains that reminded Emily of the mesas in New Mexico that they'd seen while flying out to California.

They touched down before the entrance to a deep cave. A steady stream of night dwellers were filing in.

"We have our own space in a deep part of the cave," Fawn explained. "I would like to invite you in, but, Pegasus, you would not fit in there."

"It's all right. We'd better get home as well. My dad thinks I stayed home tonight, and he's going to be worried." Emily watched as a large group of night dwellers arrived back from the Rotation Celebration. "What about Dax and Sapphire? Are they home yet?"

Fawn closed her eyes. A moment later she opened them and nodded. "They are safe underground. Sapphire is sleeping, and Dax is waiting for me." She gazed up at the increasingly pale sky. "I must go."

Emily reached out and embraced her new friend. "Don't worry, Fawn. We'll figure something out. I know Pegasus said Rotation can't be changed, but I'm going to talk to Jupiter anyway."

"Thank you, Emily." Fawn approached the winged stallion and stroked his neck. "And thank you for everything, Pegasus. This has been the very best night of my life."

Pegasus leaned his head into Fawn. His soft pink tongue licked her pale cheek. With a final wave, Fawn joined the lines of night dwellers descending into the deep caves.

As Pegasus and Emily started to walk away, Emily noticed the speed and urgency of the late arrivals. The sun was just starting to peek over the horizon and the first warming rays flooded over the land.

"Hurry—it is coming!" someone shouted from an entrance. This was the first time she'd heard a night dweller raise their voice. It was filled with genuine terror.

There were still a large number of night dwellers waiting to get into the caves before they were touched by the sunlight.

"They're not going to make it!" Emily's wild eyes looked around for anything that could shelter the remaining night dwellers, but there was nothing. Their normal quiet calm had been replaced with panic as they charged toward the narrow cave openings.

As the first rays of sun touched the exposed night dwellers, screams filled the air.

"They're going to burn up," Emily cried to Pegasus. "We've got to help them!"

Emily was desperate. She searched for something that could block the sun's rays. But there were no trees or buildings nearby, and the Temple of the Flame was too far away to offer shelter. More howls rose as the sun climbed higher in the sky.

She watched helplessly as the gentle people started to smolder. Acrid smoke filled the air. Then an idea came to her, and she prayed she had enough power to act on it.

Emily reached out with her hands and focused on the nearest mountain. She imagined a huge blade cutting a thick slice right off the flat top to make a shield large enough to block out the sun. As soon as she instructed her powers to make the cut, intense pain hit her.

Emily winced as she commanded her powers to work through the pain. She could see the night dwellers starting to burn, and focused fully on slicing off the top of the mountain.

The ground beneath them rumbled as the ancient stone was cut away from the top. Tears rose in Emily's eyes as the searing pain in her head intensified. Every instinct told her to stop. But stopping meant death to all those night dwellers being incinerated by the sun.

Screams filled the air, and Emily barely recognized them as her own. Her nose started to bleed as her powers hoisted the massive slice of rock in the air.

Higher and higher she maneuvered the rocky shield in the sky. When the slice of mountain moved into position above the night dwellers, it blocked out the sun's rays and cast a large, protective shadow on the ground.

Those unharmed by the sun charged out of the caves to assist the wounded. "Hurry!" Emily cried. "I can't hold it much longer!"

Through her cries of pain, Emily heard the faint voice of Riza calling to her.

Emily, stop. . . .

She wanted to obey. But the night dwellers weren't safe yet. The healthy were still carrying the wounded into the shelter of the caves.

"Another moment," Emily shouted. "Just one more moment . . ."

A sudden bolt of lightning seemed to tear through Emily's brain and explode through the top of her skull. The pain was unlike anything she'd ever experienced before.

Paralyzed by it, Emily could no longer control the massive sheet of rock suspended in the sky above them. Without her powers to hold it up, the slice started to tumble and fall.

The last thing she saw before the pain drove her into darkness was the sight of the massive slice of mountain crashing to the ground.

THERE WAS NOTHING. NO LIGHT, NO SOUND, no touch. But at least there was no pain. Emily was barely aware of anything as she rose to a kind of dark consciousness.

The last thing she recalled was a searing pain cutting through her head as she tried to protect the night dwellers. Then something bad had happened. "Am I dead? Is this all there is for me now?" she groaned aloud.

And then she started to hear sounds. Fragmented and confused. Voices raised in anger. Laughter mixed with the sounds of sobs.

"It is not fair! We have done nothing wrong!" A girl's voice rose loud and shrill. It was almost familiar, but it was filled with anger. It came into her mind like Riza's

voice did, but it sounded different. Riza was calm, and Emily could always feel her kind nature. This new voice was enraged. *"You cannot keep us locked in here forever. We have committed no crime—why do you imprison us? Do not walk away from me! Listen, you must let us out!"*

The anger in the voice was rising. Emily could sense a great power simmering, growing, waiting to be freed. She instantly recognized the power signature of the Flame, but it was rising within another. Had she done something so terrible, something so final, that all her powers had been transferred to someone else?

Had Riza abandoned her?

She could also sense that the girl—whoever she was—did not yet know how to release her powers, just as Emily had felt in the early days with her own. The knowledge would come. And when it did, nothing would stop this girl from getting of from wherever she was being held.

The angry voice faded away, just as a radio station does when you drive out of range. Emily tried to tune the sounds back in. But the harder she tried, the more the sounds faded, until they were gone completely.

"Riza?" Emily called into the darkness. "Can you hear me? Please, I need you. Where are you?"

After an age, or perhaps an instant, Emily heard a sound. It was a single sound, repeating over and over. But it was so faint, so weak, that she could barely understand it. Then she realized it was a name.

Over and over again the name kept repeating. There was a desperate urgency to it as it called. *"Arious."*

One by one, Emily's senses returned. She could smell the sweet fragrance of the warm breeze and felt its welcome touch brush across her fevered skin. The sound of barking was the first to cut through the haze. Her dog, Mike, jumped up on the bed and started to whine above her.

"Dad?"

"I'm—I'm here, baby, I'm right here. . . ." His voice broke.

She felt her father's hand slipping into hers. Emily opened her eyes. They felt dry and itchy and filled with sand. Her father's face was red and puffy, his eyes swollen as though he'd been crying.

"Are you all right?" she asked.

He laughed with a strange, choked sound as he sat on the edge of her bed. "I'm fine now. We're all fine now."

Pegasus was on the other side of her bed and nickered loudly. He pressed his head close and licked her with his soft pink tongue. Not an inch of her face went untouched. Emily hadn't seen the stallion this excited in ages.

"What is it, Pegs? What's wrong?" Emily lifted her hand to stroke the stallion's muzzle, but her arm felt like lead. "I feel so strange."

Pegasus left her bed and trotted over to the open window. Poking his head out, he whinnied loudly and his wings fluttered.

Suddenly a roar of cheers rose up from below her window. It sounded as though there were thousands of people outside.

"Dad, what's happening?"

Her father pulled her hand up to his lips and closed his eyes. "They're here for you, Em. They haven't left the palace in days."

"Me? Why? I don't understand."

From outside her room Emily heard the pounding

of footsteps on marble floors. Her door burst open and Joel and Paelen charged in. They looked as though they hadn't slept in days. Paelen's hair was even messier than usual.

"Em!" Joel raced to her side and threw his arms around her.

She felt smothered in his tight embrace. "It's all right, Joel. I'm fine."

As soon as Joel released her, Paelen took his place and nearly squeezed the life out of her. "You must never do that to us again!" he scolded. "Do you hear me? I nearly went insane with worry."

"Do what? Will someone please tell me what's happening?"

Jupiter entered her room, followed by Pluto and Neptune. Before long it seemed like half of Olympus was crowded around her bed. Diana gave Emily a kiss and then hugged her father in relief.

In fact, the relief of everyone in the room was palpable.

They all wore the same expression—fear mixed with hope.

"Please," Emily begged. "Tell me what's happened?"

Her father returned to her bed and took her hand. Joel was crowded in close, and Paelen was glued to her other side. He would make room only for Pegasus to stand by her.

"Pegasus told us you were trying to save some night dwellers by shearing off a piece of mountain to block the sun. He said it was working, but he could feel that you were in pain. Then you started to heat up. So much so that you burned him. Not long after that, lightning exploded from your head and you crumpled to the ground. You've been unconscious for weeks." Paelen's voice dropped. "You were barely breathing. We really thought we were going to lose you."

Emily frowned. Heating up and lightning? She looked at Pegasus. "I burned you?"

"He has recovered," Neptune said. "It is you we worry about."

Emily tried to reassure them. "I'm fine. Even my headache is gone. Yes, I'm tired, but other than that, I feel normal."

"But you were not fine," Jupiter said grimly. "And I am still unconvinced that you are recovered. Emily, you were very close to death."

Pluto, leader of the Underworld, stepped forward. "Not even my powers could halt death's approach. The Flame at the Temple all but went out. All that remained was a tiny ember that Vesta guarded with her life. There was nothing we could do to support it."

"I have just sent Cupid to the temple to see what is happening with the Flame," Diana added. "Now that you are awake, we are hopeful that it has been fully restored."

None of this made any sense to Emily. All she could recall was seeing the night dwellers starting to burn. Then she cut the slice off the mountain to shade them, but doing that made her headache worse. Everything after that was blank, except . . .

"Wait," Emily said. "I remember." She looked at her father. "I have to go to Xanadu right away."

"What?" he cried. "Em, you've only just woken up. What you need to do now is rest."

"No!" Emily insisted. "You don't understand. I didn't pass out, not really. I went to this strange place. It was dark—like the Energy Void Saturn trapped me in. But very different."

"It was a dream," Diana offered.

Emily shook her head. "No, it wasn't. I know the difference. I went somewhere. And while I was there, I heard voices. But more than that, there was a girl. She was angry, and demanding to be released."

"Em, you didn't go anywhere," Joel said. "You were right here. We've been here all this time, watching you, waiting for you to wake up."

"It wasn't a dream!" Emily insisted. She turned to Jupiter. "This girl, she has powers like mine. I could feel them. It was just like me when my powers were first awakened. She was beginning to get angry, and then her powers started to rumble. It was the Flame. I know it was. Whoever this girl is, I think she might have taken my powers from me. She is the Flame now."

"That's impossible," Joel said. "You're the only Flame of Olympus."

"He is right, child," Jupiter said. "If there were another, I am sure we would have discovered her by now."

Emily shook her head. "No, you're wrong. There is another, and she is very angry."

"All right." Joel took her hand in his. "Let's say it wasn't a dream. Who is this girl? Where is she?"

"I don't know," Emily said. "I couldn't see her. I could just hear and feel her. But this wasn't the first time I felt her. It was like she was waking up from a deep sleep. There was a woman with her. I almost caught her name, but then everything faded before I could get it. But this time the girl was much clearer—maybe because she was so angry."

"What does that have to do with going to Xanadu?" her father asked.

"I don't know," Emily said. "The last thing I heard before I woke up was the name Arious, and Arious is the supercomputer on Xanadu. I think it was Riza, trying to warn me. But I can't be sure. I won't know until I get there."

"Em, we still don't understand what that computer is. It might be dangerous for you to go," her father argued.

"Arious will not hurt me. As long as I go in alone and you stay away from me." She looked at Joel. "Especially you."

"What's that supposed to mean?" Joel looked hurt.

Emily had never told Joel or the others about her experience with Arious from the other time line. Because of the reset button, they didn't remember, and there didn't seem to be any point in explaining that Joel had almost been killed by the supercomputer. "It doesn't matter. Just know that no one must touch me while I'm in there."

"I'm sorry, Em," her father said sternly. "Until we understand what's happening to you, I don't want you going anywhere."

"But, Dad—"

"No, Em. I'm sorry. And there will be no sneaking away, either. You will stay here if I have to tie you down."

Something inside Emily told her that her life depended on going to Arious. But when her father was like this, it was impossible to change his mind.

Just as she was about to start arguing back, Cupid flew through the window. He folded his wings and landed on the floor. "We have a big problem." His face was pale as he reported back. "The Flame is there, but it is sputtering and weak. Whatever is wrong with Emily is still happening. Vesta fears the Flame may go out at any moment."

There was a collective intake of breath in the room.

"Now do you understand?" Emily said to her father. "I don't *want* to go to Xanadu. I *need* to."

WITH THE DECISION MADE THAT EMILY would return to Xanadu, Jupiter called for a meeting of those closest to her to be held at the Temple of the Flame. Emily was still weak and had to hold on extra tight to Pegasus's mane to keep from falling off the winged horse on the way to the meeting. Joel, Paelen, and Chrysaor flew close beside her for support.

They landed at the temple, and Pegasus trotted over to the plinth. Vesta stood beside it, wringing her hands. "Oh, Emily," she cried as she ran over to help her down from Pegasus. "How are you feeling?"

Emily shrugged. "Fine, I guess. But I'm really tired. I can barely keep my eyes open."

"She keeps falling asleep," Joel said. "This morning, she actually dozed off in the middle of breakfast."

"It's not that bad," Emily said.

"Um, yeah, Em, it is. Your head landed in your ambrosia—admit it."

"It did," Paelen agreed. "I saw it too."

Pegasus nodded beside her and neighed.

Emily looked sheepishly at her teacher. "Well, maybe I did. But it's not my fault. I just can't seem to stay awake."

"Of course it is not your fault." Vesta wrapped her arm around Emily and led her over to the plinth that held the Flame. Cupid was right. The Flame was there, but it was floundering. It would flash brightly, then shrink down to a very small ember, and then sputter to life again.

"It has not stopped doing that since your collapse," Vesta said. "I just do not know what I can do to support it."

Seeing the Flame so weak struck a chord of fear in Emily because, deep down inside, she felt even weaker. She held her hand over the fire. In the past, the Flame would tickle and never cause her any pain.

But when her hand entered the Flame this time, she felt nothing. No heat, no power, no tickle. Nothing.

"Well?" Joel asked.

Emily shook her head and turned to her teacher. "Why can't I feel anything?"

"I do not know. Something is happening within you, and whatever it is, it is reflected here in the Flame."

"But what could it be?" Paelen asked. "You are Vesta; you know all about the Flame."

"I thought I did, but this is beyond me." Vesta looked at Emily. "What has Riza told you?"

"Nothing," Emily said. "She's gone silent. She's done this once before. I just hope she comes back soon."

The rest of the Olympians had arrived, including Chiron the Centaur. He greeted Emily warmly: "I am pleased to see you up and about again."

Emily had a particular soft spot for the Centaur. She had fought beside him when she time-traveled back to the ancient war with the Titans. They shared many memories that had created a special bond.

"I am pleased that it has been decided that I will escort you to Xanadu," Chiron said.

"I'm going too," Joel said quickly. Before Emily could say anything, he held up his hand. "Don't try to stop me, Em, because I'm going. Don't worry, I won't touch you while we're there. I'm not sure why I can't, but I promise I won't."

"Neither will I," Paelen agreed. "I too am going, whether you want me to or not."

Emily looked at the concerned faces of her two best friends, and knew there were no others she would rather have with her. "We're like the Three Musketeers, right? Of course we're going together."

Pegasus nickered loudly in protest and nudged her.

"Sorry, Pegs. I meant to say we're the Four Musketeers."

Immediately Chrysaor squealed.

"Okay, Five Musketeers."

When everyone had gathered around the plinth, Jupiter cleared his throat. "You all know I hate duplicity and have done my very best never to lie or even mislead our people. It seems the only time I have been forced into deception is when dealing with issues concerning the Flame, and though it pains me to do so again, I must."

He approached Emily and took her hand. "We will let everyone think you are recovered. There is no point in alarming them until we know the cause of your weakness."

Neptune took over. "This means that even though we wish to journey with you, we must not." His eyes found Emily's father. "That includes you."

Steve shook his head. "Now, wait a minute. If you think I'm going to stay here, you're crazy. You want things to look normal? Me going with her would be normal."

"It's okay, Dad," Emily said to reassure him. "Everyone is used to us disappearing. We'll just go there and come right back. I promise not to do anything stupid or go anywhere without telling you. I've just got to know what's happening with me."

Despite her father's protests, it was finally agreed that Emily and her friends would journey to the ancient world of Xanadu alone. The only exception was Chiron. But with their shared past, his presence would not raise any eyebrows among the Olympians.

With plans to leave set for early the next morning,

Emily, Pegasus, and her friends returned to Jupiter's palace. Fatigue was pressing down on Emily, and she wanted nothing more than to return to her room to sleep. Instead, she spent the day cheering at the sidelines as her friends played soccer.

Pegasus refused to leave Emily as she rested on a lounge chair, watching the game. Often she would catch the stallion staring at her, and not the events on the large field.

"I'm okay, Pegs," Emily would say. But deep down, she knew it was a lie. He did too. But with everyone already stressed about her, she couldn't let them know just how much trouble she was really in.

With the warm sun shining brightly overhead, and feeling the security of Pegasus at her side, Emily shut her eyes for just a moment, but then fell into a deep sleep.

Almost immediately she heard the sounds of dripping water; loud, unsettled voices; and crying. She was blasted with an acrid smell of filth that nearly made her retch.

Emily was aware of herself and knew that she was

still Emily. But somehow she was also someone else. It was much clearer this time. She could feel a body moving that wasn't her own. She could see through eyes that weren't hers and hear a voice speaking—a voice that was familiar to her now.

"They cannot keep us here," the voice raged as its owner paced a small area.

"Calm down, my child. You will do yourself harm if you continue to rant like this. We have no choice and must accept our fate. We are trapped here until that foul monster, Jupiter, decides to release us."

"When will that be?"

"I do not know, my sweet."

"Perhaps you are prepared to accept your life here, Phoebe, but I am not. I have done nothing wrong and insist they let me out of here."

Emily felt fury grow within the girl. The Flame was starting to rumble from her core. The girl charged forward and started to pound on hard steel bars, screaming.

Her shrill voice hurt Emily's head, but then Emily realized that the girl had stopped and was now becoming aware of her.

"Who are you?" the girl demanded. *"You cannot hide from me—I can feel you in me. Tell me, who are you?"*

Something warned Emily to stay silent. There was too much rage in this girl, and the Flame within her rumbled violently.

And just as Emily was somehow inside the girl, suddenly Emily could feel the girl entering *her*.

"I know you are there," the girl called. *"Who are you? Why are you here?"*

Emily tried to drive the girl out of her head, but she wasn't strong enough. Had she been up to full power, it would have been easy. Instead, she was helpless to stop the girl from probing deeper into her mind.

"You!" the girl gasped as her powers surged forth. *"You are Emily. You stole part of me. I want it back!"*

"Stop!" Emily cried, breaking her silence. "You're hurting me."

"Give it back. Give back what you took."

The girl's rage was terrible; the Flame rose from her core and burned Emily's mind.

"Please stop!" Emily begged. "Who are you? Why are you so angry?"

"I am Lorin," the voice shouted as her Flame rose. *"Now give it back!"*

"What?" Emily shouted. "I have taken nothing from you. I don't even know you!"

"You have it! I can feel it in you!"

Lorin reached deeper inside her mind and Emily was helpless to stop her. She felt Lorin find the part of her mind that controlled the Flame and all her powers.

There was a sharp intake of breath. *"There it is. Give it back!"*

"Lorin, stop, please. You're hurting me. Stop!" Emily started to scream.

Pain across her face broke the connection. Emily opened her eyes and saw her father and Joel hovering over her.

"I'm so sorry, Em. I had to do it," her father apologized. "You were screaming and your nose was bleeding. I had to slap you in order to wake you up."

Emily sat up, feeling dizzy and disoriented. The soccer game had stopped and all the players were gathered around her. Pegasus was pressing in close, and Paelen took her hand.

"That was awful," Emily said, regaining her breath.

"What happened?" Paelen asked. "Your temperature shot up and your clothes started to smolder. We thought you were about to burst into flames."

Emily looked down at her tunic and saw scorch marks and tendrils of smoke curling in the air. "I've— I've got to see Jupiter immediately."

"I think you should go lie down and get some rest," her dad said.

"No!" Emily cried. "I can't go to sleep again. She'll get back into me. Promise me you won't let me sleep. Hit me, kick me, and bite me if you must, but I can't sleep."

"Emily, you are not making sense. Who will get back in?" Paelen asked.

Emily rose to her feet and started to run toward Jupiter's palace. "Lorin!"

Emily's headache was back, and much worse than before, as she ran.

"We have a big problem," Emily said breathlessly as she burst into Jupiter's meeting chamber. He was in a session with his main advisers.

Jupiter nodded to his guests and asked them to leave—except for his brothers and Chiron.

"What is it, child?" he asked. "What has happened?"

"I'm not sure how to explain it." Emily looked at all the ancient Olympians in the room. "Does anyone here remember someone called Phoebe? She's about my height and has blondish hair. Her eyes are bright blue and she speaks very calmly. She seems to know Jupiter, and calls him a foul monster."

"Phoebe?" Jupiter repeated. "I seem to recall that name. . . ."

"You should," Neptune said. "Phoebe was the chief adviser to Saturn before the war. You sentenced her to Tartarus with the others."

Jupiter looked alarmed. "Do you mean *that* Phoebe?"

"I don't know—maybe," Emily said. "There is a girl with her named Lorin. She's the other Flame I told you about."

"How do you know these people?" Jupiter asked.

"I don't know them," Emily insisted. "But they know you."

"Tell them about your dream," Joel prodded. He

faced the Big Three. "It gave her a nosebleed and nearly set her on fire."

Emily told them what she had experienced. "But these aren't dreams. I'm certain of that now. Somehow I am linked to this girl, Lorin. When I sleep, I seem to enter her mind. Only now she can enter mine. She insists I've stolen something from her."

"What's that?" Joel asked.

Emily shrugged. "I'm not sure. But when she was in me, she said she'd found it and was trying to take it back. It really hurt."

Jupiter rubbed his chin thoughtfully and looked at his brothers. "I wonder if Phoebe has a young daughter."

Neptune shook his head. "If it is the same Phoebe I am thinking of, she has two daughters—Leto and Asteria. There was no Lorin."

"Phoebe's not the problem," Emily insisted. "Lorin is. She has a lot of power. I think the powers she possesses were mine, but she's the one accusing *me* of stealing. She is so angry; I know she's dangerous."

Jupiter frowned at his brothers. "Who is this Lorin?"

They shrugged.

Chiron said, "I do not know. But if she is with Phoebe, she must be important." The Centaur approached Emily. "You told us about the other things you saw and heard. Do you think Lorin is in Tartarus?"

Emily nodded. "I'm certain that's where she is." She looked once more at Jupiter. "Lorin has powers. Maybe they are mine, maybe they are her own. I don't know. But I could feel them growing. She is easily strong enough to burn her way out of Tartarus."

LORIN WOKE TO FIND PHOEBE'S FACE FLOAT-
ing just above her. She was lying in the middle of the
floor of their small prison cell.

"Thank the stars," Phoebe said. "You collapsed. I
was so frightened that I had lost you once again to
that terrible sleep."

Lorin shook her head. "No, no, I am fine. But it
was so strange." She gazed around the cell. "Where
is she?"

"Who?"

"Emily."

"Who?"

"I told you about her. She is the girl I have been
dreaming about—the one who stole from me. But it

was no dream. She was right here. I am certain she is trying to take me over and control me. But I fought back and drove her out."

"I do not understand," Phoebe said as she helped Lorin to her feet. She directed her to one of the beds. "No one was here. It is just us and the other prisoners on this level. Sit, tell me everything."

Lorin sat on the edge of the bed. She shook her head. "There is not a lot to tell. While I was in that deep sleep, I dreamed of Emily. I could not see her, but I could feel her. Now that I am awake, I can still feel her. She came here and was inside my mind. But then I was inside *her* and I learned how to do this."

Lorin held out her hand and a small Flame burst into life. It flickered and danced in her palm. "There was more I needed to learn, but the connection was broken."

Phoebe stared into the Flame with wide, shocked eyes. She tried to touch it, but flinched when her finger burned. "Does this hurt you?"

Lorin shook her head. "No. It just tickles." She focused on increasing the size of the Flame, and it grew in her palm. Holding up her other hand, she repeated the command, and soon both her palms contained a pain-free Flame.

"How are you doing this?" Phoebe demanded. "Only Saturn and a few others can command the elements like this. Your parents did not have these powers."

"I do not know," Lorin said. "I know there is more I should be able to do, but I cannot because she stole it from me. I tried to find it, but Emily, she shut me down."

"What has Emily taken from you?"

Lorin gazed into the Flames and saw them surge. Finally she looked back at Phoebe. "Power. That is what she has stolen from me. My power."

"THIS IS NOT GOOD." JUPITER WAS PACING the length of the meeting chamber. "We need to understand this connection you have to Tartarus. What else do you know about this Lorin?"

"Not much," Emily said. "But whoever she is, she is growing stronger."

Jupiter looked at her with eyes that bored into her very soul. "Just as you are growing weaker?"

Emily nodded.

He looked at Chiron. "When was the Tartarus Rotation?"

"A while ago," the Centaur responded. "The last group of guards have returned and have been rewarded for their service."

Jupiter rubbed his chin. "Pluto, when the sun goes down, I want you to bring several of the most senior of the returned guards to me. Perhaps they can help solve this mystery."

Pegasus came forward and nickered softly.

"Good idea," Jupiter said. "I will speak with them when they rise. And we need to ask Fawn to reach her brother. We must know what is happening at Tartarus."

Emily, who was standing beside Pegasus, frowned. "What are you talking about?"

"Fawn and Sapphire," Paelen translated. "After the incident with the night dwellers, when you collapsed, Pegasus knew you were concerned about them. So he arranged for both girls to be moved here. Their quarters are actually beneath the palace, and they work in the gardens at night."

"You did that for them?" Emily asked the stallion.

Pegasus nickered and nodded his head.

Touched by his gesture, Emily put her arms around his strong neck and hugged him. "Thank you, Pegs. You're the best. We'll speak with them tonight."

"Not you," Neptune said. "After today's revelations,

the sooner you get to Arious, the better. I believe we should not delay. You must leave today."

"I agree," Chiron said. "It will take us a short time to prepare for our journey. We shall meet back here at the Xanadu Arch before sundown."

Emily nodded to Joel and Paelen. "Let's go get ready."

"Now, you promise you'll just go there and come right back," Steve said. "No secret journeys anywhere else."

"I promise," Emily said.

Her father went up to the stallion. "I'm counting on you, Pegasus. I know how strong-willed my daughter can be. But this is too serious for games. Bring her right back, no matter what you learn or what she says. We can take it from there."

Pegasus nickered and nodded his head.

They were gathered in the Artifact Chamber, where they could travel to Xanadu directly through the stone arch that had been created to contain the Solar Stream.

Standing before the arch, Emily shivered, remembering how she had destroyed it to protect

Xanadu from being discovered by the CRU when they occupied Olympus. But in doing so, Jupiter's palace and all of Olympus had been torn apart and had crashed through the Solar Stream right behind them.

"Hey," Joel said, catching hold of her hand. "You okay? You look like you've seen a ghost."

Emily nodded. "Just a few bad memories."

"I wish you would tell us everything that happened back then," Joel said. "Why all the secrecy?"

"There's no point in telling you," Emily said. "When we destroyed the Titan weapon, time was reset and the disaster never happened. That's why you don't remember it."

"But it did happen," Chiron said sympathetically. "I was not here for it, but I saw it through your mind. What happened to our beloved Olympus in that other time line was unforgiveable."

Her father put his hands on her shoulders. "Em, when this is over and you are back to your old self, we are going to have a long chat about everything that happened in the other time line. And I mean *everything*!"

Emily finally nodded. "All right, but let's just see what Arious has to say first."

Her father helped her up onto Pegasus. Joel sat behind her to ensure that she stayed awake during the long journey to Xanadu.

As they drew near the stone arch, Emily looked back at the Big Three. She could see the concern resting heavily on their faces.

"Journey well," Jupiter called, raising his hand to her.

"And do not take any foolish risks," Neptune added.

"I will keep them safe," Chiron promised, taking the lead. "We will return shortly."

LORIN PLAYED WITH THE SMALL FLAME dancing on the palm of her hand. With each moment that passed, she was growing stronger and more confident. Pulling the Flame back into herself, she rose from her bed and walked over to the steel bars that kept them trapped.

She looked at the opposite cell and saw the three prisoners inside, watching her closely. They had asked about the Flame, but Phoebe had no explanation.

"Phoebe, come here."

When her guardian joined her, Lorin peered down the corridor as far as the bars would allow. "Can you feel any of the guards around us?"

The effort of using powers she had not used in ages

showed on Phoebe's face as she felt for the presence of night dwellers. Long ago she had been renowned for her ability to read minds and influence people. "No. There are no guards on this level at the moment."

"Good," Lorin said. "I have an idea."

Lorin bent down to the floor where the bars joined the wall and focused all her attention on the Flame. She was not sure how to do what she wanted to do, but what she lacked in experience, she made up for with determination.

She closed her eyes and imagined the task. She needed a small but intense Flame to melt the metal bars. As she pointed her finger and concentrated, her obsession to get out and find Emily fed her power. A small blue Flame emerged from the tip of her finger. Within moments, the metal of the bar started to smoke and then melt.

Lorin was barely aware of her surroundings as she focused. But she soon became aware of sound. Or rather, the lack of it. Word of her activities had spread fast through the cells on this level, and the prisoners waited to see what she could do.

"Stop!" a voice from across the corridor cried.

Lorin looked up and saw a man of Phoebe's age standing at the bars of his cell. His hair was long and filthy, but he had a commanding elegance. A spark of life was rising in his piercing brown eyes. "I have seen these powers once before—long ago, from a girl just like you. She was responsible for our defeat and imprisonment. If that girl locked us in here, then you, child—*you*—will be our salvation. But you must listen to me. Do no more. Saturn must be informed and we must plan this very carefully. The guards cannot learn of this until we are ready."

Lorin stopped. She and Phoebe blew on the small pool of molten steel to set it and inspected the damage to the bar. It was almost burned right through. She looked into Phoebe's shocked face. "When I am through here, no bars will ever hold us in again," Lorin said.

XANADU. A LUSH GREEN JUNGLE WORLD that was once inhabited by a powerful, benevolent race known as the Xan. Highly intelligent, with powers greatly surpassing those of the Olympians, they were the creators of the Solar Stream and used it to visit countless worlds. If they encountered a dying planet, they would bring the survivors here. Xanadu was Sanctuary. But then, weary of their long existence, the Xan released themselves to the universe, leaving Xanadu to grow wild and untamed.

In the time since Emily's last visit, the jungle had reclaimed most of the clearing that had been built around the Solar Stream entrance. Although Olympians came here regularly, it was a constant battle to keep the jungle from obscuring the entrance to the arch.

Within minutes of their arrival, the travelers heard loud trumpeting and the sound of something tearing through the jungle, getting closer. All the wildlife around them hushed as the sound grew louder.

"Someone knows we have arrived," Chiron said with a grin. "Paelen, I wonder who that could be?"

"Oh no!" Paelen moaned as his eyes scanned the area.

A huge animal, more than double the size of an elephant, with two heads, long purple fur, and sharp, cutting claws, charged through the trees and ran straight to Paelen. Like an excited puppy, the creature, known as the Mother of the Jungle, danced around him and started to lick him all over.

"Emily, please," he begged. "Call her off! I do not need another bath!"

Emily laughed. "Brue loves you more than anyone. No one can call her off, not even Riza."

Joel smiled up at Emily, who was still seated on Pegasus. "It's good to see you laughing again."

Emily's eyes sparkled as she gazed down on him.

She inhaled the sweet, humid aroma of the jungle. "It is good to be back here. I didn't realize how much I missed it."

"Xanadu is part of you," Joel said. "It's like your second home."

News of their arrival must have gotten out. With each passing moment more wildlife entered the clearing to visit Emily. Before long she was covered with colorful butterflies and exotic insects, while beautifully plumed birds landed on the stallion's neck, desperate to be close to Emily, the last Xan.

"We have explored very little here," Chiron explained. "There is just so much to see, so many other continents to visit where the Xan set up sanctuaries for the species of dying worlds."

"I still want to see them," Joel said. He looked at Emily. "Don't you?"

"I do," Emily agreed. "When we're finished, we'll come back here and have a good look around."

Brue ambled up to Pegasus and grunted. She lowered her two heads to Emily's level. The purple fur on the gentle giant was soft and warmed by the sun. Her four eyes revealed nothing but devotion.

"Hello, Brue," Emily said. As she stroked the Mother of the Jungle, she couldn't help remembering how much Brue changed when she left Xanadu. The Mother of the Jungle had grown sharp, tearing teeth, coarse hair, and blazing, predatory eyes. Brue had fought loyally at their side against the Titans, and though her devotion to Paelen never wavered, she had become a terrifying monster.

But the Brue mewing for attention from Emily was anything but! She sighed with pleasure as Emily scratched her behind her ears. "I've really missed you," said Emily.

"It is obvious that everyone here has missed *you*," Paelen said.

Pegasus nickered softly and turned his neck to look up at her.

"He says," Paelen translated, "that when we make you well again, he will bring you back and we will spend time here. He knows that you retain painful memories of the other time line, but now you must put that behind you and see the beauty in this time line."

Emily nodded and patted Pegasus's strong neck. "You're right."

Chiron clapped and rubbed his hands together. "Let us get to Arious so we can solve this mystery once and for all."

Still on Pegasus, Emily led her friends deep into the chambers of the Temple of Arious. Down many stairs and around multiple bends, they made their way toward the secret chamber that housed the supercomputer.

The door to the chamber was shut.

Chiron turned to Joel. "Emily discovered how dangerous Arious is to non-Xan. We must not risk what happened to you last time ever happening again."

"What did happen?" Joel asked. He grabbed Emily's foot as it hung down from Pegasus. "C'mon, Em, isn't it about time you told me?"

"All right, I'll tell you—if only to warn you," Emily said. "In the other time line we came down here, looking for a way to help the Olympians, who were aging and dying. Riza told me about this place and said if Arious could not offer a solution, there was none to be had."

"Was I there?" Paelen asked.

Emily shook her head. "No. Only Joel came down here with me." She stopped short of saying Paelen had been too old and frail to make the journey into the depths of the Temple.

"And . . . ?" Joel prodded Emily.

"And when I hooked myself up to Arious, I started to scream. You tried to pull me away, and when you touched me, you got zapped."

"Zapped?"

"Information meant for me also went into you. It kind of blew your brains out. You collapsed and went into a coma. . . ." Emily stopped speaking as she slid down from Pegasus's back. "We all thought you were going to die."

She dropped her head as the memories pressed down on her. She vividly saw Joel lying so still that he looked dead.

"But I didn't die, did I?" Joel said. "I was fine. No brain damage, no lasting effects."

Paelen came forward and knocked on Joel's head, laughing. "That is because you are too bullheaded! Not even Arious could break through this thick skull of yours!"

"Exactly!" Joel agreed. "Nothing is getting in or out of here! Who needs a football helmet when you've got this noggin?" He laughed again. "Right, Em?"

Emily watched Joel and Paelen laugh at one of the scariest moments of her life. It helped lift a great weight off her.

"Note to self," Joel commented. "When you go into Arious, it's a 'no touchee, no zappee' situation!"

Paelen tapped Emily. "I suggest we try it again, just so I can see Joel's face when he gets zapped!"

"Let's not, but say we did," Emily said, lightening up. She approached the old stone wall and pressed the hidden spot that would open the door to Arious.

It whooshed open and Paelen peered in with wonder. "Wow. Hey, Joel, can you imagine what the CRU would do if they saw this place?"

"They already did," Emily said, feeling better about sharing the darker memories of the past. "Agent B and his men came in here. But when one of them tried to enter Arious, it killed him. After that, they stayed away."

"Serves them right," Joel said. "I wish it had killed them all!"

Chiron looked at Emily and they shared a secret moment of understanding, remembering how Agent B had changed and helped them.

Chiron cleared his throat. "Enough talk about the past—we are here to protect our future. Emily, Arious awaits you."

The room was just as bright and shiny as Emily remembered it. Polished silver walls, white tile floor, and the console to Arious, the supercomputer, resting in the very center. Within the console was an insertion area where the ancient Xan would enter the computer to upload all the things they had encountered on their explorations. This knowledge would then be shared among the people.

Joel stepped up to the insertion area. "Were the Xan a tall people?"

Emily smiled as a memory flashed. Joel had asked that exact same question the last time.

"Yes, they were. Very tall."

"As tall as the giants?" Paelen asked, also repeating a question from before.

"Not quite," Emily answered. "They were very thin, with superlong arms. Their skin was iridescent, like mother-of-pearl, and their eyes seemed to glow pearly white."

"They sound scary," Joel said.

Emily shook her head. "Oh, no, just the opposite. They were almost too beautiful to look at. I have never felt such peace as when I was in Arious. The Xan were the closest thing I can imagine to angels." Emily stepped up to the insertion area. She looked back at her friends.

"Remember, whatever happens, you must not touch me." Her eyes passed from Pegasus to Chrysaor. "Promise me you'll stop them from trying anything if I start screaming."

"You don't have to say that, Em," Joel said seriously. "If this computer zapped me once, I don't want it to happen again."

Emily nodded. Everything told her she had to do this, but as she stepped closer and raised her hands to touch the two receivers, she felt the first waves of fear. As the fear rose, so did the pounding in her head.

She gave one last smile back to Joel and then grasped the two receivers.

o   o   o

The headache vanished instantly as Arious reached into her mind to link with her. The supercomputer seemed to remember that she had been here before.

"Emily?"

Emily looked back inside herself and inhaled sharply. "Riza, is that you?"

Riza smiled radiantly. This was the first time Emily had ever seen the Xan with whom she shared her life. Her beauty stole Emily's breath. She had stunning elliptical eyes that sparkled with her love of life. Her skin was like a glowing pearl. Up close, she was even taller than Emily had imagined, and her fine, long, elegant arms ended in delicate hands. Her smile was bright and filled with mischief.

"Are you all right?" Riza asked.

Emily nodded. "I just never dreamed you'd be so beautiful."

Riza glowed with the compliment. "You have always been beautiful to me."

"Are you kidding?" Emily asked. "Beside you, I'm a mud puddle!"

Riza laughed easily in her high voice. "A very lovely mud puddle."

"Where have you been?" Emily said, growing serious. "I've really needed you, but you were gone. And how can I see you now?"

"It is Arious. She has given us the power to see each other. Emily, you must listen to me. We are in grave danger."

"From whom?"

"From us," Riza said. "Do you remember when we turned Tom into a Sphinx?"

When Emily nodded, she continued. "You were right. I was using too much power to change him. More power than we had. I was certain there was enough of me within us to do it. But I was wrong, and now I have endangered our lives."

"Is that why I've got this terrible headache?"

Riza's head dipped down. "I am sorry, but that was not a headache—it was me. It was the only way I could communicate with you. I had to warn you not to use our powers again. But I failed in that too. You used them to save the night dwellers, but at such a terrible cost to us both."

"I don't understand," Emily insisted. "What's wrong with us?"

Riza sighed, and the pain the sigh held cut through Emily like the sharpest knife. "We are dying."

"What? How?"

"Emily, when you sacrificed yourself to the Temple of the Flame, your heart opened and I was freed. I felt such joy in being with you. And then, when we could finally speak, I knew I had found a treasured sister. Time spent with you has been the happiest of my life. But you already know I am not complete. So much of me is still missing. More powers, my personal memories . . . they're all gone."

"You mean the Flame shards?"

"Yes," Riza said. "I truly believed we had enough power to turn Tom into a Sphinx. Had I been a whole Xan, the change would have been simple. But I am far from whole. Only now do I realize how much of my old self is missing."

"And . . . ," Emily prompted her.

"And then, when you used our powers to slice through that mountain and save the night dwellers, there was a fatal tear in our union. Now it is taking all my strength just to keep us coalesced—which is why I have become silent. I do not have the energy to speak with you and hold us together. Were I to stop for one moment, just one, we would fracture and break apart. But I am growing weary, and the strain is taking a terrible toll on me. I can't last much longer. Emily, we will both fade into nothingness."

A terror Emily had never known before clutched her heart. It wasn't just *her* life at stake. If anything happened to Riza and her, the Olympians would lose their Flame—their powers. "What can we do?"

"We need to find more Flame shards. I need to be restored. Only then can we survive. But time is growing short: We are both weakening—and we are facing a greater danger."

"You mean Lorin, don't you?" Emily said. "She has the power of the Flame."

Riza nodded her pale head. "As you know, when I surrendered myself to the cosmos and broke apart, a large chunk of me crashed to Olympus and became their Flame. But what we didn't know is that at the same time, an even larger piece struck Titus. It must have entered Lorin. Now that we are weakening, she is strengthening and has become aware of us."

"But that's good, isn't it?" Emily said. "If we find Lorin, maybe we can get the power back."

Riza shook her head. "The shard that crashed to Olympus contained my heart, my spirit. To keep it safe, Vesta took it and inserted it within a human girl. It has passed from one girl to another through the ages until I reached you and we were merged together in the Temple. All that I am, my emotions, my intellect—all that made me Riza, a benevolent Xan—went into you. We are two, but we are one."

"What did Lorin get?"

"What I felt from her was my power core. It is stronger than what you received, but it doesn't have Xan benevolence to govern or control it. Lorin is like a wildfire burning out of control. She knows a big part of herself is missing but doesn't understand that the missing part is my consciousness. But her powers recognized me in you, and they yearn to be joined. They are driving her to find us, to reunite."

"Then we've got to get the shard back from her."

"No! We must never meet her," Riza warned. "Emily, right now we are more vulnerable than we have ever been before. We are fighting for our very existence. Any use of power could fracture us beyond repair. But Lorin has all her powers intact. More than you ever had. Should you two meet, Lorin would draw from us our remaining energy and destroy us. She would become even more powerful, but we would cease to exist. Lorin could become Olympus's greatest threat—perhaps even a threat to the fabric of the universe!"

Emily couldn't imagine a greater danger. "So you think if we found another Flame shard, it could save us?"

"It is the only way," Riza agreed. "But there is still a risk. Even if we find a shard, we may not have enough strength left to absorb it."

"We have to try," Emily insisted. "I'm not ready to die yet. Not now, when we have so much to live for: Dad, Pegs, and everyone who loves us. We can't leave them to Lorin's mercy. I've felt her. All she knows is rage."

"You forgot someone," Riza teased as her pearl eyes twinkled with mischief. "I think on purpose. You forgot to mention Joel. He is one of the biggest reasons you are prepared to fight, is he not?"

"Yes." Emily blushed. "You already knew that."

Riza chuckled, and the sound of her laughter was like a welcome breeze on a hot summer day. "Of course I knew," she said playfully. "I love him just as much as you do. I just wanted to hear you say it out loud."

Emily smiled. In the midst of the greatest threat to their lives, Riza was teasing her. "You've been living in humans too long—you've developed a real wicked streak. So what do we do now? How do we find another shard?"

Riza closed her luminous eyes. "Arious," she said to the computer directly. "You know the danger we now face. Would you run a full cosmic scan? Search for anything resembling the energy signature of the Xan. Please help us find another piece of the 'me' that once was."

"Yes, young Riza," Arious responded with a voice that was soft and gentle.

Emily felt a surge of emotion rise from the supercomputer as it set to work. It cared. Arious actually cared! "Is Arious alive?"

"In a manner, yes," Riza said. "For countless millennia,

Arious has absorbed the psyche of the Xan. Every time we inserted ourselves into it, we left a part of ourselves behind."

"I am one of you, young Emily, but I have been alone too long," Arious said sadly. "I will not let you fade away—I will not be alone again. I will find that which you need to survive. The Xan will not end."

And, as frightened as Emily was, she could feel Arious was even more so. The supercomputer didn't want to be alone. Moments later, Arious's voice became shrill. "I have found one—I have found one!"

"Tell us," Riza demanded. "Where must we go to find the shard? How far is it?"

"It is far, but not beyond your reach. You have been there before."

"Us?" Emily asked. "Where is it?"

"A small blue planet. You know it as Earth."

EMILY STAGGERED AND STEPPED CLEAR OF Arious.

"Em!" Joel supported her as she found her balance. "Are you all right? You've been in there two days!"

Emily frowned. "No way—it's only been a few minutes."

Pegasus snorted and shook his head.

She looked around and saw the used bedrolls on the tile floor and leftover ambrosia cakes.

"We are not lying," Paelen said. "You have been in there much longer than you think. What happened? Do you know what is wrong with you?"

Emily tried to remain calm as she explained the information she had received from Arious.

"No!" Joel punched the wall with his silver fist, leaving a large dent in the once pristine metal. Paelen turned away and his shoulders slumped, and Chiron dropped his head in sorrow.

Joel shook his head. "Riza's wrong—you're not dying!"

Chrysaor trotted over to Joel and squealed softly, calming him down.

"Joel, listen to me." Emily put her hand on his shoulder to turn him around. "I'm getting weaker. You know that. I've known something's wrong for a while now."

Joel turned to face her. "Why did she do it?" he rasped. "Why did Riza have to turn Tom into a Sphinx?"

"We both wanted to," Emily said softly. "We thought we had enough power to do it. Alexis was suffering because Juno was separating them. Tom would have been left alone—just a single willow tree stranded in the desert. It would have been too cruel to leave him there."

"But then you would have been safe!" he cried.

"It is no one's fault, Joel," Chiron said. His hooves

clopped on the tile floor as he drew near. "What Emily and Riza did was a kindness. I am certain neither of them could have foreseen this outcome."

"It's not over yet, Joel," Emily said. "I'm still here. We just have to find that Flame shard."

"Find the Flame shard before you accidentally use your powers and die, or Lorin finds you and kills you," he said bitterly.

"Yes," Emily agreed. "I won't use my powers; you will all see to that. Riza will warn me with a pounding headache if I even think about using my powers again. And we have time. Lorin is locked in Tartarus. We can leave for Earth the moment we get back to Olympus. We'll retrieve the Flame shard before she even knows about it, and Riza and I will recover."

Pegasus leaned into Emily. As she stroked his strong neck, Emily could feel him trembling. She hugged him tightly. "It's okay, Pegs. I've told you before, nothing is ever going to separate us. Please help me find the shard, and then everything will be okay."

Paelen spoke softly. "We will find that shard, Emily. You and Riza will be safe—even if I have to tear Earth apart to find it."

They made their way back to the arch, anxious to return to Olympus. But when they got there, they were surprised to find a small figure draped in Pluto's heavy cloak sitting on a log beneath a leafy tree. It was definitely not Pluto, however.

"Emily, thank the stars you are here! I knew you were in the temple, but I could not risk going in and getting lost."

"Fawn?" Emily approached the figure. "Is that you under there?"

The hood nodded and stood up. "Pluto warned me of the sunlight on Xanadu and gave me his cloak to wear."

"Child, what are you doing here?" Chiron asked. He looked up at the bright sunshine filtering down through the trees. "You should be sleeping deep underground, far away from the dangers of the sun. You're too exposed here."

"I had to come to warn you," Fawn said. "You must not return to Olympus. It is under attack!"

"What?" Chiron cried.

Joel charged forward. "By who?"

"The Titans . . ."

SHOCK TORE THROUGH THE GROUP.

"Tell us everything," Chiron demanded.

Fawn started to speak. "You know my brother can speak with Sapphire and me, even though he's in Tartarus?"

"Yes, and . . . ," Emily inquired.

"Not long after he arrived there, the guards discovered a girl with powers just like yours. By the time they learned what she could do, she had freed the most powerful and dangerous Titans. They took control of Tartarus. My brother and all the other guards have been taken captive. The Titans are using the Solar Stream to enter Olympus and attack it."

She turned to Emily. "Dax says they are looking for you. You have something the girl wants."

"It's Lorin," Emily said. "She's learned to use her powers to break out, and now she wants mine." A sudden sharp pain in her head let Emily know that Riza was reacting to the news.

"Why did they send you here?" Joel asked Fawn.

Chiron answered for her. "It is because of the night dwellers' unique ability to communicate with family members across vast distances. With Fawn here, Sapphire on Olympus, and Dax on Tartarus, they are our only means of communication between the three worlds."

"Yes," Fawn agreed. "Jupiter is with my sister right now. He is waiting to speak with Emily."

"Not here," Chiron said. "Let us take you into shelter. You must not remain exposed to the sun. Pluto's cloak may protect you, but only for so long."

Fawn walked under the shade of Pegasus's wing as they made their way back to the temple. When they were safely inside, she removed the cloak. Her skin was still pale, but showed the first signs of blush, like a mild sunburn.

"Wow," Joel said, inspecting her arm. "Even covered, you still burn. How long have you been out there waiting for us?"

"I arrived yesterday and stayed under the trees. But do not worry about me. I am not burned, only singed." Fawn paused and closed her eyes. "Yes, Sapphire, we are together. Please tell Jupiter that Emily is here."

With her eyes closed, Fawn worked as a communicator between Xanadu and Olympus. Emily told Jupiter what she knew.

Fawn repeated Jupiter's words to Sapphire: "Emily, I have given Fawn the blue jewel that will open the Solar Stream. You must use it as your means of transport. We have dismantled the arch here in the Artifact Chamber as a precaution to stop the Titans from finding Xanadu."

"Jupiter, shall I come back and join the fight?" Chiron offered.

Fawn repeated the Centaur's message.

"No. We have things under control here," was the reply. "Saturn will not take Olympus. Even with Lorin under his command, we have the means to stop him. Chiron, I am counting on you to get Emily to Earth. She must merge with the Flame shard there and be restored to health."

Fawn paused and inhaled sharply as the message continued. "The Flame here is still faltering. It rallied for a bit, but then lost its strength. That has not affected our powers yet, but if you fail to find that Flame shard, we will lose our strength and Olympus will fall to the Titans."

"Emily, your father is speaking now," Fawn said. "I wish I could be with you, but I am needed here. Go straight to Earth. Don't come back to Olympus—it's too dangerous. And for heaven's sake, don't use your powers. You have a good team with you—trust each other, stick together, and find that shard. We've given Fawn your food pouch, so you'll have plenty to eat. Don't worry about us; that will only distract you. Em, you're all I've got left. Please, baby, please be careful and stay safe. You know I love you more than anything. I love all you guys, so don't delay. Get going right now. Find that shard and keep away from the CRU!"

"We will," Emily said softly to her father. "I love you too."

Fawn opened her eyes. "They are gone."

"Tell me, child," Chiron asked the night dweller. "When did the Titans attack?"

"The day after you left for Xanadu. I heard the sirens going. Just like when the Nirads first attacked. Vulcan has turned the forge over to weapons-making again."

"Has there been any fighting on Olympus yet?" Joel asked.

Fawn nodded her head. "Saturn is sending his men from Tartarus. He is commanding them from there. Venus is going to lead Hercules and Mars to Tartarus, as she knows it so well. They are gathering a team together to capture Saturn and end the attacks."

Chiron shook his head. "Mars is orchestrating that plan, I know it! He is too hotheaded for his own good. This is a foolish idea, and I am surprised Venus is supporting him. They should stay on Olympus to defend it, not go on the offensive into Saturn's stronghold. They will never get near him!"

"And we should get going to Earth right now," Joel said impatiently. "If Lorin makes it to Olympus, she may find out where we've gone."

"I agree," Chiron said. "But we do have another problem."

"What's that?" Emily said.

"When we go to Earth, we will need to arrive high in the sky so that no one sees us from the ground."

Joel nodded. "You're right. So what's the problem?"

"Me," Chiron said. "Without being boastful, I am a rather large Centaur—and I cannot fly."

DESPITE THE URGENCY, THEY HAD TO DELAY their departure long enough to make a sling large enough to carry Chiron. His horse body was not quite as big as Pegasus's, but he was much heavier. Using the strongest vines in the jungle, they braided lengths together to create a harness to hold him. This was then secured around Pegasus's deep chest, in front of his wings, then around his body.

It was decided that Fawn would fly on Pegasus with Emily, to keep her awake, while Emily could shade the night dweller with her body. When they were settled on the stallion, Emily turned back to Chiron, who was adjusting the last of the harnesses around his torso. "Are you ready?" she asked.

The Centaur gave the thumbs-up. "Whenever you are. Remember, Pegasus, take us up as high as you can. We don't want any surprises when we get to Earth."

Pegasus whinnied in agreement and started to flap his large white wings. He entered into a trot, he moved into a gallop. Chiron raced behind him, careful to keep the harness from tangling. There was barely room in the small clearing for Pegasus to gain enough speed to take off.

As the winged stallion rose in the air, Emily turned back and cringed. They were not climbing fast enough. Chiron shielded his face with his arms as he struck the dense jungle wall with explosive force. The Centaur's loud curses mixed with the sounds of breaking branches, torn leaves, and fleeing birds as he was dragged through the trees.

"Higher, Pegs," Emily called. "Chiron's hitting the trees!"

Pegasus whinnied again and Emily could feel his muscles straining to lift the heavy Centaur above the tree line. When Chiron finally burst free of the jungle, his chest was covered in scratches and he was pulling leaves and branches from his hair.

"Are you okay?" Emily called down to him.

Chiron coughed and spat out leaves. "Not something I wish to repeat anytime soon!"

Paelen laughed hysterically at the sight of the elegant Centaur trying to rub the green leaf stains off his chest. "Thank you, Chiron," he gasped. "I needed a good laugh!"

Even Joel had a smile on his face, while Pegasus nickered with humor.

"Perhaps we shall try that with *you* next time, Pegasus!" Chiron called. Then he faced Paelen. "And you too!"

Paelen shook his head. "No need—I have wings."

"No," Chiron corrected. "What you have are sandals with wings. Take them away and you are as grounded as me." When the laughter settled, he looked up at Emily. "Use the jewel to open the Solar Stream. With my weight, Pegasus will not be able to gain enough speed to enter it on his own."

Emily nodded and looked over at Joel on Chrysaor, and then at Paelen. "I'm going to open it. Are you ready?" When they nodded, Emily held up the blue jewel. "Take us to Earth!"

As they entered the Solar Stream, Emily felt the heavy drawing of sleep. She was so tired, she could barely keep her eyes open.

"Emily, do not sleep!"

Emily's eyes flashed open. Fawn was twisted around on the stallion's back and shaking her.

"I—I'm awake. Thanks. I'm just so tired."

"Hey, Em," Joel called, struggling to be heard over the whooshing of the Solar Stream. "Sing along with me." His deep voice rose loud and clear: *"Ninety-nine bottles of beer on the wall, ninety-nine bottles of beer. If one of those bottles should happen to fall, ninety-eight bottles of beer on the wall. . . ."*

Joel looked back at Paelen. "C'mon, it's easy. Sing to keep Emily awake!"

"Wait," Paelen cried. He flew closer to Joel to be heard. "Why are there ninety-nine bottles of beer on a wall? What wall? And what caused one to fall?"

"It doesn't matter—just shut up and sing!" Joel ordered.

Their voices were nearly hoarse from singing as they burst free of the blinding white light of the Solar

Stream and into a clear blue cloudless sky. A vast and seemingly endless ocean spread out beneath them, with no trace of land in sight.

Emily gazed around quickly and found the sun shining brightly behind them. Her body was working as a shelter for the night dweller. "Fawn, are you all right? Can you feel the sun?"

Pluto's hood shook. "No, I am all right."

"Okay, Em," Joel called from Chrysaor, soaring close to Pegasus's side. "It's up to you. Can you feel where we have to go?"

Emily sat taller on Pegasus and gazed at the horizon in all directions. As the moments passed, she felt . . . nothing.

The first flutters of fear settled in the pit of her stomach. What if she couldn't do it? What if Arious had been wrong and there was no shard on Earth? Everyone was watching her, waiting for her to tell them where they were going, and she couldn't feel a thing. They hadn't factored this into the plan. Earth was so big. They should have realized it wouldn't be this easy.

"Well?" Joel called.

"I don't know!" Emily cried. "Riza said I would feel it pulling me, but I don't feel anything!"

"Emily, calm down," Chiron called from beneath them. "Fear is blocking you. Relax. We have plenty of time. Just focus on what you must do. Let your powers call to each other."

Pegasus strained to look back at her and whinnied. "He says, 'Close your eyes,'" Fawn translated.

Emily closed her eyes and tried to calm down. But she still couldn't feel the shard. Suddenly there was a sharp pain in her head.

"Riza, is that you?" Emily called. "Can you hear me?"

The pain repeated, letting Emily know the ancient Xan could hear her, even if she couldn't respond in words. "Riza, I can't feel the shard. Can you?"

Once again the pain returned, and Emily had never been so grateful for it. Riza knew where the shard was; she could feel it. "I am going to look around slowly. Please pound when we are facing the direction we need to go."

Emily closed her eyes and turned to look over her shoulder. She opened them again and saw the stallion's tail fluttering out behind them as he flew in the sky. "Here we go."

Ever so slowly, Emily started to turn her head to the left. Before long she was facing directly ahead of them. Still there was nothing from Riza. But as she continued to turn her way toward the left, she started to feel a light pounding in her temples that became steadily stronger until Emily's hand shot up to her head and she squinted with the pain. "Ouch! Okay, Riza, I get it. Please stop!"

The pain subsided and Emily sighed in relief. She called forward to Pegasus. "Go to the left, Pegs." She called to the others. "We're going to be okay. I can't feel the shard, but Riza can. C'mon, it's this way!"

LORIN STOOD BEFORE THE LEADER OF THE
Titans. They were in a large chamber near the surface of Tartarus. She had been up to the surface with
Phoebe and they had tasted their first few moments
of pure freedom.

What Lorin discovered was that Tartarus was a terrible place cloaked in dark, scudding clouds. Heavy,
freezing winds battered her, and the rain quickly soaked
her to the skin. Every inch of ground was covered with
mud, as though it never stopped raining. Even though
it appeared to be day, there was very little light. Tartarus
was, in a word, miserable. In fact, she preferred being
inside the cells on the lower levels of the prison. At least
they were warmer and dryer than up on the surface.

"Where is she?" Lorin demanded. "Saturn, you promised to give Emily to me if I released everyone from their cells. I have done as you asked—we are all free."

Saturn patted her head. "You will have her. But you must be patient. Jupiter and his people are as clever as they are conniving. They will do anything to protect their 'Flame' and keep her from us. But do not fear; I promise I will give her to you. And when I do, your powers will finally be complete."

"Listen to Saturn, Lorin," Phoebe said gently, placing her hand on Lorin's shoulder. "We have time. Look around you. Everyone here has been trapped in this prison for an eternity. A few more days will not make much difference."

"But I need her," Lorin insisted. "I need to be made complete, and only Emily can do that."

"And you will have her," Saturn promised. He smiled, but the smile didn't reach his ice-blue eyes. His tone was fatherly, but it was not natural to him. "However, we may need your assistance to get her."

"What can I do?"

"My warriors have started entering Olympus, but

they are encountering great resistance. They have captured prisoners and are bringing them back here. When they do, I want you to join me for their interrogation. We want to learn everything we can about Jupiter's plans."

"How can I make them tell us anything?"

Saturn smiled. "You have great powers, powers that are growing. Show them what you can do, and what will happen if they refuse to talk."

"You want me to hurt them?"

His hand patted her head once more, but Lorin felt it wasn't a natural gesture for him. "If necessary, yes."

Lorin paused. She needed Emily. The girl had taken powers from her and she wanted them back. But her fight was with Emily, not the Olympians. Was she prepared to hurt strangers? "Perhaps if I went to Olympus, I could find Emily."

"No!" Saturn shouted. Then his voice calmed. "No, I prefer you to stay here, where you are safe. I do not want you to meet her until you are stronger. Stay here and learn to control your powers. We will bring Emily to you." Saturn paused and his face darkened.

"Now tell me. Are you prepared to do what you must to get ahold of Emily? To help free us from this wretched world and to reclaim what has been taken from us? To finally give us back Olympus?"

Lorin considered for a moment longer. How far would she go to finally feel complete?

She would do whatever she had to.

"Yes, Saturn, I will help. To get Emily, I will do anything."

ALL THROUGH THE LONG DAY THEY JOUR-
neyed over the vast ocean. The singing tapered
off as they became too hoarse to continue. As the
sun started to descend, Emily could feel the strain
Pegasus was under from carrying Chiron. She prayed
that they reached land soon so that he could rest and
regain his strength.

But they continued long after sunset. Stars shone
above them, and a sliver of moon was rising. Emily
yearned to use her powers to light a Flame to guide
them, but with just that small thought, Riza sent a
painful warning in her head that drove it quickly
from her mind.

The benefit of flying at night was that Fawn could

finally push back her hood. "I hate that thing," she complained.

"It's keeping you alive," Emily reminded her.

"I know, but I do not have to like it."

They continued in silence for many long hours until Fawn lifted a finger and pointed. "What is that over there?"

Emily squinted but could see only darkness. "I don't see anything."

"But it is right there," Fawn insisted. "It is a very big man standing at the top of a mountain."

"Pegs, can you see what Fawn is seeing?"

Pegasus whinnied, but the sound was weak. Emily reached forward and felt his strong neck. It was burning hot and covered in a film of sweat.

Paelen swooped closer. "He cannot see anything. Neither can I."

"But it is right there," Fawn insisted.

"Night dwellers have powerful night vision," Chiron explained from below. In the absolute darkness, Emily could no longer see the Centaur, but they could hear him. "If Fawn says there is a large man on a mountain, he is there."

"Tell us where to go," Emily instructed Fawn. "We need to land soon—Pegasus is exhausted."

Fawn nodded and gave them directions. Emily hoped the night dweller was right. Pegasus couldn't take much more.

"Wait. I see something!" Paelen shouted. "She is right. There is a giant man on a mountain. His arms are outstretched and there are lights shining on him."

"There are no giants on Earth," Emily said.

"It is not a giant," Chiron called. "It is a very large statue of a man. I can see him too."

As they headed toward the man on the mountain, the sky around them began to get lighter. "The sun is coming up." Fawn pulled her hood back up. "I hope we reach the man before it rises fully."

As the minutes ticked by, Emily and Joel first saw what looked like a star on the water. But as they flew closer and the sky lightened further, they were finally able to see what the others saw: a massive statue, standing at the top of the mountain. Lights from a large city were blazing beneath him. His arms were outstretched, as though offering protection to the people below.

"I know where we are!" Joel called excitedly. "We're in Brazil!"

"Brazil?" Emily asked.

"Yes! Look, that's Christ the Redeemer. It's a huge statue overlooking Rio de Janeiro. My mom and dad took us there when I was a baby. We have pictures of my mom and me next to the statue."

"The shard is in Brazil?" Emily called. "Riza, is it true?"

When there was no answer, Emily realized she'd phrased the question wrong. There was no way Riza could answer it. "Okay, can you give me one pound for yes and two for no? Is the shard near here?"

There were two brief flashes of pain in her head. "No," Emily said. "Does it still feel far away?"

One pound let her know the Flame shard was still a long way away. Emily called to the others. "We still have a long way to go. Pegs, when we're over land, find somewhere quiet to set down. You need to rest and we need to keep Fawn out of the sun."

"In Rio?" Joel asked. "Have you never heard of it? It is a busy city!"

"So is New York," Emily called. "But we found

places to hide there. Besides, look at Pegs—he's exhausted. We need to land now."

With each wingbeat, the sky lightened. Soon Emily could see Chiron suspended beneath them in the vine harness and Joel on Chrysaor with Paelen beside them.

Just as the first rays of dawn lit the horizon, they approached the shoreline of Rio. Small, rugged, peaked islands poked out of the water, and lush green mountains rose in the distance. The islands beneath them were closest, but they all looked as if they were fully inhabited and offered no protection for the Olympians.

"How about there—in the rain forest?" Joel pointed to a large area of dense jungle nestled on a mountain range directly behind the Christ statue. It was surrounded by city and homes. It wasn't ideal, but with Pegasus straining to stay airborne, they didn't have much choice.

"It's up to you, Pegs," Emily called. "Do you want to land down there?"

In answer, Pegasus started to descend and maneuver

toward a small opening in the green forest canopy. Chiron touched down first, and then Pegasus flapped his wings to avoid hitting the Centaur.

Emily was first off Pegasus and then helped Fawn down. Pegasus was panting, and his eyes were half closed with exhaustion. The powerful muscles in his shoulders, around his wings, were twitching, and he was covered in foaming sweat.

"You did so well, Pegs." Emily stroked his face, hoping that her touch would restore him, as it always had in the past. But her powers remained dormant. Pegasus's body had deep red welts where the harness was cutting into his skin, and he was too tired to lift his head. "I'm sorry my powers aren't working to heal you."

Joel and Chrysaor came up behind her. "Let's get some ambrosia into him—that should help. Just as soon as we are fully undercover, we'll make sure he and Chiron have plenty."

Chrysaor squealed softly. Joel bent down and stroked the coarse, wiry hair on the winged boar's head. "And you, my friend, will have more than you can eat."

Emily reached into her tunic pocket and pulled out the leather pouch. It was an ancient Xan relic with the capability to create whatever food it was told to. "So don't worry, Chrysaor, you'll all have enough ambrosia and chocolate ice cream to make you sick!"

Emily looked back at the Centaur. Just as it had with Pegasus, the vine harness had cut deeply into his skin. Paelen was helping him step free of the vines. "You too, Chiron. You must eat."

"Thank you, Emily. I will." As he stepped clear of the harness, he looked at it as if it were a deadly enemy. "I dread the thought of putting that thing on again. I cannot remember a time when I was more uncomfortable." He trotted up to Emily. "Do you have any idea how much farther we must travel?"

"Not really. All we know is that it's still a long way away."

Chiron gazed around the clearing. "Then we had best find cover and get as much rest as possible. I do not relish the thought of being captured and ending up in a zoo."

"You'd be lucky to end up in a zoo," Paelen said. "The CRU caught me the first time we were in New

York, and I still have nightmares about what they did to us there."

"Don't remind me," Joel said. "Let's go."

They entered the trees, and Emily gazed around. "I always dreamed of seeing the Brazilian rain forest. I just never imagined it would be like this."

"Me neither," Joel agreed. "It's a shame there's no time for sightseeing. I would love to visit Rio."

They waded deeper into the jungle and found a place to settle.

Dawn arrived with the sounds of birds singing to greet the day, while animal noises filled the trees around them. Within minutes, Pegasus was resting, with Chrysaor close beside him. Chiron sighed in contentment as he settled down next to them.

Emily produced a banquet of food from her pouch. She gave five scoops of chocolate ice cream to Fawn. Her black eyes shone as she discovered the taste of the sweet, cold treat.

While the sun climbed higher overhead and filtered through the canopy, the exhausted Olympians drifted into much-needed sleep. Pegasus fought to stay awake with Emily, but soon he, too, was lulled into a sound sleep. Fawn was wrapped up in Pluto's cloak and nestled under the cover of the stallion's large wing, a place usually reserved for Emily. But there would be no sleep for Emily—she couldn't risk it.

She stood with Joel, keeping vigil over the exhausted Olympians. "It's all right," Emily said to him. "I know you're tired too. Go get some sleep."

"I'm fine," he argued. "What about you?"

"Me? Sleep? Are you kidding? If I sleep, Lorin will be able to access me, and there's no telling what might happen then."

"But you need to sleep—everyone does."

Emily shook her head. "I'm tired now because I'm getting weaker. It has nothing to do with me *needing* sleep. Ever since I became the Flame of Olympus, I haven't needed to sleep. I did it because I thought I should, and I enjoy my dreams."

Emily hated to admit the truth, especially to Joel. It was just one more sign that she wasn't human anymore. "Riza says sleeping is a throwback to my human days. All I am now is energy in the shape of Emily."

Joel reached for her hands and held them tight.

"No offence to Riza, but you are more than just energy. I can feel your hands in mine. Smell the perfume in your hair. You are Emily, and you're a part of me. I couldn't love a ball of energy, but I love . . ." Joel seemed unable to continue.

Emily's heart started to pound. "You love . . . ," she gently prodded him.

He looked down at her hands in his and dropped them abruptly. He shuffled his feet and wouldn't meet her eyes. "Nothing . . ." His voice had lost its softness. "But you are not just energy and you know it. You're not going to fade away—I won't let you."

Emily tried to hide her disappointment. He had told her how he felt so long ago. Why was it so difficult for him now? "I may not have much choice. Riza is trying to keep us together, but she's getting really tired."

Joel walked away from her and for a few moments seemed to find the leaf of a nearby tree particularly interesting. He turned to face her again. "Are you scared?"

Emily nodded. "When I first entered the Temple of the Flame and sacrificed myself, I believed I would die, and in truth I did—well, at least my body died. I never imagined that I could become what I am now. I was frightened, but I knew I was protecting Olympus and Earth. I was sad to leave my dad. But you and I had only just met. I cared about you and Paelen and Pegasus, but what I felt then was nothing compared to how I feel about you all now. You are all the best part of my life, and I can't imagine a day without you in it. And whatever I am now, I don't want it to end. It terrifies me to think I'm fading away. . . ."

"Then don't!" Joel insisted. "You have powers, Emily. Powers I can't even imagine. There's got to be something you can do to stay alive."

"There is—and that's finding the shard. The power in that Flame shard is to me what food is to you. Without it, I'll die."

"Is there no other way?"

Emily shook her head and looked at the ground. She knew that if she looked up into Joel's eyes, she would start to cry. She had to keep strong. Joel pulled her into an embrace and held her tight. He kissed the top of her head. "Then we'll find that Flame shard and end this."

LORIN PACED THE CONFINES OF SATURN'S
new throne room, waiting for news. Tartarus was a
hive of activity as the freed prisoners plotted revenge
against Olympus. Saturn had promised to deliver
Emily to her, but she noticed that he was more interested in pursuing Jupiter than in keeping his word.

Earlier that day, warriors had charged in with news
that they were being invaded by Olympians. While
Lorin was ordered to remain in the throne room, Saturn joined the fight.

It seemed to take forever.

Lorin felt, more than heard, the arrival of Phoebe.
"Wonderful news, my child. We have captured the
invaders. They will tell us—"

"Is one of them Emily?" Lorin cut in. "Have they brought her here?"

Phoebe shook her head. "No, not Emily. It is Venus, Mars, and Hercules. They came here hoping to capture Saturn."

"Who are they?"

"Followers of Jupiter, who helped to lock us in this prison."

"What about Emily?"

Phoebe put her arms around her. "All in good time, my child, all in good time. If Emily is as powerful as Saturn says, then we will need to plan her capture very carefully. Saturn tells me she has powers enough to defeat even the strongest Titans. He believes that if we take Olympus first and capture Jupiter, Emily will be forced to surrender."

"How long will that take?" Lorin asked.

"Not long," a new voice said.

A large, powerful figure charged into the chamber. Lorin recognized him as Hyperion, one of the higher-ranking Titans that she had freed from the lowest level of the prison. He was Saturn's brother and looked a lot like him, with the same muscular build, long chestnut hair, and beard. But the big difference was his eyes. Though they were the same pale blue color, Hyperion's weren't quite as cold and threatening as Saturn's.

"Hyperion," Phoebe said respectfully, bowing her head. "What news of the invaders?"

"It was a fierce battle. But if Jupiter thought sending a team to Tartarus a second time would work, he was gravely mistaken."

"A second time?" Lorin asked.

"Long ago," Phoebe explained, "Jupiter led a team in here to free the Hundred-handers. Emily was with them. None of the Olympians' powers worked at all, but Emily's did. She was the one who freed the Hundred-handers and changed the outcome of the war."

Hyperion nodded. "Jupiter was a fool to send Olympians here again—especially without the girl. Hercules may be strong. But we have numbers on our side. He could not defeat all of us. Venus is also very strong, but she is no match for Titan strength."

"And what of Mars?" Phoebe asked.

"Subdued," Hyperion said. "Venus is in a rage at

what we have done and will not hold her tongue. She is doing her best to challenge Saturn's patience."

"Where are they?" Phoebe asked.

"Below," Hyperion said, "which is why I am here. Saturn has ordered me to bring Lorin down to the holding cells. The prisoners are refusing to talk. He feels her presence may work to persuade them."

Hyperion said the word "persuade," but Lorin knew he actually meant "torture." "What does he want to ask them?"

"Does it matter?" Hyperion demanded. "When Saturn gives a command, we obey. Even you, Lorin. You are a Titan; Saturn is your leader. You will do what he tells you to without question."

"But—"

"This is not open for discussion," Hyperion barked. He caught her by the arm and pulled her forward. "We are grateful to you for setting us free. But now the real work must begin."

Lorin realized that in the short time she'd been awake, she knew almost nothing of her people. Phoebe had explained a few things, but not enough. One thing was certain, though—when Saturn gave an order, everyone around him jumped to obey it.

Hyperion led them down to the very lowest level of Tartarus. When it seemed as if they had reached the deepest layer of the prison, he kept walking and wound his way to a hidden set of stairs going down. Almost immediately the smells around them changed. Lorin was accustomed to the general stench of the prison. But the smells that assaulted her now were enough to make her nauseous.

Farther and farther, the steep, narrow staircase descended. It ended in a long, deep puddle of water with a stink so awful, she had to plug her nose to avoid being sick.

"How far is it?" she asked in a nasal voice as she trudged through the foul water. There was no way she was going to unplug her nose. Not even for Saturn.

"Just ahead," Hyperion answered.

They entered a vast cavern—so tall she could barely see the ceiling in the darkness above them. Three massive cells lined one wall. The thick bars climbed up at least five levels, and each bar was thicker than she was.

"Who are these for?"

"Saturn kept the Hundred-handers in these cells," Phoebe answered. "Until Emily released them."

"So Emily was in here?"

"She was."

Lorin looked around with renewed interest. Emily had been here. Her eyes had seen what she was now seeing and her nose had smelled the same horrible things. It made an odd kind of connection between them.

"This way," Hyperion ordered as he drew Lorin toward the first cell.

Saturn was already there, facing the three prisoners. Peering inside the cell, Lorin saw Venus first. She was the most beautiful woman Lorin had ever seen, though her clothes were torn from fighting and her face was smudged with dirt. Beside her was a man even bigger than Saturn. He was covered in cuts and bruises, but his face was like thunder—it had to be Hercules, son of Jupiter. The third prisoner was lying unconscious on the floor.

"Ah, Lorin," Saturn said. "I am glad you are here."

"Lorin?" Venus dashed to the bars of her cell to

get a better look. She frowned. "You are Lorin?"

Lorin swallowed back the bitter bile that rose in her throat as she unplugged her nose. She nodded.

"Emily said you were young. You two could be sisters."

"You know Emily?"

Venus nodded. "She is a very dear friend of my son, Cupid. If you help us out of here, I will introduce you to her."

"Where is she?" Lorin demanded as she dashed to the bars and caught hold of Venus's hand. "Tell me—I must find her."

"Lorin, stop!" Saturn shouted. "We will find Emily. Right now we need to concentrate on taking Olympus." His gaze fell on Venus. "Do not try to sway Lorin to your ways. She is a true Titan and serves only me. Now tell me, what defenses does Olympus possess these days?"

"We will tell you nothing," Hercules spat. "We defeated you once, Saturn, and we will do so again. You will not destroy Olympus as you tried to do before. It has taken generations for Titus to be able to support life again after you destroyed it developing your weapon. Olympus will not suffer the same fate."

Saturn shrugged. "You can make this easy on yourself, or difficult. The choice is yours. Just remember, while you have your Flame of Olympus, I possess the Flame of Titus. Lorin has all the powers that Emily has—perhaps even more. She is mine to wield as I choose."

"You would use this child as a weapon?" Venus cried.

Saturn laughed. "Of course!"

"Time here has driven you mad!" Venus turned to Hyperion. "You are fools to follow him. Not long ago, Jupiter and the council agreed to return you and your people to Titus, now that it can sustain life again. This *was* going to happen. But after this, it will not. Saturn has ruined your chances for freedom. You will remain on this desolate world for all eternity."

"Empty words, Venus!" Saturn barked. "Let us see how empty your words will be when I have shown you the power of my Flame!"

Saturn put his hand on Lorin's shoulder. "If you wish to find Emily, this is what you must do." He walked with her to the neighboring cell, which held the captured Olympian guards. Lorin looked at the strange people Phoebe had called night dwellers. Sensitive to light, they lived only in darkness.

"Lorin, summon your Flame. Show Venus and Hercules what you can do. Burn the night dwellers."

Phoebe gasped.

"You wish me to hurt them?" Lorin asked.

"You heard me. I command you to summon your powers and burn them."

Lorin's eyes landed on the youngest night dweller in the cell. He was a boy not much older than her. His hair was white and his eyes dark. He was shaking his head and pleading softly, "No . . ."

"I am to kill them?"

"If necessary, yes," Saturn said. "You will stop when I tell you to."

Hercules started to shout. "Saturn, do not do this! She is just a child! You must not force her to kill!"

"Then tell me what I want to know."

"Phoebe," Venus pleaded. "You cannot want this. You have known motherhood. Think of your grandchildren—Diana and Apollo, in Olympus. Do not let Saturn use Lorin this way. It is wrong, and you know it!"

Phoebe was shaking as she turned to Venus. "He is my leader. Just as you serve Jupiter, I must do as he commands."

"Lorin, listen to me," Venus called. "You do not have to do this. There is another life for you, far away from here, where you can know the sun and true freedom. Come to Olympus with us. You will be welcomed there."

"She has everything she needs here," Saturn spat. He caught Lorin roughly by the shoulders. "Do not listen to Venus. That is her power. She will seduce you into thinking she cares. It is a lie. I am the only one who truly cares for you, as if you are my own child. Not Phoebe, not them. Just me. I want you to find Emily and finally gather all your powers together. But to do that, we need information—information that they hold. You must do this if you ever hope to be made complete."

Complete. That was all Lorin wanted to be. *Needed* to be. She had to reclaim her powers from Emily. She had promised to do anything necessary for that to happen. But she never imagined it would mean torturing or killing people.

"Please tell him," Lorin said to Venus. "Do not make me hurt these people. Tell him what he wants to know."

"Do not speak!" the night dwellers shouted to Venus and Hercules. "Olympus must be protected. Do not think of us."

Lorin's eyes passed from Venus and Hercules to the night dwellers. "You must tell Saturn what he wants to know . . ." She inhaled deeply and raised her hands, which burst into Flame.

"Please!" Venus begged. "Stop—they are innocent!"

Lorin closed her eyes and released her powers.

"NO! DAX!"

The camp was awakened by Fawn's cries. She writhed on the ground beneath Pegasus's wing and howled in pain. "It burns. Stop! Please, it burns!"

With a final cry, Fawn curled into a tight ball and wept.

"What is it?" Joel pulled her from beneath the stallion's wing and helped her to her feet. "Fawn, talk to us. What's happening?"

Fawn threw her arms around his neck and started to cry. "I think Dax is dead. . . ."

"What!" Emily cried. "How?"

The night dweller clung to Joel. Her shoulders

shook as grief overcame her. "L-L-Lorin killed him. She—she k-killed all the guards."

Chiron prized Fawn's arms away from Joel and caught hold of her hands. "I am sorry, child. I do not mean to be harsh. But you must tell us everything. What has happened on Tartarus?"

Fawn gulped down air, trying to regain control. After several deep breaths, she repeated what she had heard from her brother, down to his final agonizing moments, when Lorin unleashed the Flame on all the night dwellers trapped in the cell.

"She—she did it to force Venus and Hercules to talk," Fawn concluded. "But they would not. So she killed them."

Chiron released Fawn's hands and walked away, rubbing his chin. "This is very bad indeed." He turned to Emily. "She is just a child—how could she do this to those innocent people? I cannot conceive of such horrors. What kind of monster is she?"

"The kind who's not afraid to use her powers for evil," Joel said.

Chiron shook his head. "If Lorin can do that,

there is no telling what else she will do for Saturn. Olympus is in very grave danger."

"Lorin does not want Olympus," Fawn said weakly. "She only wants Emily."

Paelen corrected her. "Not Emily, just her powers. If she is prepared to kill to gain information for Saturn, there is nothing she will not do to get Emily."

"Fawn, did your sister feel what you felt?" Joel asked. "Does Sapphire know about Dax? Has she told Jupiter?"

Fawn sniffed and nodded. "She heard and felt everything. Diana is with her, but she is crying too much to tell them what has happened."

"Talk to her," Chiron said. "Tell her you will be back with her soon, but she must tell Diana everything. Jupiter must be informed that Venus, Mars, and Hercules have been captured and are in grave danger."

"You don't think they'll torture them?" Emily asked.

Pegasus was on his feet and standing beside Emily. He nickered softly.

"I agree, Pegasus," Chiron said. "Saturn is insane.

He will stop at nothing to get his revenge against Jupiter—including torturing his own daughter."

"Daughter?" Emily asked.

Chiron nodded. "Venus is Saturn's child. But Saturn does not perceive family the way we do. He locked his children in Tartarus, after all, fearing that they might one day overthrow him."

"And that's what they did," Joel said.

Pegasus gazed up through the canopy of trees and the sunlight flickered down. He nickered and Paelen translated. "The sun will be setting soon. We must be ready to leave the moment it is dark. Please get the harnesses ready."

A heavy silence fell on the camp as Emily, Joel, and Paelen helped get Pegasus and then Chiron into the vine harness. Lost in grief, Fawn was settled in the cover of the thick trees to avoid the sun's rays.

"I wonder if we have time to go into town to get a better harness, or at least some cushioning," Joel offered as he inspected the vines. "These vines are strong, but they're cutting into the both of you. Another solid night of flying will be agony."

"A bit of pain is a small price to pay to help recover

that Flame shard," Chiron said. His eyes landed on Emily. "I fear that very soon you will have to go up against Lorin. That battle will not be easily won. You must have all the power you can before you face her."

Emily nodded. "I know. I can feel it coming too. I just hope we find the shard before she finds us."

Pegasus nickered again and pressed his head to her. She welcomed his support, but as she stroked his thick neck, Emily knew it would not be enough when she finally faced Lorin.

Getting into the air proved more difficult than it had on Xanadu. For one, the clearing was small and offered less room for takeoff. But the second, bigger problem was how stiff and tired Pegasus was. They were just starting the night's long journey, but the moment the vine harness settled into his back, he whinnied in pain.

Chiron gritted his teeth as the harness settled into his cuts. Emily prayed they wouldn't have far to fly.

They followed a straight northwestern line, but by dawn they were still no closer to the shard. With Olympus in increasing danger, they risked flying through the day. Emily shielded Fawn from the sun with her body, and with only the jungle beneath them, there was, hopefully, little chance of being seen.

On and on they traveled, over the dense, tree-filled rain forest. Halfway through another long night of flying, Emily saw starlight sparkling on another large body of water, lying just ahead of them.

"Pegasus, everyone—we have to land!" Emily called.

"What is wrong?" Joel called.

"Look, there's water ahead. We know the shard is that way, but we don't know how far over water we have to go. Pegasus and Chiron are exhausted. I think we should land and rest one more day before we take on another ocean."

Pegasus whinnied and Chiron called from beneath them, "No. We must keep going! We do not know what is happening on Tartarus. We must not waste a precious moment."

"No, Em's right. The sun will be up soon anyway," Joel said. "I think we should land. You need to rest."

Under protest, Pegasus settled on a place to land. It was a sandy beach with sharp, rocky mountains rising up behind it. After a quick search, they found a cave cut deep into the mountain face.

As they freed the stallion and Chiron from the harness, Joel said, "When the sun is up, Paelen and I will head into the village we saw on the way in."

"Why?" Emily asked. "We don't need food or water—my pouch can supply that."

"Don't you think it's more important to find out where we are?" Joel snapped. "It's not like the pouch can tell us that. For all we know, we're in the middle of Mexico or just about anywhere else! You say Riza's telling us to go over *another* ocean—don't you think we should find out how far that could be?"

Joel's sudden change in mood felt like a slap in the face to Emily. They were all under stress; they were all tired. There was no need for him to snap at her. She walked over to Pegasus and stroked his neck. In the darkness, she could barely see the stallion. Pain and fatigue had removed his bright, healthy glow. Only the stars sparkling on the water and the sound of the low waves brushing the shore told her where the ocean was.

"Come on, Pegs, let's go cool you off in the water.

It'll clean out those cuts from the harness. Joel and Paelen can do whatever they want."

"Emily, wait . . . ," Joel called after her. "I'm sorry. . . ."

Chiron trotted up to them and carefully entered the water with Emily and Pegasus. "Do not be too hard on Joel," the Centaur said. "He is terrified of losing you."

"He has a funny way of showing it," Emily said. "He didn't have to bite my head off!"

"That is very true. But you must understand, Joel is a very strong young man. Right now, however, he feels powerless, and it is frustrating him. He has found something very special with you and fears it is slipping away. He does not know how to tell you what he is feeling. Give him time. I am sure he will work it out."

Emily nodded. Chiron was right. Joel was frightened. She just wished he would talk to her.

The healing waters of the ocean did wonders for Pegasus. They walked into the water until their bodies were submerged.

"Ahhh . . . ," Chiron sighed, enjoying the cool

water. "I needed this, though I doubt the scars on my flanks will ever heal."

Emily stayed in the water with Pegasus and Chiron until daybreak. When the sun slowly appeared, they made their way into the dark sea cave. Joel, Paelen, and Fawn were clearing away debris and gathering up seaweed to form a soft bed for Pegasus.

"Em," Joel said softly when she approached the entrance. "Can I talk to you for a minute?"

Emily nodded and let Joel lead her out of the cave and closer to the water.

"I'm really sorry. I didn't mean to snap at you."

"I know." Emily sighed. "We're all stressed. And you're right. We should know where we are." She gazed out over the ocean. "There's a lot of water out there, Joel. What if the shard is in the ocean?"

"I really don't know," he said. "But if what Riza says is true, you can't drown. It would be up to you to go get it."

The sound of barking shattered the stillness. They looked down the beach and saw two black Labradors running in the surf. Their owner, a short, stocky middle-aged man, was jogging along the shoreline.

When the dogs saw Emily and Joel, they came charging over.

"Hi there," Emily said, scratching the closest dog.

The man followed, and Emily felt self-conscious when she noticed him taking in their Olympian tunics and Joel's silver arm.

He started to speak to them in Spanish, and Joel managed to answer him, gesturing with his real arm and keeping his silver one very still. He was pointing to the water and then to the area around the cliffs. Whatever he was saying, the man seemed very interested and offered his own comments as he too pointed to the water. Eventually the man smiled, nodded at Emily, and jogged away with his dogs.

Joel caught her arm. "We've got a problem. Let's get back to the others."

Back at the cave, Joel explained what the man had said. "The guy was a bit freaked at first, but I told him our parents brought us here on holiday after I lost my arm in a car wreck. He seemed to believe me. I'm just glad he didn't ask where we were staying!"

"Did he give you any idea where we are?" Paelen asked.

Joel nodded. "We're in Ecuador."

This announcement was met with blank expressions from the Olympians. "Ecuador," Joel repeated. "Don't you get it? This is the last bit of land for a thousand miles. That's the Pacific Ocean out there. If we follow the same course, we'll hit the Galápagos Islands. After that, it's just open water until we find the Hawaiian Islands, and then Japan."

"How do you know this?" Paelen asked.

"It's called geography. It was my favorite subject at school. The Galápagos were first on my list of places I wanted to run away to. Then Japan. I researched where they were and saw they were in a straight line. The Galápagos are in the middle of the ocean."

Joel looked at Emily. "Riza, do we still need to go northwest?" he asked.

One painful throb in Emily's temples made her wince. She rubbed her head and frowned. "She says yes."

"Well," Joel said. "It looks like we're going toward the Galápagos, then Hawaii, Japan, and maybe even China."

LORIN SAT ON THE EDGE OF HER BED, FEEL-
ing sickened by what she had done. At what Saturn
had made her do. She never imagined it would be so
simple. Just command the powers to be released and
people died.

What wasn't so simple was dealing with the
sounds, sights, and smells of what happened after
that. In the instant before she opened fire she saw the
older night dwellers push the younger boy down and
jump on top of him.

They shielded him with their bodies. Why would
they try to save one boy?

It had worked. While many of them seemed to
vanish in a puff of smoke and ash, some farther back

in the cell survived, but suffered horrendous burns. The sounds of their moans would haunt her for the rest of her life. She could see that the boy had survived, but he too was badly wounded and unconscious. She wanted to help him, but Saturn refused her request. He'd told her not to let the weakness of emotion in. Night dwellers were nothing. They were trash to be swept away.

But the boy's eyes, the pleading in his black eyes right before she unleashed the Flame on those poor people—she couldn't get that out of her head.

Lorin rose and started to pace the confines of her cell. The door was open; she could leave anytime. But go where? Where could she go to get away from the horrors she had committed?

And then there was Phoebe. It was as if she did not care. Phoebe said the survivors would be moved into the cell with the Olympians, to act as a reminder of what would happen if they continued to defy Saturn, but she showed no regret. Lorin wanted to go back down there to check on the boy. But Saturn had put guards on the stairwell and had ordered her to stay away.

"This is all Emily's fault," she said bitterly to herself, as though placing the blame on someone else would ease her guilt. If it weren't for Emily, she would have all her powers, and would not have had to hurt those people. She had to find Emily to become complete. Then she wouldn't have to obey Saturn and hurt people. With or without Saturn's permission, Lorin would track Emily down. But how?

Focusing all her energy on that, Lorin drove the memories of what she'd done from her mind. She had heard of the Solar Stream that the guards used to transport food and supplies from Olympus. Now that the Titans had full run of the prison, perhaps she could use the Solar Stream to finally find Emily.

EMILY STOOD AT THE ENTRANCE OF THE cave, watching the sun cross the sky. Deeper inside, everyone was sleeping soundly. Fawn had tried to stay awake to keep her company, but exhaustion and grief over her brother pulled at her until she couldn't keep her eyes open.

As late afternoon arrived, Fawn woke up and started to scream: "Dax? Dax, speak to me—tell me what happened?"

Emily ran back to her. "Fawn, it's all right. You were just dreaming."

"No, it was not a dream. Dax is alive, I can hear him. I am awake and I can still hear him!" She threw her arms around Emily as everyone in the cave awoke. "Emily, he is alive!"

"He has just gone back to sleep," Fawn explained after she had closed her eyes and listened to Dax. "He told me he is in a lot of pain. He is alive because the elder night dwellers protected him with their bodies while Lorin attacked."

"How many survived?" Chiron asked.

"Not many. The wounded have been moved into the cell with Venus, Hercules, and Mars. They are tending to them as best they can. But Dax and the others need proper help."

"But he's alive!" Paelen cheered.

Fawn screamed in happiness, louder than Emily had imagined she could. Feeling her joy, Emily, too, started to shout and laugh with the others. The news that Dax was alive seemed to energize everyone and give them hope. Joel whooped and danced around the cave with Chrysaor, while Pegasus, despite his exhaustion, flapped his wings and whinnied in celebration.

Emily pulled out her pouch and produced a celebratory banquet. There were ambrosia cakes, a full

Italian meal for Joel, and bucketloads of chocolate ice cream and chocolate bars.

As they ate, Emily had an idea. She pulled out the small blue jewel. "Chiron, this jewel," she said. "It opens the Solar Stream and lets us cross the universe, right?"

"That is correct," Chiron said.

Emily rolled the gem in her hand. "Would it work for shorter trips? Like to the Galápagos? And then to Hawaii and maybe Japan?"

"I believe it might," Chiron answered.

Joel suddenly caught on to what she was thinking. "So we use the Solar Stream to get us to each point so Pegasus won't have to fly all the way!" He ran over to Emily and hugged her. "Em, you're a genius!"

Emily laughed. "Only if it works."

When night arrived, they walked to the beach.

"I must say, I am not looking forward to this," Chiron complained as he moved the strong harness vines into position on his open wounds. "I doubt my skin will recover."

"I just hope Em's idea works," Joel said. "I doubt

any of us could make it over a thousand miles of ocean otherwise."

"It has to work," Emily said. "It *will* work!"

She helped Fawn up onto Pegasus and then climbed up behind her. She looked back. Chiron was ready and gave her the thumbs-up. Joel nodded and Paelen grinned.

"All right, Pegs," Emily said. "We're ready. Get us in the air and I'll use the gem."

Emily and Fawn felt every muscle in Pegasus's body tense in protest as he started to trot stiffly down the dark beach and finally enter a gallop. He flapped his wings and, with a mighty leap, took off.

Behind them, Chiron leaped high in the air at the same time, which reduced the drag on the stallion. Soon they were high in the night sky.

"Ready?" Emily shouted. She held out the jewel and called, "Take us to the skies over the Galápagos Islands!"

The swirling Solar Stream opened and they flew into it. In less than a blink of an eye, they flew right out again. Emily frowned. "Did we just go anywhere?"

Fawn looked around. "Yes. The land behind us is gone. Up ahead I can see islands. Some are small and some are large." She screamed, "It worked! We are at the Galápagos!"

Joel shouted and cheered while Paelen clapped his hands. When they flew closer, Joel called, "Em, can you feel the shard?"

Emily closed her eyes. "Riza, is it here?" After a moment, there were two bursts of pain in her head.

"It's not here!" Emily called. "We'll try Hawaii next."

The second journey through the Solar Stream was a fraction longer than the first. The moment they exited the blazing, swirling lights, Emily felt a slight tingling sensation. Then, just as suddenly, pain started in her head and she rubbed her temples.

"Are you all right?" Fawn asked.

"Yeah. It's just a small headache. I wish I had some painkillers. . . ." It was only after she said it that she realized she had a *headache*!

"Riza," Emily called, excited, "is that you making my head hurt?"

A single, painful throb pounding in her temple said yes.

"Are we close? Is that the shard I'm feeling?"

Emily thought her head would explode from the single shooting pain in her temples.

"Everyone, listen—we found it!" Emily shouted. "Pegasus, can you hear me? Riza says we're here! Can you take us down lower?"

After a moment, Joel called ahead, "Fawn, can you see Hawaii?"

Fawn leaned farther forward. "I do not know, but I can see some islands."

"How many?" Joel asked.

Fawn counted. "There are eight. How many does Hawaii have?"

Joel whooped. "Eight!"

THE HAWAIIAN ISLANDS LAY DEAD AHEAD.

As they approached the first and largest island, the tingling Emily felt changed. It became a strange drawing sensation pulling her onward. "I feel the shard!" she cried. "Pegs, it's just ahead of us, calling to me."

Emily also felt the light pounding of Riza's celebration inside her head. But when they were over the Big Island, Emily sensed that the shard wasn't there. Disappointment crushed her. "It's not on this one. Maybe it'll be on one of those middle islands."

With each wingbeat Pegasus was faltering. He had pushed himself hard, but carrying the weight of Chiron over long distances was taking a heavy toll. He shrieked as his left wing tucked in fast and then flashed out again, and they almost stumbled in the sky.

"He is getting wing cramps," Paelen cried. "We must land. He will not make it much farther."

"He doesn't have to!" Emily called. "Down there, Pegs—I feel the shard! It's right down there on that smaller island in the middle, the one with the clouds covering half of it. Take us down!"

It was not a smooth flight. But it became much worse the moment they entered the gathered clouds above the island. Rough winds tore at them, and torrential rain made it impossible to see more than what was right in front of them.

Weak from the long flight, the stallion was swept up in a powerful gust of wind that blew him sideways. Pegasus shrieked and screamed, fighting to stay on course. Behind them, Chrysaor squealed as he was buffeted by the winds. Chiron swung dangerously in the harness, destabilizing Pegasus further.

"Chiron, hold on!" Joel called.

"I am trying," the Centaur called. "Pegasus, we need more speed—I can feel the tension on the vines increasing!"

Deeper into the storm they descended. Emily's hair whipped into her face, and rain blurred her vision. The rain seemed to be blowing in every direction as they fought to stay airborne.

"Fawn, hold on!" Emily cried.

Fawn tucked herself into the stallion's neck and clung to his whipping mane while Emily kept her arms tight around the night dweller's waist.

Paelen flew up to the stallion's head. "Hurry, Pegasus—one of the vines just snapped. They will not hold much longer!"

Emily turned back and in the weak light saw a second line snap.

A gust of wind caught Chrysaor and flipped the winged boar over, casting Joel off his back.

"Joel!" Emily howled. She instinctively reached out with her powers, but a flashing agony in her head stopped her. "Riza, no, I need to get to him!" But the pain would not let up.

Joel somersaulted in the sky. Just as he fell past the Centaur, Chiron kicked his back leg out. "Joel, catch my leg!"

Joel's silver hand shot out and caught hold of one

of Chiron's back hooves. His added weight put too much strain on the stretched vines, and more started to break.

"Pegs, take us down now before they fall!" Emily shouted.

They were still high above water but approaching the shoreline. Buildings with blazing lights had been constructed all along the beach. There was nowhere private or secluded to land.

With the added weight of Joel, Pegasus could take no more. He whinnied and started to fall out of the sky. He stretched his wings fully and tried to glide. But when another gust of wind struck them, Pegasus was too exhausted to fight it.

They half glided and half fell past the beach and toward the roof of a tall rectangular building. Lights shone from the windows and the sides were lined with balconies. With his last bit of energy, Pegasus gave one final, mighty flap of his wings to get them closer to the building.

They were coming down fast. Emily closed her eyes and braced for impact. Pegasus hit the roof and tumbled, his descent uncontrolled. Behind them came the explosive sound of shattering glass.

Emily and Fawn were thrown from the stallion's back and hit the rooftop several yards away. They rolled to a stop, and when Emily sat up she found she was facing what looked like the entrance to an apartment with sliding glass doors. They had landed in the penthouse apartment's patio area. The windows were dark, and she prayed no one was home. But their crash had been noisy. Had anyone else heard them?

"Chiron!" Fawn cried. She was on her feet and running toward the railing that circled the rooftop.

The harness! Emily realized.

It was dangling over the side of the building. She looked at the vines still around Pegasus and watched as he was dragged slowly toward the edge of the roof by the combined weight of Joel and Chiron.

Emily ran to Fawn, who was at the railing. Chiron was swinging against the side of the balcony on the floor beneath them. He was looking down at Joel and trying not to move.

"Joel, hold on!" Chiron called. He looked up. "Paelen, get down here. Help Joel!"

Joel was clinging to the Centaur's hoof and dangling

at a fourteen-story fall. He had a gash on his forehead that was bleeding into his eyes.

Paelen flew down and was by Joel's side in an instant. He wrapped his arms around him. "Joel, I have you. Let go."

Emily held out her hand to use her powers to draw them up, but a shooting pain in her head drove her to her knees. "Riza! Please, I need to help them."

But the pain would not stop.

"Up!" Paelen commanded his sandals. "Take us to Pegasus!"

The tiny wings on the sandals obeyed. Paelen carried Joel up so that Fawn could help haul him over the railing. As soon as they were safe and on their feet, they leaned over and pulled the vines to lift up Chiron. But for all their strength, and with the whipping rain making everything slippery, the Centaur was too heavy for them to lift.

"Joel, look!" Emily cried as another vine snapped. There were now only four vines holding the Centaur. As another started to fray, Chrysaor flew down to Chiron so that he could catch hold of his rear legs.

"Go!" Chiron cried to the winged boar. "Fly!"

Chrysaor squealed and flapped his wings, straining to lift Chiron. From above, the others struggled to pull up the vines. But their combined strength wasn't enough to pull the Centaur up to the roof.

"You are not strong enough," Chiron called. "Secure Pegasus!"

"He's going to fall!" Joel cried.

"No, he's not! Stay here and hold on to him!" Emily ordered. She ran back to Pegasus. The stallion was barely conscious and lying on his side. Rain splattered his face and closed eyes. "Pegs, please get up! Chiron is going to fall. We're not strong enough to lift him. Please, you've got to pull; you're his only hope. Get up and pull before the last vines break!"

Pegasus lifted his head, and Emily saw he was close to collapse. Blood poured from his nostrils. At first she thought the blood was just from a cut, but the flow was too heavy. The strain of the long flight was too much, and his heart was on the verge of bursting.

But hearing that Chiron was in danger was enough to get Pegasus to rise. As he climbed to his feet, Chiron's weight pulled him toward the edge of the roof.

Joel jumped between the railing and the stallion's

rump and started to push Pegasus away from the edge and back toward the middle of the rooftop.

Paelen flew back over the side of the building and hovered beneath the Centaur to support his weight.

With Emily, Fawn, and Joel now pushing Pegasus from behind, the stallion started to pull.

Little by little, Chiron was lifted up closer to the railing. Emily dared to steal a look back and saw the Centaur let go of Chrysaor and catch hold of the lowest bar on the railing.

"Almost there." Chiron strained as he climbed the railing. "Just a bit more . . ."

"Keep going, Pegs," she cried. "It's working. He's almost here!"

Pegasus whinnied against the strain. The sounds of his screams mixed with a twanging sound as another vine snapped. Paelen cried from below as he pushed the Centaur up. But with one final heaving shove, Chiron made it over the top of the railing and fell onto the roof.

"They're safe!" Joel panted.

With those final words, Pegasus screamed and collapsed.

23

"PEGASUS!"

Emily dashed to the stricken stallion. Pegasus was crumpled on the roof, completely still. Chrysaor was squealing to wake him up, but the stallion was unconscious.

"Joel, Paelen, help me with him!"

Everyone gathered around Pegasus. He was still breathing, but his breaths were labored.

"He used his last reserve to save me," Chiron said. "He needs a safe place to rest and recover."

Now that the immediate danger was over, they were able to take in their surroundings. They were on the large roof of a building. Other buildings rose higher around them. Some still had their lights on, and they all seemed to have balconies. But with the high winds and heavy rain, no one was out in the storm.

Emily rose and peered through the glass doors of the penthouse. "It doesn't look like anyone's home. If we get this door open, maybe we can move Pegasus inside before the sun comes up."

Chiron clopped over to the glass door. "We must never assume we are alone," he said. He reached for the handle and grunted. The lock snapped and the door slid open. "Paelen, you are an excellent thief. Go in and see if there is anyone inside. But be careful. If there are people, try not to be seen."

"I am no longer a thief!" Paelen uttered angrily. "Why will no one believe that?" But he slipped past Chiron and entered the apartment.

Outside, Emily looked around. "I really hope no one heard or saw us. That wasn't a quiet landing. All we need now is to have to face the police!"

"We will deal with that as it comes," Chiron said. "Pegasus is our first priority."

Paelen reappeared. "It is empty. We are alone."

"All right, everyone," Chiron said. "We must get

Pegasus inside. Paelen, tie one of those vines to Chrysaor. The rest of you, get ahold of another vine. We are going to have to drag him in."

While everyone was straining to move Pegasus, Emily wished more than ever that she had her powers back to help lift the stallion.

After much effort, they succeeded in getting Pegasus inside. Paelen closed the glass door and shut the curtains before Joel switched on the lights.

"Uh-oh," Joel said. He was standing by a desk. "This isn't an apartment." He held up a welcome folder. "It's the Outrigger Reef on the Beach Hotel."

"So?" Paelen said.

"It's a hotel room. Anyone can book in here at any time."

"As I said, we shall deal with it if they do," Chiron said darkly. "But right now, Pegasus is our main concern. Emily, Fawn, please see if you can find something to cover him. Joel, Paelen, help me settle Pegasus's wings so he is not lying on them. We do not want to worry about broken bones as well."

Emily soon discovered that they were not just in a hotel room, but in an exclusive suite that was larger than her New York apartment had been. There were three bedrooms, a kitchen, two bathrooms, and the large living area where Pegasus and Chrysaor were lying. Emily put two large pillows beneath the stallion's head and carried in a pan full of warm, soapy water to wash the blood from his nose and muzzle. Without her powers to heal him, this was all she could do to help him feel better.

While she worked, Joel, Paelen, and Fawn went back out on the patio area and cleaned up the mess they'd made with the crash landing.

"Well, we've got great ocean views here," Joel said, returning. He looked at Chiron. "You did a number on the room beneath us. You bent the railing and smashed the glass doors on the balcony. How hard did you hit it?"

"Hard enough to give me a pounding headache," Chiron said, rubbing his bruised forehead. "And I have no doubt I will be pulling glass from my flanks for some time."

"At least you're okay," Emily said. "I'm thankful we all are."

Joel nodded. "But for how long? By the looks of

it, we couldn't have crashed in a busier tourist area. Keeping hidden is going to be tough."

"Hopefully, we won't be here that long." Emily stood, carried the pot of used water to the kitchen, and emptied it. "I can feel the pull of the shard. We are very close to it. I'm sure tomorrow we'll find it. Then I'll heal Pegasus and we can go."

"Until then I suggest we rest," Chiron said. "That last bit was very difficult. We are all exhausted." The large Centaur settled himself in front of the hotel room door. No one was going to get in with him lying there.

Joel and Paelen refused to go to a bedroom, and settled on one of the sofas in the living area. They turned on the television, but after a few minutes, Joel was sleeping soundly.

Fawn was fascinated by the moving pictures and listened with great interest as Paelen explained about television. But as with Joel, fatigue quickly overcame them and they were soon asleep.

Emily was lying on the floor beside Pegasus. She was listening to his breathing. It was still labored, and sounded like he had inhaled half the ocean.

She feared that his lungs had filled with water or blood. The journey had been too long for him and he had pushed himself beyond his limits. What had it cost him?

Watching the flickering television as fear and worry pressed down on her, Emily soon drifted to sleep. . . .

LORIN WAS ANXIOUS TO SPEAK WITH VENUS to learn more about Emily. But every attempt she made to visit the prisoners was blocked by security. In fact, Saturn had posted even more guards on the route leading to the lowest level of Tartarus to stop her from descending. He instructed them not to talk to her about the prisoners or the fate of the wounded night dwellers.

With nothing left to do, Lorin made her way back to her cell. She noticed that guards were posted everywhere she went and watched her constantly. Everyone called her a Titan—said that she was one of them. But she wasn't being treated like one. In fact, she began to feel like a prisoner among her own kind.

She wasn't even allowed up to the surface anymore.

Saturn had said he had a special plan just for her and that she was crucial to the retaking of Olympus, so she must be protected—hence the guards. But he wouldn't say what that plan was or outline her part in it.

Lorin tried talking to Phoebe about the restrictions, but her guardian kept insisting they were for her own good. But what good was coming from keeping her all but trapped in her cell? What's more, Phoebe had changed. It wasn't anything she'd said or done; it was the way Phoebe looked at her. Almost as if she was frightened of her.

Lorin settled down on her bed. She needed to find Emily more than ever. She had to find a way out of here. Closing her eyes, she tried to block out the noise of conversation and the sounds of others moving around. Before long, she had slipped into sleep.

Emily!

From the moment she fell asleep, Lorin felt the connection again. Emily was also sleeping—she could sense it. But in her own sleep, she felt Emily's fear. Something was very wrong.

Lorin followed the strand of connection and was soon deep inside Emily's mind. As the connection solidified, she recognized another presence within her. It was a small and fading light, but held echoes that were so familiar to her.

Echoes that *were* her!

That was it! That was what Emily had taken from her. Not just power, but all the things that made her whole. As Lorin probed deeper, a name came to her. A name she recognized—the name of the "someone" she used to be.

"I was Riza. . . ."

Suddenly it all made sense. She was once someone else. Someone very ancient and very powerful.

"Give her back!" Lorin demanded of Emily. "You cannot keep her!"

"I didn't take her," Emily cried. "Riza is part of me; I was born with her. You can't take her—she is me!"

"Then I shall find you and take you, too! I need to be whole again."

"Why?" Emily challenged. "So you can kill more people? I know what you did, Lorin. The night dwellers were innocent—you had no right to hurt them."

"I did as Saturn commanded," Lorin said, shocked that Emily knew what she had done.

"Saturn is a monster. He ruined his own world and killed many of his own people in the hope of destroying Olympus. Ask Phoebe. She'll tell you. All he wants is power. And now you've killed for him. That makes you just as much a monster as he is!"

"Stop it!" Lorin shouted. "You are just trying to confuse me. Saturn is not evil. He cares for us. Jupiter is the evil one. He imprisoned us here. He is the one who would destroy us if he could. I want Riza back. I need to be complete."

"By killing people?" Emily cried. "You may have Riza's power, but you are not her. She is gentle and kind. The Xan protected lives; they did not destroy them. You will never be her!"

"Yes, I will!" Lorin cried. "I will find you, Emily; I will find you and I will free Riza. We will be whole again, and you will be gone forever!"

Lorin pressed deeper into Emily's mind. She pushed through a barrier Emily fought to protect, and she saw—Pegasus.

"Pegasus." Lorin inhaled sharply at the sight of the

winged stallion. "He is beautiful. When I am whole, Pegasus will be mine!"

"No!" Emily shouted. "Pegasus belongs to no one. He is free. He will never be yours—I will stop you."

Lorin probed even deeper into Emily, and saw memories and a life that fascinated her. She saw Emily's mother, her father, Diana, Joel. . . . But then she saw a face that stopped her in her tracks. A face with a crooked grin and dark eyes that sparkled with pure mischief.

"Who is that?" Lorin asked.

"Get out of my head!" Emily shouted.

"It is *my* head, Emily. All the things you have, all the people you care for, should be mine, not yours."

Lorin pushed further. "Paelen . . ."

"Leave me alone!" Emily shouted.

Now Lorin was more determined than ever to find Emily. She had a family and friends who cared for her; she had everything that Lorin desired most. "Where are you?"

"I'll never tell you."

Lorin fought through Emily's defenses and discovered that she and Pegasus were looking for something very important. Lorin inhaled. There it was!

"You want that Flame shard, but it belongs to me!" Lorin cried.

"You can't have it!" Emily exclaimed. "It's part of Riza, and she's part of me. All you have are her powers. Her heart and consciousness reside within me. I will fight you to protect her!"

"I know you have no powers left," Lorin said. She saw the long journey that Emily and the others had taken. They'd gone to a world called Xanadu and then to Earth. After a long flight, they had made it to a place called Hawaii.

"Outrigger Reef on the Beach Hotel . . . ," Lorin said slowly, reading from Emily's mind. "See? You cannot hide from me, Emily. I see everything. You are in Hawaii and I am coming for you. Then Riza, Pegasus, and Paelen will be mine!"

"NO!" EMILY HOWLED.

A painful slap across her face pulled Emily from her slumber. Her face felt hot and wet. She wiped her nose and saw red, then gazed up into the concerned faces of Joel, Paelen, and Fawn. She started to rock back and forth, chiding herself. "I shouldn't have slept. Why did I fall asleep? I've been so careful. But now I've ruined everything."

"Em, calm down." Joel handed her a towel for her nosebleed. "Talk to us. What happened?"

"Because I slept, Lorin got into my head again. She knows everything, including why we're here."

The others were waiting patiently for her to tell them more. Emily turned back to them. "Her strength is growing. I couldn't stop her. She knows I have no powers now and that I need the shard to survive. She said she's coming here to get me and free Riza." Emily paused. "She's also coming here to take Pegasus and . . ."

"And?" Chiron asked.

Emily's eyes settled on Paelen. "And you."

"Me?" Paelen cried. "What do you mean, me?"

"She saw you in my mind. She saw all of you. But the moment Lorin saw you, that was all she would focus on."

"Me? But—but why?"

"I'm not sure. All I know is that she wants you," Emily answered darkly. "And she's coming here to kill me and take you."

"Well, she cannot have me!" Paelen insisted. "I do not want this Lorin—especially if she wants to hurt you."

"She won't care what you want, Paelen. She has so much power. More than I ever had. I don't think she even realizes what she can do. But one thing is clear. She doesn't understand that killing the night dwellers was wrong, because Saturn told her to do it."

"This is very disturbing indeed," Chiron said, rubbing his chin. "You say she does not yet understand all her powers? If Saturn does, and if he can control her enough to make her kill, that makes Lorin the ultimate weapon against Olympus and all the other worlds along the Solar Stream."

Emily heard echoes in her memory of being called the same thing. Agent B once claimed that she was *the ultimate weapon*. But she had been raised to care for others and see all life as precious. Lorin hadn't. Saturn was teaching her. And that meant she was more dangerous than could ever be imagined.

Emily shook her head. "It's so strange. While I was with her, I had the impression that Lorin was like a very young child who was never taught right from wrong. She just follows Saturn's orders. It's lucky she still doesn't know how to use her powers fully. She is obsessed with finding me and taking Riza back. I can't reason with her. She just wants what she wants without considering the damage she can do."

Chiron nodded. "Then we still may have some time. If she does not understand her powers, she will need to use the Solar Stream to get here."

"Then we've got to find that shard!" Joel said. He focused on Emily. "You need to be up to full power when you face her."

"I know," Emily agreed. "But even so, I'm frightened she'll still have more power than I do."

Pegasus remained asleep on the floor. His breathing was steadier but still sounded like his chest was full of fluid. Chrysaor had recovered much faster, and was awake and hungry for all the ambrosia Emily could pull from her pouch.

While Chrysaor ate, Emily and Joel stepped out onto the patio area to check what damage they had done during the night. Emily shielded her eyes from the sun, which was directly overhead. "I thought Las Vegas was hot. But this place is crazy hot."

"At least the breeze helps," Joel offered as his dark hair blew into his eyes. He inhaled deeply. "It's beautiful here. I wish we were here for a different reason."

The only sign of their struggle was a large dent in the railing around the edge of the patio. From where they stood, leaning over the side, they couldn't see all the damage Chiron had caused to the balcony or the glass doors on the floor beneath them, but what little they saw was bad.

The ocean sparkled below them. Small boats, surfers, and bathers dotted the clear blue water. A shallow beach with palm trees and people lounging in the sun was adjacent to the building. Toward the right they overlooked a flat roof that was another part of the hotel.

They stood watching the activity on the beach below them. A young family was playing in the sand, and the children's laughter could be heard. The air was fresh and clean and the ocean calm after the raging storm the night before.

To the far right, the beach continued beyond their hotel until it stopped at a marina containing large sailboats. To the left, the beach circled around and ended at a mountain. Everywhere they looked there were hotels. There was an area on the beach where tourists could rent surfboards. The whole shore was filled with people. Lots and lots of people.

"You were right," Emily said. "We couldn't have picked a busier place to land." She turned and went to the other side of the patio, which gave her a view farther inland. "Those mountains behind us would have been easier to hide in."

Joel nodded. "We're lucky we made it this far. I thought for sure Pegasus was going to crash into the ocean. But this hotel isn't safe. We were lucky the suite was empty, but I checked the hotel brochure. This place is a resort. This suite won't be empty for long. We've got to get out of here before we're caught."

They heard children's laughter and the sounds of footsteps behind them. On their guard, Emily and Joel turned instantly to see a boy and girl running along a narrow path that ran between their suite and the railing along the roof's edge. The children rushed past Joel and Emily and climbed up onto the first rung of the railing at the end.

"Gregor, Elsa, be careful. Get down from there!" A young American woman ran up behind them. She slowed down when she saw Emily and Joel. "I am so sorry to disturb you. We've got the suite behind yours, and these two monsters wanted to see the ocean. They're not happy with our view of Honolulu."

"Of course," Joel said. "We do have a beautiful view here."

Emily saw the woman frown as she took in their tunics. She looked as if she was about to say something when her son distracted her.

"Mom, look," he squealed. "There it is. There's Diamond Head!"

The boy must have been about ten, with a sweet round face and warm chocolate-brown eyes that were flashing with excitement. His sister had the same eyes, but had long blond hair. She couldn't have been older than five or six.

"That's Diamond Head," the boy said knowingly to Emily. "It's a volcano."

Emily followed his pointing finger to the strange mountain rising beside the ocean. It did look different from the other mountains behind it. The top came to a sharp peak on the ocean side that sloped down along the uppermost rim of the crater. It was only a short distance from their hotel. "Really, that's a volcano?"

The boy nodded. "We're going to see it tomorrow, aren't we?" he asked his mother.

"Of course we are. But it's not really a volcano anymore. It won't erupt. We'll be perfectly safe." The woman approached her two children and shooed them away from the railing. "C'mon, you two, let's get away from here. If you put on your swimsuits, we can head down to the beach."

Gregor cheered and ran back the way he had come with his sister in tow. Their mother smiled again. "I am sorry if they've troubled you. Enjoy your stay."

"We will, thanks," Joel said.

Emily closed her eyes and lifted her face to the hot sun. The pull of the shard was very strong. She looked back to the left and opened her eyes. "It's that way. The shard is there."

"How far?" Joel asked. "Is it before or after Diamond Head?"

Emily shook her head. "Neither. The shard is *in* Diamond Head."

"THE SHARD IS IN A VOLCANO?" PAELEN CRIED.

Emily nodded. "I can't explain how I know. I just do."

"It makes perfect sense," Chiron said. "When Riza tried to follow her people and surrendered herself to the cosmos, one of the shards landed here, on an island prone to volcanoes. Perhaps the shard was the cause of them. After all, Earth is a relatively young world. Olympus no longer has active volcanoes, but I'm sure if we did, the power of the shard crashing could have activated one."

"So you're saying the shard created Diamond Head?" Emily said.

"Possibly," Chiron said. "We cannot know for certain."

"One thing we do know," Joel said, looking at the welcome folder from the hotel. "If the Flame shard really is in Diamond Head, then it's in one of Hawaii's top tourist attractions. Look . . ." He offered the folder to Emily while Paelen peered over her shoulder. "They have tours there all day long. You can go into the crater and even climb up to the ridgeline."

Emily looked at the photographs of the dormant volcano. In one shot, taken from above, it was clear that the mountain actually was a volcano. The photo showed a wide, deep crater encircled by a tall wall that ended in the high ocean-side peak they could see from the hotel roof. It was large and, judging from the diagram, took up a good percentage of this part of the island.

"It says that this island is called Oahu and that it has several volcanoes," Emily said, reading from the folder. "There's another one not far from here called the Punchbowl—it's now a military monument. So how are we supposed to get the shard out of Diamond Head if it's a tourist attraction?"

Joel pointed down to the information sheet, which he had taken out of the folder on Diamond Head tours. "Look, it says it closes at six. We'll wait till dark and head over when everyone is gone."

Emily looked around the room and saw a clock. "It's almost three. That's a long wait. Every minute we waste gives Lorin time to get here."

"I do not like waiting either," Chiron said, "but I cannot see what choice we have."

The long afternoon slowly ticked away, and eventually Pegasus woke up. Emily was there at the moment he opened his eyes.

"Take it easy, Pegs. You're safe. Thanks to you, we're all safe," she whispered in his ear.

Chiron settled down on the floor beside the stallion. "You have done us all proud, my friend. You brought us to the shard. Soon Emily will claim it and we can return home. Just lie still and regain your strength."

Pegasus nickered softly and looked meaningfully at Emily.

Emily leaned forward and kissed the stallion's

cheek. "I'm fine. It's you that has me worried." She reached over for the plate of ambrosia cakes she had summoned for him. "Here." She offered him one. "Please eat as much as you can; they will help you recover."

Pegasus sat up and ate the entire plateful of cakes. Then he drank a large bowl of nectar. When he could take no more, he settled down again to rest.

As they waited, Emily grew more and more worried. Would they be discovered? Would Lorin find them before they could get the shard?

News from Olympus only added to the strain. Fawn was in constant touch with her sister. Sapphire was being kept safe in the tunnels beneath the palace with Emily's father and aunt while the fighting raged aboveground.

More and more Titans were moving into Olympus. Jupiter's forces were doing what they could to defend against the invaders, but the Titans were using stealth and planning in their attacks. Little damage was being done to the buildings of Olympus, but many of its citizens were being captured and taken back to the prison world.

The news from Tartarus was no better. Though Dax was recovering, Venus, Mars, and Hercules had been dragged from the cell. There was no word about what was happening to them.

Chiron cursed. "I should be there."

"We all should," Joel added. "Olympus needs us." He turned to Emily. "The moment we get that shard, you've got to take us back there."

"I will," Emily promised as she started to pace, waiting for the moment when they could move.

By the time night fell, Pegasus was strong enough to stand. He wandered around the suite and tested his wings. He was sore from the long flight, and his skin was still raw and cut open from the harness. But his strength was returning.

Just after two in the morning, they turned off all the lights and walked out onto the dark patio.

"That's Diamond Head." Emily showed Pegasus, Chiron, and Chrysaor the mountain. "That's where the shard is."

"We should get moving," Joel said. "It's going to be a long walk."

Pegasus nickered softly.

"You are not going," Paelen said. "Pegasus, you have had a very long, exhausting flight. You must stay here and recover. We can go there and come back."

The winged stallion shook his head and snorted.

"They are right," Chiron said. "You have been greatly tested; you must stay here with me. They will not do anything foolish."

Pegasus would have none of it and continued to protest.

"Pegs, please," Emily said. She stroked his soft muzzle. "You can barely move. I can't ask you to carry me there."

Pegasus shook his head again and dropped his wing to invite Emily up onto his back. When she didn't move, he nickered at her and fluttered his wing impatiently.

Paelen translated. "He says he has carried you this far; he will not stop now. He will not be dissuaded. He is ordering you up on his back."

Chrysaor nudged Joel with his snout.

"Not you too," Joel said. "You're in no better shape than he is!"

"Pegasus, you are being stubborn," Chiron chastised.

"This is foolish, and you know it." After a long series of sounds from Pegasus, Chiron shook his head. "There are times when you are more stubborn than your father!" The Centaur turned to Emily. "He says if you try to walk there without him, he will follow you anyway."

Emily knew he would. Reluctantly, she climbed up on his back while Joel settled on Chrysaor. Fawn stayed at the hotel with Chiron, to keep in close communication with Olympus.

"Please be careful," Chiron said. "Do not take any foolish risks."

"We won't," Emily promised. "The same goes for you. Don't answer the door to anyone."

"Agreed," Chiron said.

The Centaur and Fawn stood back as Pegasus tested his wings. He stretched them wide and flapped them until they moved with ease. When he was ready, he trotted across the large patio area and leaped confidently over the railing. Pegasus sailed out over the beach and then over the ocean. They didn't want to fly over the coastline and risk being seen by late-night strollers on the beach.

"Are you all right?" Emily called to Pegasus, patting his neck. The stallion's head bobbed in the air and he nickered back to her.

Chrysaor was gliding easily in the ocean winds close beside them. After a few minutes, Pegasus maneuvered in the sky and started to head back inland. Diamond Head's dark mass loomed directly ahead.

"It looks ominous in the dark," Joel called. "Almost like a big mouth waiting to bite down on someone."

"Let's hope it doesn't decide tonight's the night it's going to erupt," Emily called back.

As they drew closer to the massive crater, Pegasus tilted his wings. He touched down lightly on the narrow ground at the ridgeline of the volcano. The terrain around them was rocky and uneven. Grasses and weeds grew along the rim, and short trees dotted the sides.

Pegasus shook his head and snorted.

Paelen and Chrysaor landed beside them. "He has asked you to check your senses," Paelen said. "Can you feel the shard?"

Emily sat up tall on the stallion's back. She closed her eyes and reached out with her senses. She was overwhelmed by the nearness of the shard. But as she filtered through all the feelings, she sensed that it was down on the actual crater floor.

"It's down there," she said. "Right in the very center."

"How is this a volcano?" Joel asked. "Look down there—there's a parking lot and lighted signs everywhere. It's just a big tourist attraction."

"Remember what that woman said this afternoon," Emily said. "It's not really a volcano anymore."

"This is just too weird," Joel offered. "Let's just get in there, get the shard, and get out."

Pegasus flapped his wings and glided down into the crater, landing in the center of a paved parking area.

Emily discovered that the lights they'd seen from above were from the public toilets and also on a very big wooden sign that read DIAMOND HEAD STATE MONUMENT. She slid off the stallion's back and stood beside him. "I can feel it—it is right around here."

"Where, exactly?" Joel said. "Look around—this crater is bigger than three football fields! How are we ever going to find it in here?"

The crater was not only large; it looked like a nature park. There were long grasses and trees growing all around, and it was full of wildlife. They heard the sounds of crickets and small scurrying animals. Bats danced in the air, chasing flying insects drawn to the lights. There were paved trails winding through the trees, and even a few squat buildings surrounded by fences. It couldn't have looked less like a volcanic crater if it tried.

"I'll find it because I have to," Emily said. She closed her eyes and could feel the power of the shard everywhere—it seemed to glow from the volcanic rocks and boulders around them; it rained down from the leaves in the trees and shot up from every blade of grass. The Flame shard had become an integral part of the life in Diamond Head.

But as the moments ticked by, the Flame shard called to her from a specific spot. Emily walked away from the stallion and moved across the parking lot.

She opened her eyes. "It is everywhere, but strongest right here, beneath us." Inside her head, she could feel Riza's excitement mixing with her own.

"Everyone, stay back," Emily warned. "I'm going

to summon it. It feels as if it's really deep, so I don't know how it will find its way out."

Pegasus and the others moved back as Emily stood in the very center of the parking lot. She held out both her hands, closed her eyes, and lifted her face to the stars. "Come," she commanded.

At first nothing happened. But then the ground beneath them rumbled ever so slightly.

"Whoa," Joel called, steadying himself. "Did you feel that? Was it an earthquake?"

"Come!" Emily repeated, louder. Again the ground rumbled in response, but the Flame shard remained trapped beneath them. "It's not working! I can feel it there, but it's like something is holding it down. Maybe I'm not strong enough to call it up."

Her temples pounded, and Emily knew Riza was trying to reach her. "Can you call it, Riza?" Emily said aloud. A single painful pounding in her temple was the answer: yes.

Emily lifted her arms. Her hands trembled as they stretched above the ground where the Flame shard was trapped. This time she did nothing and let Riza summon the shard. But although the ground rumbled and shook harder, nothing else happened.

Emily wiped sweat from her brow. "It's right here. I can feel it. But it can't move. Not even Riza can summon it."

"Try again," Joel ordered her. "It's got to work. You need that shard."

"I know!" Emily replied angrily. "But something is holding it."

Pegasus nudged her gently. He nickered softly. "He would like to try," Paelen said. "He will break up the ground for you to summon the shard." Paelen started to walk backward. "He warns us to move away."

Emily followed Paelen and Joel and moved away from Pegasus. She had seen him do this once before, at Area 51, when he had used his powers to return water to Groom Lake. Back then the earth beneath his hooves had cracked and opened like an egg.

"Good luck," Emily called.

Joel took Emily's hand as they stood back to watch Pegasus. The winged stallion shook his head, snorted, and then raised himself high on his hind legs. With his wings open wide, he brought his front legs down with a force that shook the ground.

The sounds of deep cracking rolled out of the ground like rumbling thunder. Pegasus rose and smashed down on the ground a second time with his sharp front hooves. The rumbling intensified.

With Pegasus's third and final attempt, the pavement beneath their feet cracked. Giant fissures opened and chased through the parking area, spreading across the entire surface of the crater.

The ground shook with the force of a mighty earthquake. Emily could see Joel calling to her but could not hear what he was saying over the explosive sounds. Before she could ask him to repeat himself, a huge geyser of water shot up through the crack closest to Pegasus. It continued up into the sky and rained down on them with a force that knocked everyone to the ground.

"Emily, get the shard before Diamond Head erupts!" Joel shouted as he helped her to her feet.

The roaring of water rushing through the fissures was deafening as the ground beneath them heaved. They were all knocked down again.

Emily climbed to her knees. She held her hands out and summoned the Flame shard.

"Well?" Paelen cried.

"It's not working!" she shouted. "It's still trapped!"

Joel knelt beside her. "Has the water put it out?"

Emily felt the draw of the shard just as powerfully as ever. "No—it just can't move!"

The rumbling increased and the ground heaved. More cracks appeared as the roaring sounds of a second, third, and then fourth geyser erupted. One caught Pegasus in his underside and lifted him into the air. Pegasus tried to use his wings, but the water pressure was too forceful. He was cast aside and crashed back down to the ground.

"We must go," Paelen shouted. "The crater is going to blow!"

They ran over to Pegasus to help him up. Joel lifted Emily onto the stallion's back and slapped his rump. "Go, Pegasus! Get Emily out of here before we drown!"

Paelen was already in the air and shouting down at Joel, "Hurry!"

Chrysaor appeared beside Joel, squealing as the water level rose up to his snout. Joel jumped on his back and the boar flapped his wings and struggled to take off.

The ground rumbled and shook as the volcano

erupted—not with lava, but with water. Pegasus and Chrysaor flapped unsteadily from above as a piercing warning siren rang out all over the island.

Police and fire sirens competed with the larger warning siren as the ground continued to tremble and shake. Windows in the buildings closest to the volcano shattered and rained glass down on the streets. People flooded out of their hotels and ran farther inland in blind panic.

As they flew over downtown, the streetlights flickered and went out. Electrical boxes shorted out and started to burn. They watched a car tearing through an intersection crash into a taxi going in the opposite direction. It was pandemonium on the ground as Honolulu suffered the large earthquake.

As they reached the patio area of their suite at the top of the Outrigger Reef, Chiron was waiting for them. "What has happened? The earth is shaking. Did you do this?"

"We couldn't get the shard," Emily explained breathlessly. "Pegasus used his powers to open the ground. But that started an earthquake and the crater filled with water."

Joel and Paelen ran into the living room and switched on the television. News reports flashed on all the networks, advising the public to remain calm—but due to the large earthquake and aftershocks centered in Honolulu, tsunami warnings were now in effect for all the Hawaiian Islands. Everyone was advised to move inland to seek higher ground.

"A tsunami?" Paelen asked.

"It's a tidal wave," Joel explained. "That must have been the loud siren we heard. It means a big wave is coming. It will destroy the coast if it hits. We've got to evacuate."

"We can't," Emily said. "We still haven't got the shard."

"How do we get it?" Joel said desperately. "Especially now that the whole crater is filled with water!"

"This is not good," Chiron said. "We have endangered all these people." He turned to the stallion. "Pegasus, I fear you have underestimated your powers. Now that you have drawn water from the ground, it will not stop. The shard is even further from our reach."

"Wait," Emily said, looking around. She held out her hand. It was steady. "The earthquake has stopped. Maybe it's not so bad."

"Em, we filled the whole crater with water!" Joel said. "That's just about as bad as it gets!"

"If only Neptune were here," Paelen said. "He could clear the water from the crater in no time."

"Good idea," Joel agreed. "And maybe Jupiter could open the ground to get the shard. Can we call them to Earth?"

Chiron rubbed his chin. "We could try. But with Olympus under attack, Jupiter may be hesitant to leave."

"He's going to have to," Joel said. "Emily's life is at stake."

Chiron nodded. "Fawn, please speak with your sister. Tell her what has happened and that we need them here as soon as possible."

As Fawn started to reach out to her sister, the door to their suite burst open.

Standing in the doorway was a young woman wearing a long, straight floral dress and finely tooled sandals. She had waist-length black hair and a wreath of white flowers around her head. And if her face was anything to go by, she was livid.

"What are you doing here?" Her dark eyes flashed, moving from Chiron to Pegasus, then down to Chrysaor and finally to Fawn. She frowned. "And just what is a night dweller doing on my Island?"

"WHO ARE YOU?" JOEL CHALLENGED THE
stranger. "That door was locked. How did you get
in here?"

"I am Pele, and these are *my* Islands!" The woman
stormed up to Chiron. "Answer my question, Centaur. Who are you?"

Chiron stood tall and bowed elegantly in respect.
"I am Chiron of Olympus. It is a great honor to
finally meet you, Pele."

"Chiron," the woman repeated. "The Olympians
left this world millennia ago. What are you doing
back?"

"Indeed, dear lady, we did leave. We have returned
for a very good reason. I assure you we intend no

disrespect and come here in peace. We do not seek trouble with you."

"And yet your presence here has caused a disaster. Look what you have done to Oahu!"

Emily was fascinated by this strange, exotic woman. Her dress appeared to be alive. All the flowers on it moved as though in a gentle breeze. Hummingbirds were woven in the pattern, but were drinking nectar from the flowers and flying all around the fabric. As Emily watched, one flew over Pele's shoulder and disappeared down her back.

Pele's fiery eyes landed on Pegasus. "It was you, wasn't it? You did this—I can feel your guilt. You flooded Le'ahi."

"Hey, wait a minute," Emily said, snapping out of her enchantment with the dress. "You leave him alone!"

"You would do well to show me some respect."

"I'll give respect when I get it," Emily replied. "When we *all* get it. This is Pegasus of Olympus. You will be nice to him—"

Pele challenged her: "Or what?"

Pegasus nickered and stepped quickly between

Emily and Pele. He bowed his head before the Hawaiian beauty.

"Pegs, what are you doing?" Emily asked.

"He is doing what you should!" Pele paused, and her black eyes pierced Emily's. "What is this I feel from you?" She moved closer. "Two in one?" Her fine hand reached out and grasped Emily's chin. "This makes no sense."

Emily tried to pull away, but the grip was unbreakable.

Pele leaned in close to peer into Emily's eyes. "Hmmm . . . not human and not Olympian. Tell me, what are you?"

Joel jumped to Emily's aid. "Get your hands off her! Who do you think you are, storming in here and making demands?"

"Joel, it is all right," Chiron said soothingly. "I know who this is. Let me speak with her." He turned to Pele. "Emily is part of the Xan—an ancient race older than all of us. Long ago, an important part of her crashed on these Islands and became trapped in the Diamond Head volcano."

"That was you!" Pele snapped, turning to Emily.

Her eyes flashed, and for a moment flames blazed in their dark depths. "You are the one responsible for this ceaseless pain in my side. For an age I have used all my powers to keep your invading Flame from harming me. It does not belong here." She gazed around the room. "None of you belong here!"

Emily's temples pounded as Riza responded to Pele's words. "So it's you who is stopping me from removing the Flame shard from Le'ahi, or Diamond Head, or whatever it's called."

"It is Le'ahi," Pele said. "British sailors changed the name to Diamond Head long ago. But that is not its Island name."

"Diamond Head or Le'ahi, it doesn't matter right now. What *does* matter is that you are keeping the shard prisoner. When I tried to remove it, it couldn't move."

"That's because I have put protections around it to keep myself safe."

"Look, I don't know who you are, lady," Joel exclaimed. "But you have to release the shard. Without it, Emily will die and the Titans may gain control of Olympus."

"Why should I care about this girl?" Pele demanded. "Or that ridiculous struggle between the Titans and the Olympians?" Her accusing eyes flashed at Chiron. "Your foolishness nearly destroyed this world ages ago. We all breathed a sigh of relief when you left."

"I understand your anger," Chiron said calmly. "But you yourself just said that the shard has been causing you pain. If you help us release it, we will take it far from here and it will trouble you no further."

"I would be happy to have that thing removed from me. But thanks to you, I can't."

"I do not understand," Chiron said. "You are Pele, and these are your Islands. You can do anything here."

"Yes, I can," Pele agreed. "But not while waters continue to flood *Diamond Head*"—Pele stared at Emily defiantly—"is that name easier for you?"

Emily was about to say yes, but a warning look from Chiron stopped her. Chiron obviously knew who this woman was, and they were going to have to trust him.

"Pele, please," he continued. "There is more at stake here than you know."

The Hawaiian turned on him. "If you truly know me, Chiron, you would understand why I can't go near that volcano now. Those waters give access to my ocean sister. I can't risk it."

"Are you two still fighting?" Chiron asked.

"What business is it of yours?"

Emily had no clue what that exchange meant, but whatever it was, they would still need Pele's help. "Then we're stuck," she said to Pele. "I can't remove the shard, because you've put a spell around it. You can't remove it, because there's water in the crater."

"Pele, hear me," Chiron pressed. "You may not care about our struggle against the Titans. But you must realize what Saturn will do if he has his way. What transpired here in the past will be repeated, only it would be much worse. This squabble you have with your sister will mean nothing."

Chiron paused and took her hands. "If Saturn conquers Olympus, he will not stop there. You know him—he will set his sights on Earth once again. You will all be enslaved if we are not there to fight for you."

Pele pulled her hands free and focused hard eyes on him. "What are you suggesting?"

"Make peace with your sister—if only for a short time during this crisis. After we remove the shard, you can go back to warring as you always have."

"I doubt that Nā-maka-o-Kahaʻi will care. Should Saturn come here to conquer Earth, the seas and oceans will remain intact. She will stay safe. It is the rest of us who will be enslaved."

"Or worse," Paelen added.

Pele nodded. "Yes, or worse." She walked to the windows and threw back the drapes. "I have stopped the earthquake you started. There will be no tidal waves." She turned and faced Emily. "But you have chosen a bad place to hide your shard. This is Oahu— it has the largest military presence in the Pacific."

"Military?" Joel asked, flicking a nervous look at Emily. Military often equaled CRU.

Pele nodded. "Have you heard of Pearl Harbor? It is not far from here. It was bombed during the Second World War. After that, Oahu became the biggest military base in the Islands—which is why I live in Kilauea, on the Big Island."

"You haven't heard of the CRU, have you?" Emily asked, hoping the answer would be no.

"Of course I have heard of them. I would be a fool if I had not. I have managed to stay 'under the radar,' as the saying goes. My family and I remain safe by masquerading as humans. We draw no attention to ourselves. Even so, we do not risk exposure by living on this Island. But this earthquake and the flooding at Diamond Head will not go unnoticed. You must be on your guard."

"What do we do?" Joel asked. "Where can we go?"

Chiron answered. "We wait to see if Nā-maka-o-Kaha'i will cooperate and remove the waters in Diamond Head. Then we get in there, get the shard, and get away from here as quickly as possible."

"And if she refuses?" Pele said.

"Then we wait for Jupiter, Neptune, and Pluto to arrive. Neptune will no doubt have the power to halt the waters, which will free the volcano for you to open."

"You already know how I feel about Olympians," Pele said. "You expect me to welcome more to my Island?"

"If you want that shard out of your side, you will," Emily said.

Pele looked around. "I don't think I like you very much, or your attitude."

Emily opened her mouth to retort, but Chiron stopped her with a raised hand. "Pele, please," he said, ever the diplomat. "Without your help, we will have no choice but to ask the Big Three to come."

Pele sighed heavily. "Fine, I'll talk to my sister. I am assuming none of you have checked into this hotel?"

"No," Joel said. "We don't have any money. We thought we'd get the shard and go. We didn't expect this trouble. But we've been lucky so far—no one's discovered us."

"This is Honolulu in the tourist season. It's unlikely this suite will remain empty for long," Pele said. "I will arrange for you to stay here. You will not be disturbed."

"You can do that?" Emily asked.

Pele nodded. She walked up to Pegasus and pulled a floral lei from around her neck. She placed the wreath of bright red flowers around the stallion's white neck and kissed his muzzle. "Aloha, Pegasus. I welcome you to my Island and place you under my protection. This lei is part of me. If you need my help, I am bound to give it to you."

Emily was fascinated by Pele. She held the respect of the Olympians in the room, but spoke like an ordinary modern woman. She also appeared to be wearing only one lei, yet each time she gave one away to the Olympians, there was always one still around her neck.

Pele approached Joel. She lifted herself onto her toes, pulled the lei around his neck, and kissed him lightly on the lips.

Joel blushed bright red and smiled at Pele. "Thank you."

"You are most welcome, Joel."

Pele stood before Emily now. "As you are the cause of my pain, I don't feel inclined to welcome you. I wish you no ill, but offer no protection."

Emily shook her head. "But that's not fair! This isn't my fault."

"Maybe not, but the shard is yours. Until it is removed from my side, I can feel no warmth toward you." She started toward the door. "I will try to reason with my sister and will let you know the outcome.

You will be safe for the time being. But watch your-selves—there are military eyes everywhere. And I warn you, don't abuse my generosity."

Pele waved her hand and the door magically opened. It slammed shut after her. When she was gone, Emily shook her head and asked Chiron, "Who is that woman, and why did you bow to her?"

Chiron looked down on the lei resting against his bare chest. He sniffed the fresh, fragrant flowers. "I have known of her, but this was our first meeting. She is Pele. The simplest way to describe her, for you to understand, is that she is the most powerful god of these Islands. Volcanoes are her domain and, just as with you, Fire is her power. She and her kind have been on Earth since the beginning of time."

"So you're not the only gods?" Joel said, confused.

Chiron shook his head and chuckled. "Oh heavens, no. Each culture has its own gods. We are one kind. Pele, her ocean sister, and their family are another. But unlike Jupiter and his brothers, as you heard, Pele and her sister do not get along."

"Why?" Fawn asked.

Chiron sighed. "Like many family squabbles, this

one starts out simple and then escalates. In this case, they were fighting over a man. It was said that Nā-maka-o-Kaha'i saw him first and fell instantly in love with him. But then Pele saw him swimming with her ocean sister and used her powers to charm him away from her.

"After that, the fight grew. Now, if Pele creates a volcano, Nā-maka, as we knew her, stirs the oceans to extinguish it. This is why Pele resides in the Kilauea Volcano. She used to live in Diamond Head. But it was too close to the shore, and Nā-maka extinguished it. Her current home is too tall for her sister to reach with her waves—though she does cool the lava that reaches her shores."

"No, no, no," Joel insisted, shaking his head violently. "Volcanoes are caused by gases building up in the liquid core of our planet. It's science. Pele can't create them. That's just a myth."

Pegasus nickered and seemed to be laughing. Chiron joined in. He patted Joel on the back. "Joel, you do amuse me at times. Not everything has a scientific explanation. Yes, volcanoes are formed by gases and lava building up and leaking through breaks in a planet's crust. But it is Pele who makes that happen here."

Emily frowned. "Does that mean Pele creates all the volcanoes on Earth? Like the one in Italy that destroyed Pompeii, or even Mount St. Helens, which erupted in the United States?"

Chiron shrugged. "I do not know. Those of us with power tend to respect each other's territories and do not interact. But I do not believe her powers would extend to all the volcanoes in the world. Pele is a Hawaiian god."

Paelen elbowed Joel. "What she is, is beautiful."

"She sure is." Joel grinned and lifted the lei around his neck to sniff the flowers. He tried to lift it off his head, but it would not budge. "Hey, it's stuck."

Chiron nodded. "These are Pele's promise of protection. No one can remove them but Pele."

"Really?" Joel asked. "But she came in here only wearing one. Where did these others come from?"

"They came directly from Pele," Chiron said. He looked at everyone in the room. "I need each of you to remember your manners around her. Pele is known for her power, passion, jealousy, and capricious nature.

She has a ferocious temper! This is her Island, and we are only visitors here. We must respect her laws."

"What if she doesn't respect us?" Emily said.

Chiron sighed. "Then we could have a very large problem."

EACH DAY SATURN'S FIGHTERS DELIVERED more captured Olympians to Tartarus. Lorin often sneaked into their cellblocks to peer curiously at them.

Olympians looked just like Titans. They weren't the monsters she had been led to believe. They came in all shapes and sizes, just like the Titans—and on more than one occasion, she discovered that there were many Titans among the prisoners who were actually fighting on the side of Olympus. When she'd questioned Phoebe about it, her guardian spat and called them traitors, saying that some foolish Titans actually preferred Jupiter to Saturn. Those traitors would face the harshest punishment of all.

None of it made any sense.

Not long after another group of prisoners arrived, Lorin was summoned to the throne room. She tried to ask her escorts what the summons was about as they passed through the maze that was Tartarus, but they said nothing. They wouldn't even look at her.

"He's waiting for you in there," one of her escorts finally said as they stopped before the throne room.

He was anxious to get away from her, like the rest of the Titans. Those who did speak to her used short, clipped sentences and ended the conversation as quickly as possible. Even Phoebe was starting to avoid her and had moved out of the cell they shared. When she asked why, Phoebe would only say that as servants of Saturn, they must do as they were told.

It was then that Lorin realized the truth. She wasn't like the other Titans.

"Ah, child," Saturn called when he saw her at the door. "Come in, come in."

A line of wounded Olympians was standing before the throne in chains. One satyr looked far too young to be fighting. His eyes were filled with terror, and he was shaking.

"I want you all to meet my servant—Lorin, the Flame of Titus!" Saturn said with relish. "She is infinitely more powerful than your Flame of Olympus. And unlike Emily, Lorin does as she is told."

By the look on the Olympians' faces, they knew of her reputation. Some showed fear, but others looked at her with pity.

"Lorin, come closer," Saturn commanded.

As Lorin stepped up to Saturn's throne, a feeling of dread deep inside her warned her that something very terrible was brewing in their leader's mind.

Saturn stood and put his arm around her possessively. It was a show for the Olympians, nothing more. Lorin wished he'd continued to ignore her, as he had been doing recently.

"Look here, Lorin. Look at these filthy traitors who betrayed me. See how they refuse to kneel before my authority. They serve my ungrateful son. But not for long."

Saturn called to one of his guards. "You there, bring that young satyr to me."

No! thought Loren. *Not him!* It was as if Saturn had picked the youngest, most vulnerable prisoner on purpose. She wasn't going to do it. He couldn't make her hurt him.

The guard raced forward and undid the chain connecting the satyr to the other prisoners. The boy's face filled with terror as he was dragged away from the others and delivered to Saturn. "Please," he begged.

Saturn mocked him: "Please? You wish to die with the others?"

Gasps escaped the prisoners as Saturn escorted Lorin and the satyr closer to the line of Olympians, his hard eyes focused on the satyr. "Watch this, boy," he spat. "Watch and learn."

With his arm still around her, Saturn looked down on Lorin. "Show them what you can do."

Lorin frowned and did nothing.

"Show them!" Saturn commanded. "Use your Flame. Burn them up! They are traitors and must be punished!"

"You want me to kill them?"

"That is what you do to traitors!" Saturn shouted. "Now do it!"

His hand started to tighten around her shoulder

and squeeze it painfully. Lorin looked up into Saturn's wild pale eyes and then over to the line of Olympians. "Why must they die?"

"*Why?*" Saturn boomed. "You question my authority?"

"No, but—but I do not understand why I must harm them."

"Because I am your leader and I command you to do it. Now show them!" he boomed. "Jupiter must be taught that he cannot win against me. I have the power, and I possess the Flame of Titus!"

Lorin had never seen Saturn like this before. His eyes were crazy with blood lust. His hand on her shoulder shook with rage and squeezed her even tighter.

"If I do this, will you give me Emily?" she managed to choke out.

"Do not bargain with me!" Saturn boomed. "I am your leader. You will do as I command, when I command! Now kill them!"

Lorin was trapped. If she didn't do as he ordered, she was certain he would turn his rage against her. She had power—but did he have more? He was her leader; Phoebe said she had to obey him. But she didn't want to kill these people. All she wanted to do was to find Emily and become whole.

"Now!" Saturn cried.

In a fraction of a second, Lorin weighed her options. She considered what *she* needed as opposed to what Saturn wanted. What she needed was to be whole—to have friends like Paelen and Joel, and to possess Pegasus. If she defied Saturn now, he would hurt her, and she would never fulfill that dream.

That could not be allowed to happen.

Lorin closed her eyes and raised her hands. She had to do this to become complete. But she did not wish the Olympians to suffer. As the Flame rumbled in her stomach and flowed up her body and down to her hands, she unleashed a blast so intense, it instantly vaporized the Olympians. There had been no time for terror, no pain. They were simply turned to ash.

Saturn boomed with laughter, a sick, triumphant sound, as he struck the satyr and knocked him across the room. When the boy rose, she saw the horror on his young face. Silent tears streamed down his cheeks as he stared at the space where his people had been standing.

"Boy," Saturn called. "You will go back and tell Jupiter what you have witnessed. He will surrender to me or I will unleash the Flame of Titus on Olympus and burn it to ash!"

The satyr fell to his goat knees and let out a howl so filled with pain that Lorin knew it would haunt her for the rest of her life. Unable to bear the sound a moment longer, she didn't wait for Saturn to give her permission to leave. She ran out of the throne room, shoved past the guards in the corridor, and raced down the steps to her cell.

Curled up into a ball and rocking herself on her bed, Lorin was horrified by what she had done. Why did she do it? Those people were innocent. Why had she let Saturn bully her into killing them? She knew it was wrong, but she hadn't been able to stop herself.

It was Emily's fault! If she had been complete, if Emily hadn't stolen her power and Riza from her, then she would have family and friends. She would have Pegasus. She would be more to Saturn than just a weapon. She would be loved.

Lorin ached to talk to someone about her feelings, but Phoebe was lost to her. There was no one she could speak to. She was completely and utterly alone.

"Never again," she promised herself as she rocked. She now knew for sure that Saturn was a bloodthirsty monster who took pleasure in pain. She would not serve him. She would never serve anyone but herself again.

Late in the evening, Lorin made her move. If Saturn wasn't going to bring Emily to her, she would go out and find her herself.

It had taken her some time to learn the details of how the Solar Stream worked, but after threatening a guard with her powers, Lorin now knew how to use it. She rose from her bed while the guards at the end of her cellblock changed shifts and were too occupied with reporting their status to notice her. Then she slipped out of her cell and escaped through the corridor at the end opposite to the guards' station.

She crept into a stairwell and started to climb

quietly until she heard troops entering the stairs beneath her. She ducked into a corridor and hid until they passed. As she waited, Lorin recalled everything she had seen and heard when she had been linked with Emily.

Emily was on Earth in a place called Honolulu, Hawaii. After the connection had been severed, Lorin had asked Phoebe about Earth and, specifically, Hawaii. But her guardian had said that the Human World was off-limits to her until Saturn defeated the Olympians. Further questions about Earth were cut off.

When the coast was clear, Lorin crept out from her hiding spot. She knew she didn't have much time. Soon someone would notice her absence from the cell and start to look for her.

At the uppermost level, Lorin stayed hidden in the stairwell and watched the activity at the entrance of the prison. A crowd of Titan fighters was trying to get out through the large prison doors, but at the same time others were returning from Olympus with more prisoners. The doors were wide, but there were too many people trying to get through, and with the congestion building on both sides, no one was getting in or out.

The growing chaos gave Lorin an idea. She had learned that the Titans were impatient and extremely short-tempered. Seeing the congestion building, she knew it wouldn't take much to set them off.

Focusing her thoughts, Lorin used her powers to shove an exiting Titan against a fighter trying to get in. Then she used her powers again to push a group of fighters on the outside against those on the inside. After that, she let the Titans do the rest.

Shouting started first, then more pushing and shoving. This was followed by the first punch. A second punch was thrown and then more blows exchanged as the Titans began to fight each other.

Lorin smiled as a devious idea entered her head. She opened the shackles on the Olympian prisoners and set them on the Titans. In an instant there was a full-blown riot.

Lorin took this opportunity to slip quietly around the chaos.

Outside the gates she turned around to look back. Most of the prison was underground, so there wasn't much to see except for the growing pandemonium at the entrance of the roughly cut stone building.

Titan versus Titan versus Olympian. It no longer seemed to matter who fought whom. It was just one big brawl. The muddy ground outside the prison made everything worse as the fighters slipped and fell into the muck. This caused even more rage as the fighting increased.

The nighttime winds were up and the driving rain was even harder than the last time Lorin had been to the surface. The temperature was freezing, compared to the stifling heat and stuffiness of the lower levels of the prison. She pulled her shawl tighter around herself and began to run.

Despite the foul weather, Lorin inhaled deeply and savored the first taste of freedom that she had had in an age. Keeping low, she picked her way through the dark, rocky terrain to the large arch that had been built to contain the transport device to Olympus.

Back when Lorin was still allowed to wander freely around Tartarus, Phoebe had brought her here to watch the first fighters heading to Olympus. She hadn't told Lorin how the arch worked, but after some quiet investigating on her own, Lorin now knew what she had to do.

Excitement and nerves bunched up in her stomach as she carefully approached the arch. She looked around and couldn't see anyone near. Lorin inhaled deeply and called out, "Earth, Oahu—Honolulu."

The arch burst into life. Stealing one last glance over her shoulder, Lorin steeled herself and stepped into the blazing white light of the Solar Stream.

29

LATE INTO THE NIGHT EMILY STOOD ON THE patio overlooking the ocean. Pegasus was at her side. The air was almost as hot as it was during the day, but there was an ocean wind that made it comfortable. The tsunami warning siren had stopped and people were slowly returning to their hotels. Police and fire sirens wailed in the distance.

News reports claimed that the epicenter of the large earthquake was in the Diamond Head crater, but the quake had caused only minor damage to downtown Honolulu and the surrounding areas. There were no building collapses, little structural damage, and only broken glass to be cleared up.

Seismologists were studying the results and said

that the public should be aware that some aftershocks might still be felt but that the tsunami warning was canceled. They warned that until they could get into the volcano, they couldn't be sure if Diamond Head was facing imminent eruption.

The news reported that the scientists were stumped. Diamond Head sat directly on the shore. Yet the water filling the crater was pure, clean, fresh water and not ocean water. Were it not for the entrance tunnel cut through the side of the volcano, leading into the crater, the crater would have completely filled. Instead, the water flowed through the tunnel and was flooding the neighborhoods surrounding the volcano.

Emily lowered her head, saddened by the damage they had caused. From the little she'd seen of the island, it was beautiful and didn't deserve this.

"Emily?" Fawn joined her and Pegasus. Fawn was wearing her Olympian robes, having left Pluto's cloak inside. The wind whipped back her long white hair, and her eyes glowed with their night vision.

"You should be asleep like the others," Emily said.

Fawn laughed lightly. "A night dweller that sleeps

at night? It would not be much of a life, considering night is the only safe time for us to be out."

"You know what I mean," Emily said. "You've been up most days too. You need your rest." She stroked the stallion's neck. "You too, Pegs. You're still recovering from the long flight."

Pegasus nickered softly but shook his head.

"I am fine also," Fawn said. "But thank you for your concern." She put her hand on Emily's shoulder. "This is not your fault."

Emily frowned at her. "Is mind reading also one of your powers?"

Fawn shook her head. "No, but I have come to know you. You are blaming yourself for this."

Once again Pegasus nickered.

"It is not your fault either," Fawn said to him. "Neither of you should blame yourselves for what happened at Diamond Head. It was an accident. Pele put protection around the shard. None of us could have foreseen what would happen."

Emily shook her head. "Even so, look at the mess we've made. Olympus needs us. Instead, we're here and I'm completely powerless."

"Pele will convince her sister to empty the crater. I know it. Then you can free the shard and reclaim your powers, and we can go home. Sapphire says that if Pele fails, then Jupiter and his brothers have agreed to come here. One way or another, this will be over soon."

Emily nodded, but said nothing. Fawn smiled softly, and her dark eyes sparkled as her white hair blew back in the breeze. She held up her hands, enjoying the sensations of the wind on her skin. "I have heard from Dax. He is feeling better. There are more Olympians imprisoned with him now. The wounded night dwellers are being well cared for."

"I'm so glad to hear that," Emily said, genuinely happy for the bit of good news.

The three leaned against the railing, gazing out over the dark ocean. Fawn sighed. "When this is over, I would like to come back to Earth. I have seen so many wonders here. I want to see more."

"I hope we can," Emily agreed.

As the final hours of darkness slipped by and dawn broke on the horizon, the others in the suite started to stir.

Paelen ran out onto the patio. "Emily, you must come. There is someone at the door!"

By the time Emily, Pegasus, and Fawn ran back into their suite, Chrysaor and Chiron had slipped into a bedroom to hide. Pegasus and Fawn followed behind them.

"Okay," Emily called softly to Joel, "all clear. You can answer it."

Joel had pulled on one of the hotel robes to hide his arm. "Coming," he called as he tied it closed and plunged his silver hand into the large pocket. He reached the door, gave the room a final check, and turned the knob.

A hotel employee stood there holding a large manila envelope. "Good morning. I am sorry to disturb you so early, but I was told to get this to you as soon as possible. I understand your aunt checked you in late last night just after the earthquake. On behalf of the Outrigger Reef on the Beach, I want to welcome you to our hotel and let you know that we suffered very little damage and you are quite safe."

"Yes, our aunt," Joel agreed, stealing a glance at Emily.

"Where is she?" Emily asked.

The hotel employee entered the room. "She's been called away this morning, but said she would be back. She wanted you to have this." He handed over the large envelope and a folded card to Emily. Inside the card were three white plastic hotel-room keycards.

"Thank you," Emily said, smiling sweetly and trying to act normal when she felt anything but normal.

"You're welcome. I'm Michael Grove—my friends call me Mickey. I'm with hotel services and will be your personal representative during your stay. If you need anything at all, just call reception and ask for me. Your aunt has set up a charge account for you in the shops downstairs. The card is in the envelope. You need only to ask for something and it will be delivered to your room."

"Really?" Paelen asked, greedily rubbing his hands together. "Anything?"

Mickey nodded.

"Thank you, Mickey," Emily said. "We'll call if we need something."

Mickey nodded again and exited the room. When

he was gone, they opened the large envelope. Emily poured the contents onto the dining room table.

"Wow!" She stared at a large wad of cash.

"I had heard that Pele can be generous. It appears this is true," Chiron said as he and the others returned from the bedroom.

Joel read the note that came with the money. "Pele's gone to meet with her sister and says it could take some time. She wants us to buy some human clothes. We can reach her, if we need to, by going to Diamond Head and calling her name. She will hear us there and come back."

"How?" Paelen asked. "It is flooded, and I still have not learned to dive yet."

Emily nodded at her friend. "Let's just hope we don't need to."

After breakfast, Emily and Fawn went down to the hotel shops to buy clothes for Joel and Paelen. They could get away with wearing Olympian tunics, but the boys couldn't.

"Fawn," Paelen said, taking on the role of a teacher before they left the suite. "This is your first time among humans. Just act normal." He paused. "No, wait. Do not smile or talk to anyone. Your teeth are not human."

Fawn's eyes sparkled with excitement. "I understand."

"She'll be fine as long as we keep out of direct sunlight." Emily grabbed the charge card from Pele and one of the room keycards. "We won't be long."

When the elevator doors slid apart to reveal an open-air lobby, Emily suddenly felt very exposed. They were under the cover of the building, so they were safe from the sun, but there were people everywhere; there was a crowd around the reception desk checking in and out of the hotel. Porters were rushing around, pushing trolleys of suitcases and wearing shorts with bright floral shirts and seashell leis. Vacationers were relaxing in the lobby lounge, dressed in wild, colorful clothes and beachwear.

"Come on, Fawn, let's look around."

Emily laughed at Fawn's incredulous expression. The night dweller had obviously never seen anything like this before and stopped to stare at everything.

A bell rang, making Fawn jump. The elevators

behind them opened and out poured a group of men wearing army fatigues. Soldiers. Emily flinched as she thought of the CRU. She remembered Pele's warning about the large military presence on Oahu. But these soldiers seemed much more carefree than the serious CRU agents she had encountered before. She watched them laugh with each other as they carried their army bags over to another large gathering of soldiers, who were drinking coffee and waiting to board a shuttle bus.

"This way." Emily pulled at Fawn's arm and lowered her head as she led Fawn in the opposite direction.

They were in a beautiful resort hotel. It wasn't like any place Emily had stayed at before. A gentle wind blew through the open lobby, and the fragrance of suntan lotion, an ocean breeze, and flowers mixed pleasantly together. The reception desk area was mostly covered, but then it opened up and she could see the blazing blue sky above them. Every hotel employee they encountered offered a friendly greeting. This should have made Emily relaxed, but it had the opposite effect. She didn't want to draw attention to either of them.

They followed the sounds of children's laughter to a pool area where splashing could be heard. To the left of the large pool was a kiosk where a man was handing out bath towels to swimmers, while to the right there was an open-air restaurant where guests were enjoying an outdoor breakfast around the pool.

Fawn looked longingly at the pool and the palm trees that surrounded it, but fear of the sun kept her in the shadows.

"Come on, we'd better keep moving," Emily warned. "Let's find the shops."

The far end of the large ground-floor area opened directly to the beach and ocean. Although it was still early morning, sunbathers were lying on the yellow sand, while others splashed in the blue ocean.

After a bit more exploring, they found a shop that sold Hawaiian-style clothes, with baggy shorts and colorful floral tops or dresses that looked very much like the clothing Pele had worn—though obviously without the moving pattern. Fawn devoured the racks of brightly colored clothing. Each time she thought she'd settled on an outfit, another would catch her eye and she would squeal with excitement.

Emily couldn't keep from smiling at the night dweller, but warned her to cover her mouth when she spoke. Her sharp, pointed teeth, extra-pale, almost gray complexion, and elliptical eyes made her stand out from the tanned vacationers.

Emily imagined how strange it must be for Fawn, who, until now, had lived her whole life only at night. She was now walking around during the daytime, exposed to all the vibrant colors of the world that can be seen only in daylight. Emily wondered if it would be difficult for her to return to the dark.

Emily chose an outfit for herself, and Hawaiian shorts and shirts for Joel and Paelen. She made sure to buy Joel a long-sleeved sweatshirt to cover his arm. It had *Honolulu* blazoned on the front. As an after-thought, she picked up some diving gloves to cover his hand and they were set.

Fawn couldn't wait to change into her Hawaiian clothes and did so as soon as they were back in the suite. Joel was less impressed with his new outfit and hated having to wear a heavy sweatshirt in the heat, but he pulled it on anyway.

Paelen paraded around the suite showing off his

bright floral shirt and large, baggy shorts, but refused to surrender his winged sandals for normal footwear.

"Okay, now we're dressed like tourists—I think we should get moving," Joel said. "Fawn, call the Big Three and get them here now. Emily's in too much danger for us to wait around much longer."

Chiron shook his head. "Olympus is under attack. We must try to work this out ourselves if we can." He moved to the windows and opened the curtains just enough to peer out. "I cannot see Diamond Head from here. We have no way of knowing if Pele has convinced her sister to drain the crater."

"Perhaps if we . . ." Fawn stopped in midsentence. Her eyes became distant as she received a message from her sister. Her hand shot up to her mouth. "No! When? Where?"

Everyone was instantly on alert. They could see from Fawn's face that the news from Olympus was not good.

Fawn turned to Emily. "A young satyr has just returned from Tartarus. He was captured by the Titans, but Saturn sent him back with a message for Jupiter. If he and his brothers do not surrender immediately, he will have Lorin turn Olympus to dust. To prove it, he had Lorin kill a group of prisoners right in front of him. He said she turned them to ash with no effort!"

"They can't surrender," Joel cried. "It would be suicide!"

"They will not," Chiron agreed. "The Titans cannot defeat Jupiter. We have the Hundred-handers on our side. They put down Saturn once, and they can do it again."

Emily shook her head. "The Titans might not be able to defeat the Hundred-handers, but Lorin can. She has the power of the Flame, remember."

A heavy silence filled the room.

"Where is Jupiter right now?" Chiron asked.

Fawn relayed the message. "He is meeting with his brothers, the Sphinxes, and his best warriors. The Big Three are preparing to merge their powers against Lorin if Saturn brings her to Olympus. Sapphire says the fighting is getting intense."

"Lorin's powers alone can easily defeat the Big Three." Chiron's voice was grave.

"But that is not possible," Paelen said.

The Centaur's eyes settled on Emily. "Remember when you were captured by the Gorgons? They knew you were the only one powerful enough to destroy Jupiter."

Pegasus whinnied and pawed the floor. His sharp hoof cut a deep trench in the expensive carpet.

"He's right," Emily said. "I've known it for some time. I have . . ." She paused and corrected herself. "I *had* the power to destroy Jupiter and his brothers if I'd wanted to." Her eyes landed on Pegasus. "But you know I'd never do it. All of you are my family. I couldn't even imagine it."

"But Lorin can," Chiron said. "That was the point of the demonstration. You, Emily, were raised with loving parents who taught you right from wrong. All Lorin knows is the poison that Saturn has fed to her. She has no conscience, and will do what he tells her to."

"We should be there." Emily cursed and shook her head. "We can't wait any longer. I'm going to Diamond Head. Joel and Paelen will come with me. We've got to call Pele and tell her what's happened. I need that shard now more than ever. If Lorin has the same powers as me, then I'm the only one who can fight her."

"But you haven't got your powers anymore," Joel said.

"Maybe not now, but I will—when I get that shard!"

"It's my fault," Emily told Joel and Paelen as they closed the door to the suite.

"Don't you dare!" Joel said. "If you think this has something to do with you losing your powers . . ."

"It has everything to do with that," Emily said. The mild pounding in her temples told her that Riza was thinking the same thing.

"How?" Paelen asked.

They stepped into the elevator and pressed the button for the lobby. "I sensed this from Lorin when we were merged. She's been asleep for most of her life. But when Riza and I turned Tom into a Sphinx and we used too much of our power, it somehow called to Lorin and woke her up. Each moment she has been awake, her powers have grown. When she was in my mind, she learned how to use them. If Riza and I hadn't turned Tom into a Sphinx, Lorin would still be asleep."

"You couldn't have known," Joel said.

"I know," Emily agreed softly, dropping her head. "And we would never have done it if we'd known. But now, because of us, Saturn is free and he's going to use Lorin to kill the Big Three and destroy Olympus."

"And Earth," Paelen said. "We all know he will not stop with Olympus. He will try to rule all the worlds along the Solar Stream. Those who oppose him will be destroyed."

"He'll never get this far," Joel said as the elevator reached the lobby. "Because we're gonna stop him!"

Getting to Diamond Head was their next challenge. They found a taxi driver willing to take them as far as possible, but the whole area around the volcano had been closed off.

"You'll have to walk the rest of the way. But you won't get into the crater, not with all the water pouring out of it. 'Course, I could take you to the side facing the ocean. It hasn't got the best views of Diamond Head and you can't get into the crater now. But the ocean is beautiful, and you can visit the lighthouse."

"That would be perfect, thank you," Emily said as they settled into the back of the taxi.

Joel looked at her and frowned. Emily pointed down to Paelen's winged sandals. His eyes grew wide when he understood what she planned. He mouthed, "No way. Not in daylight!"

"We must," Emily mouthed back.

When Paelen finally caught up with the conversation, he cried aloud, "You expect me to fly up there in the middle of the day? Are you mad?"

Emily elbowed him sharply and nodded toward the driver, who was eyeing them in the mirror. "No, not until we ask Mom and Dad if we can go up in the helicopter," Emily said, exaggerating every word.

"I still think you're crazy," Joel said loudly. "Besides, helicopters frighten you."

"But I really want to see Diamond Head!" Emily insisted.

The journey from the hotel took only fifteen minutes. They had to drive through a steady flow of water running down the road as they got as close to the volcano as they could. The driver turned and took a road leading to the ocean highway.

To the right, the ocean was calm and blue. Emily wondered whether Pele was with her sister and whether they were fighting or working together to help the Olympians.

On their left, the ocean wall of Diamond Head loomed. The closer they got to it, the less like a volcano it looked. There were tall, leafy trees, shrubs, and long grasses growing all the way up the side, giving the viewer the impression that it was a simple mountain slope. It wasn't smooth, either. There were deep grooves sliced into it, as though water had been pouring down the side and had cut trails into the mountain.

The driver pulled into a parking area by a large white lighthouse. "Here you go, kids. This is as close as you're going to get. That's Diamond Head over there, but like I said, you can't reach the crater from here. From what I heard, they are going to seal the tunnel into the crater on the other side and let it fill up. Then they're gonna direct the water down here and into the ocean. The highway and all this area will be flooded."

"When will they do that?" Joel asked.

The driver shrugged. "I haven't heard. Hey, you want me to stay here while you look around?"

Emily shook her head. "No thanks. We're going to spend some time exploring."

"Suit yourselves," the driver said as Emily paid him.

"Now what?" Joel asked as he watched the taxi pull away. They looked at the rising mountain across the highway. "Pele's note said we could call her from Diamond Head, but she never said if we had to be *in* the crater."

"She knew about the water," Paelen suggested. "I am sure she knew we could not go inside."

They crossed the highway and walked up to where the incline started. Emily gazed up the side and squinted. "Wow, it doesn't look like a volcano from here." She looked back at Joel and Paelen and then focused her full attention on the side of Diamond Head. "Pele, can you hear me? We really need your help. Please come."

They expected Pele to magically appear. But there was nothing except a gentle breeze, birdsong, and an occasional car passing along the highway. They looked back at the lighthouse and beyond it to the calm ocean.

"I wonder if she's out there," Joel said.

"Maybe we need to be higher." Emily looked back at Paelen. "If Joel and I keep watch, will you fly up the side and call for Pele? She might hear you better from up there."

"I don't know, Em," Joel said. "That's kind of risky."

No sooner had the words come out of his mouth than a squadron of military jets blasted past their location.

"Soldiers—quick, get down!" Joel grabbed Emily and they ducked down into some bushes.

"They're moving too fast to be looking for us," Emily said as she stood and brushed dirt off her new clothes. "Besides, the CRU use black helicopters."

"I do not like this island," Paelen said as his eyes followed the fighter jets soaring along the coastline. "There are too many soldiers." He looked back at them. "I will do it. I will try anything to get us out of here."

"Just keep close to the ground," Joel suggested.

"Try to look like you're climbing it. But go as high as you can."

Paelen nodded and said to his sandals, "Take me up the side of Diamond Head, but keep us close to the ground."

The tiny wings flapped in acknowledgment and Paelen was lifted off the ground.

"The way is clear," Joel said, checking the road. "Go now!"

"Go!" Paelen ordered his sandals.

As Paelen ascended the side of the mountain, Emily and Joel kept watch.

"He looks as if he's climbing," Joel commented, following his progress.

"I just hope Pele hears him."

Paelen returned a few minutes later, his face flushed. "You would not believe it! It is not a crater anymore, but a big lake. There are people on the opposite side and there is actually a boat in there. It was filled with people."

"Probably scientists," Joel suggested. "Or military."

"What about Pele?" Emily asked.

"I called to her many times, but she did not respond. I even called into the lei she gave me, but it was as though she could not hear me. I wanted to shout, but I feared being overheard."

"What do we do now?" Joel asked.

Emily considered their options. "We're out of time. Fawn must call the Big Three and get them here as soon as possible. Without them, we can't get to the shard."

Joel shielded his eyes from the blazing sun and gazed around. "Maybe we should have asked the taxi to wait. It's a long walk back to the hotel, and it's getting hot."

"If we see one on the way, we can stop it," Emily said. "C'mon, I don't like leaving Pegs and the others alone too long."

The sun grew hotter and climbed to its highest point as they made their way back to the hotel. They noticed traffic in the sky. There were still a few tourist helicopters, but most were the large, heavy twin rotors of military helicopters flying low over Honolulu.

They looked at each other uneasily. "You don't

think they could have seen Paelen and alerted the CRU?" Joel asked.

"No way," Emily said, but she lacked confidence. "Pele said this was a military island—they're probably training or something."

"Yeah, that's it," Joel agreed, a little too quickly.

"They are not looking for us," Paelen insisted. "The CRU cannot know we are here. We have done nothing to draw attention to ourselves."

"No, of course not," Emily agreed. "We didn't cause the earthquake or open Diamond Head to all that water. And we didn't crash on the roof a couple of nights ago, making more noise than a bomb. No, we didn't do anything at all!"

"All I meant," Paelen said, "is that we have not been seen. I was very careful this morning. No one saw me."

The more they tried to convince themselves that they were safe, the faster they walked. Soon something funny settled in the pit of Emily's stomach.

That "something" was confirmed the moment they turned a corner and reached the driveway of their hotel. Dark green military trucks were pulled up in front of the Outrigger Reef, and armed soldiers filled the lobby. Hotel guests were being lined up and their identification checked by men in dark suits wearing grim expressions.

"Please tell me this is just a drill," Joel whispered as they joined the curious crowds gathering across from their hotel.

Suddenly a loudspeaker rang out. "Put down your phones and cameras. No photographs permitted! Clear the area immediately! This is a military order. You are instructed to clear the area."

The sound of rotor blades from above was deafening. They looked up and saw a large black helicopter approaching the roof. Emily's heart skipped as it hovered right above their suite. "They're black," she whispered tightly. "It's got to be the CRU!"

A heavy cable was lowered from the helicopter and a large green tarpaulin was hoisted off the roof. They could see movement in the tarpaulin, and even from this distance, Emily could hear the sound of Pegasus's screams.

"No!" Emily wailed. She lifted her hand to use her powers, but Joel threw his arms around her and pulled her hand down. Pain tore through her temples as Riza pounded her warning.

"You can't help him," Joel whispered urgently. "Em, stop, they'll see you."

"But they've got Pegs!" Each scream from the winged stallion cut through Emily's heart like a knife. She cursed herself for not having the power to stop them. All she could do was watch the helicopter pull away, taking Pegasus with it.

Soldiers crossed the street and approached the crowds. "Move along. There's nothing to see here. Just keep moving."

A second black helicopter moved into position and another heavy cable was lowered down to the hotel's roof.

As they were forced away with the crowds, a second tarpaulin was hoisted into the air. They watched two hands shoot out of the top of the tarp, followed by hooves and a head with a flash of long chestnut hair. Chiron was trying to climb up the cable.

"Look! There's a man in there!" a woman called. "What are they doing to him?"

"I don't know," her husband said, "and we don't

want to know. Let's just do as they say and get out of here." He caught her by the hand and drew her quickly away.

Emily felt sick with helplessness. Pegasus and the others were being taken and she was powerless to help them.

"Kids, this way . . ." A hand closed around Emily's arm. She looked up into the face of Mickey, their hotel representative. "Quickly, before they see you."

"What's happening?" Emily said.

"You already know," Mickey said. "Soldiers are tearing the hotel apart, looking for you. It won't take them long to check the surrounding area. Come with me if you want to stay free."

Paelen gripped Mickey's wrist. His face was dark and threatening. "We are not going anywhere with you until you tell us what you know of this." The hotel worker winced as Paelen squeezed his wrist. "Tell us!"

"Answer him before he breaks your arm," Joel threatened. "Who are you? What do you know about us?"

"I serve Pele," Mickey said quickly. "She told me to keep an eye on you. She's with her ocean sister and commanded me to keep you safe. She said you are under her protection."

"Pele?" Emily cried. "We tried to call her today, but she didn't answer."

"She won't, not if she is with Nā-maka. Now hurry. We only have moments. My car is parked down the street. I must get you away from here."

With soldiers searching the area, they had only a second to decide. "All right," Emily said. She looked from Paelen to Joel. "We don't have a choice."

Keeping their heads down, they moved quickly away from the hotel without looking back. Each step was a pain tearing through Emily. Her worst nightmare had been realized.

Pegasus was back in the hands of the CRU.

30

MICKEY'S HOUSE WAS SEVERAL MILES FROM Honolulu. He showed them into a lounge area and left them alone to get refreshments.

Joel grabbed the TV remote. "Let's see if there's anything on the news."

But there was nothing at all about the events at the hotel.

"It was the CRU, wasn't it?" Emily asked.

"Looks like it," Joel said heavily. "Same black helicopters and men in suits."

"Can this get any worse?" Emily exclaimed. She got up and started to pace the room.

"Em, calm down—don't blow a gasket!" Joel warned. "We'll find them."

"How?" Paelen asked.

"Okay, everyone, think," Emily said. "We've gone up against the CRU before; this is no different. So where would they take them? This island isn't that big. Could the CRU have an underground facility here?"

Joel shrugged. "I don't know. There are mountains in the middle of the island. Maybe they've got a place there."

"Or perhaps they have taken them off the island," Paelen added.

Emily hated to admit it, but Paelen could be right. It would be more logical to take the Olympians away from Honolulu. She flopped down on the sofa and moaned, "It's starting all over again. They'll make more clones, just like in Las Vegas."

"No they won't, not this time," Joel insisted. "Fawn is with them, she'll get a message to Jupiter. I bet he knows already. They'll be here any moment."

"Then what?" Emily asked. "The Big Three will do to Hawaii what they did to Las Vegas?" She looked back at her friend. "Do you realize that wherever we go, we cause destruction? Here, in Greece, in Las Vegas, even in New York."

"We've never been to Greece," Joel said.

"Yes we have!" Emily snapped. "You just don't remember it. I lost control of my powers at the Acropolis Museum and accidentally destroyed Athens."

"Em, stop," Joel said. "That won't happen. I promise."

"I want to know how they knew about us," Paelen said. "We were careful. No one saw anything at the hotel."

Joel shrugged. "I don't think that family saw Pegasus or Chiron. Gregor was hanging around the balcony a lot, but he was cool."

"And he was more interested in the ocean view than us," Emily said.

Mickey returned with a tray of drinks. "Here, everyone drink up. It'll help."

They each took a glass and drank down the cool fruit juice. "How long have you been serving Pele?" Emily asked.

"Oh, it seems like forever." Mickey took a seat beside Emily. She could feel him trembling.

"Are you all right?"

He nodded. "Just a bit nervous."

"What have you got to be nervous about? We're the ones they're looking for," Joel said.

"I know, but I might have been seen helping you. My job is on the line. Maybe even my life, if I'm not careful."

"So," Emily said, changing the subject, "how is it that you serve Pele? I mean, you don't exactly look . . ." She stopped.

"Hawaiian?" Mickey said.

"Well, yes," Emily admitted.

"You don't have to be from the Islands to serve the gods. I was born in Los Angeles but raised on the Big Island. When I was young, I was visited by Pele."

"Really? That must have been something," Emily said as she finished her drink.

"It was the worst day of my life," Mickey said. "There's a legend here in the Islands that the tour guides tell visitors. It's more like a warning, really. But basically it's said that if you visit the Kilauca Volcano on the Big Island, you must never take away any of the black rocks on the ground. If you do, it will anger Pele and bring bad luck. In fact"—Mickey rose and looked out of the windows nervously—"there's actually a special post office around here that returns the rocks tourists take home with them and then send back when the bad luck starts. Those rocks are all returned to Kilauea."

"So why was meeting Pele your worst day?" Joel asked.

"Because Pele is mean-spirited, vicious, and power mad. Before I knew about the legend, I visited Kilauea and took a large piece of black rock. I thought it was pretty and wanted it for my mineral collection. But Pele appeared. She was furious and threatened me. If it hadn't been for Nā-maka intervening on my behalf, I'm sure Pele would have killed me. I was just a dumb teenager. I didn't know any better, but that didn't matter. She said I'd disrespected her and stolen from her home. From that day forward, I swore service and devotion to her sister. Pele is a monster, just like you and the Olympians."

"Wh-what?" Paelen said. He stood and staggered, looking at his empty glass. His eyes grew foggy and heavy. "What was in this?" The glass fell from his hands and shattered on the tile floor just as he collapsed.

"It is a special drink, prepared just for you by Nā-maka. I hope you like it."

Just then, Joel fell back on the sofa.

"Joel, Paelen!" Emily cried. She reached over and checked the pulse in Joel's neck. It pounded steadily and his breathing was normal. But he and Paelen were out cold. Her eyes flashed to their drink glasses. "What have you done to them?"

"What I was commanded to do." Mickey looked at her empty glass and frowned.

Emily stood. "Whatever you put in our drinks won't work on me. Now, who are you really?" she demanded. "Are you working with the CRU?"

"Those idiots?" Mickey rose and backed away from the sofa. "Don't be stupid. I told you already. I serve Nā-maka." He reached his desk and opened the top drawer. He pulled out a gun and pointed it at Emily. "I don't know what you are, if the drink didn't work on you. But I'm sure you're not bullet-proof."

"Actually, I am," Emily said darkly as she advanced on him. She raised her hand to summon the Flame, but even before the thought was finished, Riza shot a pain through her temple. If she was going to survive this, Emily needed a good bluff.

"Stop!" Mickey cried. He turned the gun on Joel. "I'll bet he's not bulletproof."

"If you fire that gun, it will be the last thing you ever do." Emily pushed past the pain and summoned a very small Flame in her palm. Riza had to understand this was necessary and know she wouldn't summon any more. "Now drop the gun before I lose my temper."

Fear rose on Mickey's face. "You're just like Pele— a fire demon."

"I'm no demon," Emily said. "But I will do anything to protect my friends. Believe me, Flame is the least of my powers. Now tell me, why have you done this to us?"

"You really wanna know? Fine, it won't change anything. For years, Nā-maka has been waiting for the chance to overpower her sister. Your coming here has provided the first opportunity she's had in a very long time. We are not going to waste it."

"Now who's being stupid?" Emily challenged. "You have no idea what's happening here. There's a war going on out there. A big one. The Titans versus the Olympians. If the Titans win, they won't stop with Olympus. Their next move will be to come here and conquer Earth. They will enslave everyone, including the Hawaiian gods. Pele and Nā-maka must stop fighting and unite to help us defeat Saturn. He is their enemy too."

"Empty threats," Mickey said. "Nā-maka-o-Kaha'i is much stronger than your Olympians or Titans. She has promised me eternal life for my service. I will not betray her."

"You betrayed us for eternal life?"

"I would do much more than that," Mickey said darkly.

"So what does she want you to do?" Emily asked.

"I am to hand all of you over to her."

"What does she want with us?"

"You're the one who doesn't understand what's going on. Let me spell it out for you. Pele put you under her protection, so her word and honor are at stake. Should anything happen to you, it will weaken her position as leader of the gods, because she couldn't keep her word. These gods are all honor-driven. If her promise is broken, she will lose the respect and support of the others. It will completely upset the balance of power, and she will be replaced."

His eyes lit up with a strange kind of madness. "I can't wait to see it! Once she is gone, Nā-maka can take control."

"You're wrong. Pele didn't offer protection to me. Do you see any flowers? If you really want to hurt her, you need to get Pegasus and the others away from the military. Those are the Olympians she has under her protection."

The gun in Mickey's hand wavered and then pointed at Paelen and Joel. "No, they're wearing Pele's lei. They're under her protection too. Besides, I can't reach the others; they've been taken to the Honolulu Zoo."

"The zoo?" Emily cried. "How do you know?"

"Who do you think called the military in the first place? When they arrived at the Outrigger, I overheard them talking. The Olympians were being taken to the zoo instead of the base at Pearl Harbor. The zoo is a trap and the others are bait. It's you they're really after."

"It was you who betrayed us?" Emily cried. "You moron! You don't know what you've done!"

"I did as I was commanded," Mickey said. "If they'd taken the Olympians to Pearl Harbor, it would have been easy. That's right on the water, and Nā-maka could have claimed them already. But they're at the zoo, and that's too far inland for her. I now have two choices. Either I offer to trade you to the military in exchange for Pegasus or that Centaur, or I make do with you three. If the military wants you, Nā-maka may want you too."

Mickey paused and looked at her strangely. "Why is the military more interested in you than the others?"

"I'll tell you if you put the gun down," Emily said.

"Now who's being stupid?" Mickey spat. "I don't care what you are. Just sit down and shut your mouth."

Emily stood before the armed man, weighing her options. She could try to summon whatever was left of her powers, but would they work? How much could she use before she destroyed herself and Riza? Would it be enough to save Joel and Paelen? What would happen then? Lorin would get the shard and then there would be no stopping her or the Titans. Could she risk it?

No.

Emily lowered her hands and sat down. "Please, Mickey, listen to me. If you do this, Nā-maka may defeat her sister, but to what end if the Titans enslave Earth? Please, help us stop them. Then Pele and her sister can go back to their own war."

The madness returned to his eyes as he pulled a roll of duct tape from a drawer. "You're so convinced that your Olympians and Titans are more powerful than the Hawaiian gods. But you're wrong. Nā-maka can raise a wall of water to drown these Islands if she wanted. She commands all the oceans."

Emily was tempted to say that Neptune could do the same thing, or that the Big Three could destroy Earth without even coming here. But she chose to stay silent.

She sat still as Mickey bound her arms behind her back. She hated surrendering to him, but with Joel and Paelen unconscious and her powers all but gone, there was little she could do on her own. She would use the time to think up a plan.

Emily watched Mickey bind Paelen's hands and then move on to Joel. But when he pulled off Joel's glove to reveal the silver hand, he frowned. "What's this?"

"Vulcan made it for him. The Olympians are very clever and generous. If you help us, I'm sure Jupiter will grant you eternal life. You don't have to do this to us."

His eyes grew dark and stormy. "Are you asking me to betray my oath?"

Emily shook her head. "I'm asking you to think. You are in the middle of two big fights: the Olympians versus the Titans and Nā-maka-o-Kaha'i versus Pele. If it continues, no one will win."

"I told you to shut up." He came back to her and put a strip of tape on her mouth. He leaned in close to her face. "You are *not* changing my mind."

The angrier Mickey became, the rougher he was with Joel and Paelen as he put tape around their hands and then legs. He hoisted Paelen up on his shoulder and carried him away. He then did the same with Joel.

When he came back, he lifted Emily onto his

shoulder. She mused on how easy it would have been to defeat him with her powers. But now she couldn't even stop him from carrying her through the small house. She felt completely helpless as they passed through a door and into the garage. Emily was deposited roughly in the back of an old white van between the unconscious bodies of Joel and Paelen.

Mickey showed her the gun as he slipped it into his waistline. "Listen to me. Don't go trying any of those fire tricks. If I smell even the tiniest smoldering, I swear I will put a bullet in Joel's head. Do you understand me?"

Emily nodded as Mickey climbed into the driver's seat and started the engine. Soon the automatic garage door opened and the van was pulling out of the driveway.

Emily struggled to sit up and peered out the front window as the van made its way through the neighborhood. There were lush green mountains directly ahead of them as Mickey maneuvered the van onto a highway. Wherever he was taking them, it was away from Honolulu.

Mickey reached for his cell phone and dialed a

number. "Yeah, Kono, it's me. I've got 'em. Two of them are out cold. The girl is still awake. . . ."

A voice at the other end asked a muffled question.

"Of course I gave it to her, but it didn't work. I don't know what she is, but I don't think she's normal. She can make fire just like Pele. It doesn't matter anyway. If Nā-maka won't take her, we can trade her for one of the other animals—either that flying horse or the pig. I doubt they'll let that Centaur go. But she's the one they're really after."

Another muffled comment came from the cell phone. "Yeah," Mickey answered. "I'm on Highway Three right now, crossing the island. We should be there within the hour. Get the boat ready. I want to go the moment we arrive."

So Mickey wasn't working alone. Emily nudged Joel, trying to get him to wake up. When that failed, she tried Paelen. But he remained unconscious. Whatever Mickey had given them must have been powerful if it was strong enough to knock out Olympians.

Time stood still as Emily lay in the back of the van. They were in deep trouble. Mickey and his accomplice planned to hand them over to Nā-maka-o-Kaha'i. If her temper was anything like her sister's, then what the CRU was doing to Pegasus and the others would pale in comparison to what they were facing.

Emily heard Paelen start to stir. She leaned close to his face and his eyes fluttered open. Emily shook her head, warning him not to move. She nodded toward Mickey in the driver's seat.

Paelen nodded and closed his eyes again. But though they were closed, she could feel his subtle movements as he tore through the tape binding his hands behind his back.

Once free, he slipped his hands beneath her and used his power to stretch out his arms. He reached for the tape binding her hands. With little effort she was freed.

Just as Emily reached for Joel, they felt the van turn off the highway. It slowed and turned onto what sounded like a gravel road and then bumped onto a softer surface that Emily guessed was sand. She lifted her head to look out the window again, and gasped. The ocean was in front of them. A rowboat was bobbing on the shore, and a large Hawaiian man was standing beside it.

Mickey stopped the van, then turned back and looked at her. "Remember," he said, showing her the gun, "you try anything and I'll start shooting. Don't move a muscle—I'll be right back."

As soon as he left the van, Emily turned back to Paelen. He reached forward and gently pulled the tape away from her face.

"He's working for Nā-maka," Emily quickly explained. "He's going to hand us over to her to use against Pele."

"He is going to try," Paelen said darkly. "But he will fail. I do not think he understands who we are or what we can do."

"I can't do anything now," Emily said.

"Why do you say that when you know you can fight?" Paelen said. "You are more than just your powers. Diana has trained you well. You just have to believe in yourself."

"But I've never put my training into practice. I hardly even paid attention!"

"You did not have to. Now you do." Paelen gave

her a crooked grin and his eyes sparkled. "You will be amazed at what you can accomplish. Look at me. I am small for an Olympian, but fighting humans is easy—they are so squishy." He reached past Emily and started to shake Joel. "Wake up, Joel. There is a fight coming!"

"Whatever he gave us to drink, it's really powerful. I don't know if Joel will wake up anytime soon. I'm just so glad you're awake," Emily said.

Paelen grinned again. "So am I."

They heard voices as Mickey and the other man returned to the van. "They're all tied up in here, Kono."

Emily and Paelen immediately lay back down. Emily remembered to put the tape back on her mouth. When the van door opened, she squinted at the bright sunshine pouring in.

Kono reached for Joel, roughly hauled him out of the van and carried him over to the boat. When he returned, Mickey caught hold of Emily. "Your turn—out you come. We don't want to keep the lady waiting."

In the same instant, Kono reached for Paelen. "What the—"

Paelen struck with a blow so fast and powerful, it knocked the Hawaiian against the inside of the van. Paelen leaped out and grabbed him. He lifted him easily over his head and slammed him down to the sand.

As Mickey looked on in shock, Emily used the opportunity to turn her anger on him. Pulling the tape from her mouth, she roared like Diana and kicked out at him with a surprise blow to his stomach that knocked him down to his knees. Emily tried to remember everything Diana had taught her, and tested out her fighting moves.

Before Mickey could land one punch on Emily, Paelen appeared and gave him a bone-crushing jab to the chin. "That is for Joel!" The blow was hard enough to lift Mickey off the ground and send him flying several feet in the air before crashing down on a sand dune.

"See, Emily?" Paelen grinned. "Humans are squishy!" After another punch, Mickey collapsed onto the sand, unconscious.

As Emily and Paelen crossed the beach to the rowboat where Joel lay, the ocean stirred and started to swirl, and a large waterspout rose high in the air. A beautiful woman emerged from the side of the spout. Her hair was as green as the clearest ocean waters and her face was pale, like sea foam. She had webbing between her long fingers and wore a gown of seaweed that had tiny fish swimming in the air around her. Her eyes were as black as Pele's. Around her neck was a lei of pearls and tiny colorful seashells.

She held out her arms to them. "Come to me!"

Paelen caught hold of Emily's hand and held her back. "Who are you?"

"I am Nā-maka-o-Kaha'i! You, who wear the lei of my sister, will come with me now. Pele will know my wrath!"

Emily's eyes moved from the ocean goddess to Joel in the rowboat, just yards from her powerful waterspout. "Please, listen. I know about your rivalry with your sister, but we're all in terrible danger. We need your help. You must command the waters in Diamond Head to recede so Pele can open the surface and I can retrieve what I need to save Earth."

"From the Titans?" Nā-maka-o-Kaha'i laughed. "Pele told me, but I know it's a trick—a foolish trap designed by my sister to contain me within the springwater filling the Diamond Head crater. Without me to oppose her, Pele will have free rein over these Islands and the oceans. I don't know what she promised the Olympians in exchange for their help, but they will never see their reward."

"I swear it's no trick," Emily said. "If Saturn isn't stopped, he'll invade Earth."

"The Titans do not frighten me."

"They should," Paelen said. "They frighten all of us."

Nā-maka shook her head. "The Titans tried to subdue Earth many thousands of years ago and failed—"

"They failed because I went back there and helped stop them," Emily cut in. "But my powers have been trapped in Diamond Head. If I do not free them, the Titans will succeed."

"You overestimate their abilities—and your own. This fight is between them; it means nothing to me."

The ocean goddess raised her hand and a large wave of water shot toward Emily and Paelen. Paelen immediately wrapped his arm around Emily's waist.

"Up! Now!" he ordered his winged sandals, and they lifted into the air, missing the attacking wave by inches.

"Come back here!" Nā-maka-o-Kaha'i commanded. Her waterspout spun furiously close to shore, but did not touch the dry sand.

Paelen ordered his sandals to lift them higher, away from her reaching ocean hands. "You cannot follow us onto land, can you?" Paelen challenged.

"There is no need. I already have one of you, and I see by the red lei that he is under my sister's protection. He will do nicely."

Before Paelen could make a move, the ocean goddess used her water hands to catch hold of Joel. Still unconscious, Joel was lifted out of the rowboat by the swirling ocean water and carried over to Nā-maka-o-Kaha'i.

"Joel!" Emily howled. "Let him go or I swear you'll regret it!"

"Are you threatening me, child?"

"Yes!" Emily shouted. "These may be your Islands, but if you don't release Joel right now, I promise you, the moment I get my powers back, you'll pay for what you've done to him!"

"No one threatens me!" Pounding waves of fury rose up around Nā-maka-o-Kaha'i and crashed noisily to the beach, crushing the rowboat into splinters and throwing wet sand in the air. The small fish swimming around her ducked into the protection of her seaweed dress.

Nā-maka-o-Kaha'i moved as close to the shore as she dared and spat at Emily with ocean foam. "You listen to me, you insolent child. Tell Pele she will surrender to me or I will drown this boy in my depths and let the ocean life feed on his bones! You have one day!"

She rose higher above her waterspout before diving down into its swirling center. Joel was sucked in after her as the waterspout spun across the ocean surface before disappearing into its depths.

"Joel!" Emily cried.

Paelen landed on the beach, and they watched the spot where Nā-maka-o-Kaha'i had vanished.

"How can she be so blind?" Emily raged.

"Her hatred of Pele has obscured everything else. If we hoped to reason with her and get her help, we must forget it. Our only chance now is the Big Three. Come, we must find Fawn to get the message to Jupiter to meet us at Diamond Head."

But Emily remained still at the shore, staring at the sea.

"You cannot help him by staying here." Paelen sighed, gently drawing her away. "Only when your powers are restored will you be strong enough to face her. Joel is safe for now."

"Safe? How can you be so sure?" Emily raged. "You saw her—she's insane!" Emily kicked sand in the air and collapsed to the ground, punching it with both fists. "If she hurts him, I swear she'll regret it."

"Emily, please," Paelen cried as he knelt beside her. "You will not do Joel or the others any good if you lose your temper and accidentally use your powers. You could hurt yourself. Do you not understand that? You could die if you do not control yourself!"

Emily was so tired of it all. Her increasing weakness, her aching body, and the constant need to sleep. And now, when she needed her powers the most, they were gone.

She sighed heavily and sat back. "You're right, I know. It's just that . . ."

"I understand," Paelen said as he drew her up. "I feel the same." They walked back up the beach to where Mickey and Kono still lay unconscious. Paelen lifted Kono away from the van and threw him down on the sand beside Mickey. He started to shake the men. "Wake up!"

"What are you planning?" Emily asked.

"They must tell us where the others are."

"Mickey already told me. They're at the zoo. He said it's a trap for us. They're using Pegasus and the others as bait."

"Trap or not," Paelen said, "we do not have much choice. We cannot leave them to the mercy of the CRU. We must do what we can to free them."

"You're right. We've got to rescue them." Emily gazed toward the ocean a final time, knowing that Joel was out there somewhere. "If she hurts him . . ."

Paelen put his arms around her and held her tight. "She would not dare."

Emily gazed up into his eyes and she could see a trace of sadness there.

"I know how you feel about Joel and how he feels about you," Paelen said softly. "I have known for some time and I accept it. Please know this. If she does hurt him, she will answer to me as well."

Emily clung to him, grateful to have such a precious friend.

When he released her, he bent down, searched through Mickey's pockets, and pulled out the van keys. Then he reached for the man's baseball cap and pulled it on. "We must not be seen using my sandals in daylight, but we cannot wait until dark."

"Are you thinking about taking the van to the zoo?" Emily cried. "Paelen, we don't have a license!"

"We do not have much choice."

Emily reached for the van keys. "I think I should drive."

"I will drive," Paelen said.

"You? You've never driven a car. I have. My mom used to let me practice in a parking lot when we drove out of the city."

"I have watched Joel closely—I know what I am doing. And I have the baseball cap. That is all I need."

"Hats don't make you able to drive!" Emily argued.

"Of course they do," Paelen said. "I have watched

humans closely. Most drivers here wear these hats."

"No, Paelen, *practice* makes you a good driver. Now give me the keys."

Paelen grinned and climbed in behind the wheel. "Do you wish to keep arguing, or are we going to the zoo to free our friends?"

Emily huffed, but climbed into the passenger seat. Almost from the start she regretted it. Within minutes Paelen had driven into a palm tree, knocked over a fence, crushed trash cans, and got the van trapped in a sand dune. He had to lift the van out of the sand trap.

When he sat behind the wheel again, he shook his head. "Joel makes it look so easy!"

"Now can I try?" Emily asked.

When they switched seats, Emily sat behind the wheel. She checked her mirrors as her mother taught her and then put the van in gear.

At first the van lurched forward and then stopped. But after a couple of false starts, Emily managed to pull the vehicle away.

Paelen cheered and pulled the cap off his head and put it on Emily. "Here, you have earned it. Now get us to the zoo!"

Emily stopped the van and looked at him. "Where is the zoo?"

Paelen shrugged. "You are Flame of Olympus, the last Xan. You should know."

"How?"

"I do not know," Paelen insisted. "I thought you could feel Pegasus, with or without your powers."

"I always have a connection with him," she said, "but not enough to tell me where he is."

With little idea where they were going, Emily inched the van down the road. When they came upon a gas station, she carefully pulled in. "Stay here. I'm going to find out where we are."

She returned with a map showing the whole island. "The guy said we are here on this side of the island and that this circle over here is the Honolulu Zoo." She traced her finger on the map. "It doesn't look too difficult. If we just follow the coastline, we'll go around the bottom of the island and come up the other side, where the zoo is. Simple."

Paelen looked up at her, raised his eyebrows, and grinned. "Oh, really?"

Emily punched him. "Cut me some slack. My

powers are gone, a crazy mermaid has kidnapped Joel, and I'm freaked that I'm going to get caught driving this stolen van."

Paelen's grin grew wider. "Then drive carefully and do not get caught."

Within minutes they had plotted their route, and Emily pulled the van back out into traffic. The sun was starting to set on the horizon, casting a beautiful golden glow on the Hawaiian mountains.

"I would like to visit this place again when we are finished." Paelen held his hand out the window, feeling the warm wind between his fingers.

"You mean if Saturn doesn't conquer it?"

The crooked grin on his face always made her feel better. "Exactly!"

Emily followed the coastline around Oahu. She was glad that they were far enough from the shore that Nā-maka-o-Kaha'i couldn't reach them. When they arrived at the southern tip of the island and started the journey north, Emily saw a familiar sight rising in the distance.

"There's Diamond Head! The guy at the gas station said the zoo isn't far from it. We're almost there."

Nerves settled in the pit of her stomach. They were about to enter the lion's den, but they had no clue what they would find there. What had the CRU done to the Olympians? Were they even still there?

As they got closer to Honolulu, commuter traffic increased. Cars cut her off and horns blared around them as Emily drove much slower than the speed limit.

"Perhaps you should drive faster," Paelen suggested.

Emily shot him a dirty look. "Do you want to drive?"

He held up his hands. "No thank you! You are doing fine. But might I suggest we try a less busy route?"

Emily nodded. Her knuckles were white from clutching the steering wheel as she tried to maneuver the vehicle off the main highway and onto a less busy road. She indicated a right turn, but miscalculated as she turned the van around the corner and grazed a red sedan waiting at the light. Emily turned the wheel sharply in the other direction, but lost control and smashed headlong into a lamppost.

Steam rose from under the hood and the engine chugged and then died. Emily looked over at Paelen. "You okay?"

Paelen grinned. "Well, that is one way to turn a corner. Not the best way, but still . . ."

Cars pulled up around them and drivers were getting out.

"What are we going to do now?" Emily grimaced.

"Play it cool." Paelen opened his door and climbed out of the van. Emily took a deep breath and did the same. The driver of the red sedan was walking toward them. He looked around forty and wore a light linen business suit. "Are you both all right?"

"Yes, thank you," Emily said carefully. "Are you?"

He nodded but then registered that there was no adult with them. "How old are you kids? Do you even have a driver's license?"

"I am older than you could ever imagine," Paelen answered boldly.

The man was just about to retort when a woman ran up to them. "I've just called the police and they'll be here in a moment."

"The police!" Emily cried. "Why did you do that?

It's my dad's van. He'll pay for the damages. There was no need to call the police!"

"Hey, calm down," the man said, growing even more suspicious. "We'll let the cops sort this out. But I think you two are in a bit of trouble. I doubt you've got insurance."

Paelen took hold of Emily's arm. "I think we should be going."

"Oh, no you don't," the man said, catching hold of Paelen's shirt. "You're not going anywhere until the cops get here."

Paelen grabbed the man's hand and squeezed. "I say we are. I am very sorry about your car, but there is nothing we can do about that now. If you do not release me right now, I shall break your hand."

The man was driven to his knees as Paelen's grip hardened.

"That's enough," Emily said as she pulled Paelen free. "Let's go!"

They took off running as the wail of police sirens sounded in the distance. At the corner they turned left into a suburban-looking area with houses that stood away from the road.

"This way!" Paelen shouted to Emily as he led her down a long driveway. They kept low behind a couple of large SUVs, ducked around the side of the house, and moved into the open backyard, where they continued to run. At the rear of the yard, they climbed over a fence and ran through another yard.

They dipped and dodged through streets and yards until they could no longer hear police sirens. Then they stopped to catch their breath, huddled behind a large flowering bush growing up against a house. They took in their surroundings. They were in a built-up residential area. They saw the odd person walking a dog, but otherwise the area was quiet.

Emily cursed. "I left the map in the van!"

"I am sure we are not far from the zoo," Paelen said.

"That's not what I'm worried about. The zoo was circled on the map! If the police see it, they'll know where we're going."

Paelen started to laugh. "Emily, we are going to the zoo—a place that we already know is a trap for us. There are CRU agents and soldiers with guns waiting to shoot us the moment we arrive. And you are worried about the police because of the stolen van?"

Emily paused and then broke into a big smile. "Okay, you're right." She rose and peered above the bush. "The sun is almost down. Maybe we should wait here until dark. Then we can go save Pegasus."

31

LORIN WAS SURROUNDED BY BLAZING WHITE light. She heard sounds like nothing she'd ever heard before. But then, her only experience of sounds was from deep inside Tartarus. Here in the Solar Stream there was no screaming or crying, just a loud whooshing in her ears.

Shivers of excitement coursed down her spine. Soon she would come face-to-face with Emily. Then she would find the shard and finally be complete.

The bright lights faded as her journey ended. Her eyes adjusted and she looked around in awe. It was dark out, but the air around her felt fresh and full of sounds and wondrous smells. A gentle, warm breeze blew on her face, and she could taste salt on her lips.

The ground beneath her feet was not solid like it was on Tartarus. As she turned around, it seemed to move beneath her and pour into her sandals. She reached down and picked up a handful of sand, and it slipped through her fingers. The bits that were left were small and gritty.

Lorin's eyes widened as she faced the largest body of water she had ever seen. It went well beyond her vision and was lost to the dark horizon. There was water in the prison, but it was only for drinking and was not to be wasted. But here the water seemed endless. It rolled to shore with a soft swishing sound that stroked her ears pleasantly.

She looked up and was awestruck by the millions of stars in the night sky. When Phoebe had first taken her to the surface of Tartarus, a storm had been blowing. But Phoebe had described in detail the night sky on Titus. Lorin imagined it must be just like this.

Behind her were tall structures. Candlelight shone through most of the windows, and she could see people on some of the open balconies. Farther down the beach, she heard laughter. She stood still as a man and woman approached. They were holding hands and gave her only a passing glance.

The woman was wearing a long floral skirt and a white T-shirt. Lorin looked down at her own garments. They looked like filthy rags, barely held together. She looked back at the water. Without hesitation, Lorin walked into the ocean and had her first bath.

The sensation of the cool water on her skin was indescribable. She laughed and splashed in the light surf. Lorin discovered that she could float on her back and stare up at the stars. This one moment was the happiest she had known since waking.

Soon Lorin became aware of something else. A gentle drawing sensation was rising from the pit of her stomach—almost as though something was calling to her.

She stood in the water and gazed around. It seemed to be pulling her from one specific direction. At first the feeling frightened her. But then, as the moments passed, she seemed to understand what it was.

"The shard," she said aloud.

Lorin followed the feeling. By the light of the stars and the moon, she saw a giant dark shape looming in the distance. The feeling was coming from there. She emerged from the water onto the shore and started to walk in the direction of the shard.

With each step, she felt more excited. Walking was just too slow. She started to run, but even that wasn't fast enough. Lorin had to get there. The shard was calling her.

She focused everything she had on the shard and the next thing she knew, she was rising from the ground. Her powers! Lorin laughed as she began to realize what she was able to do. She started to fly in the direction of the shard.

She wasn't sure what was making her more excited: the proximity of the shard or the absolute freedom she felt in flying under a clear, open sky. To her left, she saw strange vehicles moving along the ground. She watched one stop and saw people climb out. She laughed even louder, excited at the idea of riding in one of these things.

Within minutes she was rising up the steep side of the mountain that housed the shard. She approached the summit. But just as she sailed over the top, her heart sank. It was full of water.

Lorin landed on the upper edge and gazed down into the black depths. The shard was there—she could feel it—but it was deep beneath the surface. How was she going to free it?

She held out her arms to summon it the way she made Flame shoot from her hands. She could feel the shard. It was right there, but something was blocking it. Lorin fed more power into her command. The ground beneath her started to shake. The harder she tried, the harder the ground shook.

Lorin looked up into the star-filled sky and shouted, "I will have the shard! Do you hear me, Emily? I will have it and I will be complete!"

Rage made Flames blaze in her hands. Lorin looked down into the black water and fired two powerful blasts of Flame at it. They sizzled and smoked on the surface. She added more power, hoping to burn her way down to the shard, but no matter how much power she added to the Flame, all she accomplished was the creation of a large plume of steam. Water was filling the crater faster than she could burn it away.

"You there—don't move. Stay where you are!" She was so focused on the shard that she hadn't noticed soldiers shouting and running toward her along the path that circled the rim of the volcano.

Lorin pulled the Flame back into herself and waited for them to get closer. They would tell her where Emily was.

"Drop your weapons and put up your hands!" one of them shouted.

"I do not have weapons," Lorin said.

"We saw you using a flamethrower. Where is it?"

Lorin held out her hand and it burst into Flame. "Do you mean this?"

The men gasped and stepped back. They raised the items they carried in their hands. "Who—who are you? How did you get up here?"

Lorin studied them closely. They were young men wearing strange clothes and they had serious expressions on their faces. They almost looked like Titans, but there was something very different about them. It was more a feeling than anything physical.

"Answer my question," one of them demanded as he stepped forward. He looked older than the others and appeared to be in charge. "How did you get up here?"

"I flew," Lorin answered. "Where is Emily?"

"Flew?" the man repeated.

"Yes," Lorin said. "Like this . . ." She used her powers to lift herself off the ground. "It is wonderful. You should try it. Now will you tell me about Emily?"

The men's mouths hung open.

"How do you know Emily?" the one in charge asked.

Lorin tilted her head to the side. "She is the reason I came here. She has stolen something from me and I want it back."

"Well, now, miss, if you come with us, I—I'm sure we can help you find her."

Lorin landed back on the ground. "You will take me to her?"

"Yes, yes, of course we will. Just come this way."

Lorin smiled and started to walk with the men who surrounded her on all sides.

"What are you?" she asked.

"I'm a sergeant," the one in charge said. "Sergeant Walker."

"Sergeant Walker," Lorin repeated. "I am a Titan. You all look like Titans, but you are different—smaller. You speak differently too."

"Titans, miss?" the sergeant repeated. "I don't understand."

"Neither do I," Lorin admitted. "This is all very strange to me. I have never been to Earth before . . ." She paused. "This is Earth, is it not? Honolulu—Hawaii—where Emily is?"

"You've never been to Earth . . . ," the soldier repeated. He stopped and studied her closely. "Where do you come from?"

"Tartarus," Lorin answered. "But Phoebe told me I was born on Titus. It was Jupiter and the Olympians who locked us in Tartarus. But we are free now. Soon Saturn will claim Olympus and I will go there."

"You know about Jupiter and Olympus?"

Lorin nodded. "Yes, Saturn is attacking Olympus right now. He wants me to kill Jupiter, but I do not want to do it. I came here to find Emily and become whole, not to kill anyone else."

"I'm glad you don't want to kill," the soldier said carefully. "If you come with me, maybe we can help you find her."

Lorin continued to follow the men when her sandal caught in a weed and she stumbled. Before she fell, the sergeant caught her and steadied her. "Careful there. It's easy to trip up here."

Lorin smiled at him. He was so nice and friendly and was only a little bit scared of her. "Tell me, do all Sergeant Walkers dress like you? I saw others down there by the water that looked very different."

The sergeant gave her a curious look. "We're soldiers—this is how we dress."

"Soldiers," Lorin repeated. "You said you were a Sergeant Walker."

The man started to chuckle. "No, my name is Walker. I'm David Walker. I'm a sergeant in the United States Army. But you can call me David."

"Oh," Lorin said, just as confused as ever. "I am Lorin." Her eyes landed on the item in his hands. "Is that a weapon?"

"Yes," David answered, looking at his rifle. "A very dangerous weapon."

"Why do you need it?"

"We're assigned to keep trespassers away from here."

"What is a trespasser?"

"Someone who does not belong here."

"Like me?"

The sergeant nodded. "But don't be frightened. I won't use it on you. We'll just help you get down from here."

"And then we can find Emily?"

"Yes." He nodded. "Then we'll find Emily."

The soldiers accompanied Lorin down a long set of stairs. David Walker stayed at her side and helped her down.

At the bottom, Lorin was escorted into a building and then into a large room. She saw other men in there, watching her with interest. There were two men who were different from the rest. They were dressed in dark clothes and had angry expressions on their faces. Their eyes landed on her and studied her intently. There was something about them that Lorin didn't like one bit.

The men in dark clothes stood before them. "Report."

"This is Lorin," Sergeant Walker said. "We found her at the top of Diamond Head. She is very special, and is looking for Emily. She says she is from Tartarus."

Lorin watched the exchange with interest. David

Walker was a bit scared of her. But he was even more scared of them.

"We'll take it from here, Sergeant," the older of the two men said.

The sergeant nodded. "Yes, Agent G." He looked at Lorin. "These two men will take you to Emily."

Lorin looked into the predatory eyes of Agent G. She smiled back at the sergeant. "No, I prefer you to take me to her."

"That's quite impossible," Agent G said. He grabbed her arm roughly.

"No!" Lorin's temper flared, and she used her powers to drive the two men across the room. They hit the wall with an explosive contact and crumpled to the floor. "I will stay with David Walker!"

The soldiers in the room raised their weapons at her.

"Stand down!" the sergeant ordered. He turned to Lorin. "You calm down too! You can't go doing things like that. You'll get into trouble."

She felt his fear increasing. Was it fear of her, or for her? "Do not be frightened of me, David. I would never hurt you. But tell them to stay away from me."

Lorin walked deeper into the room, ignoring the

soldiers who watched her every move. She was fascinated by her surroundings. There were so many strange things here. Lights blazed in the ceiling and on a desk. She held her hand above the bulb and smiled at him. "This is not fire, but it is hot?"

Sergeant Walker nodded to his men as they carried the two unconscious CRU agents out of the room. "It is a light," he said to Lorin. "It uses electricity, not fire. Now, would you like to come and sit down beside me?"

Lorin did as she was asked and sat beside the desk. She watched in fascination as Sergeant Walker held a strange device up to his ear and pressed several buttons on a small box. Then he started to speak. She could hear the whole conversation. He was talking to someone called Colonel James and they were discussing her. He told Colonel James that Lorin had just arrived from Tartarus and had flown up to the top of Diamond Head. He said she was looking for Emily, who had stolen something from her. He also added that the CRU agents were being taken to the hospital. Colonel James ordered the sergeant to get Lorin to the Honolulu Zoo as quickly as possible. Priority *Alpha, Alpha One.*

"What is Honolulu Zoo?" she asked when Sergeant Walker disconnected the call. "And what does 'Alpha, Alpha One' mean?"

The sergeant frowned at her. "You heard all that?"

Lorin nodded.

"My colonel—that is, the man I serve—has asked me to bring you to the zoo. It is a very special place, and he really wants to meet you."

"And 'Alpha, Alpha One'?"

"That means that you are a very, very special and important girl and he can't wait to meet you."

Lorin could sense something from him. He wasn't telling the whole truth. "Is he angry at me because of what I did to those two men?"

"No, of course not." David leaned in closer to her. "I don't think the colonel likes them much either."

"Will Emily be there?"

"I hope so. I do know that they have some very special animals there. In fact, I heard that they have a horse with wings."

"Pegasus is there!" Lorin cried.

The sergeant looked at his men and then back at Lorin. "You know about Pegasus?"

Lorin nodded. "I saw him in Emily's mind. She thinks he belongs to her. But he does not. He is mine."

As she spoke, Lorin sniffed the air and became distracted by the most overwhelming fragrance. The smell made her stomach rumble. She realized she hadn't eaten anything in ages and was starving. She rose. As she did, the men at the door stiffened and grasped their weapons. Lorin noticed this, but once again took no indication of it. Instead, she walked over to a nearby desk. The smell was coming from a large, flat white box.

"I said stand down," Sergeant Walker said to his men. He walked up to Lorin. "Are you hungry? Do you want one?"

When the sergeant opened the box, Lorin almost cried with excitement. She snatched up a small round treat and took her first bite. Flavors exploded in her mouth.

"These are called doughnuts," he explained. He smiled at her. "I see you like them."

"They are wonderful," Lorin said as crumbs flew from her mouth. Before she'd finished the first one, she was starting on a second doughnut. "I have never tasted anything so good."

The sergeant went to a white cupboard and pulled out a tin. He opened the top and held it out to her. "Here, drink this and slow down a bit—I don't want you to choke."

Lorin looked at the tin and frowned. But when Sergeant Walker took a sip, she understood. She took the can and tossed back a large mouthful. More sweet flavors danced in her mouth. Her eyes went wide with excitement as she reached for a third doughnut.

One of the men came forward. "Sir, Colonel James is waiting for us."

"Colonel James can wait," the sergeant snapped. "Let Lorin enjoy her meal."

WHEN IT WAS DARK, EMILY AND PAELEN
moved out of their hideout. They had made so many
twists and turns to escape the police, they had no idea
where the zoo was and had to ask a woman walking
her dog.

"It's just three blocks from here," she said. "Just go
down to the end of this street, then turn right and
take the first left, and in two blocks you're there. You
can't miss it."

They thanked her and were on their way. As they
got closer to the zoo, Emily's connection to Pegasus
grew stronger. She stopped. "Something's wrong with
Pegs. He's not in pain, but he's very angry."

Concern for Pegasus and the others quickening their pace.

Soon they were standing across the street from the Honolulu Zoo. In the dark there was very little they could see. But from what they could make out, it didn't look anything like a zoo. There was a very tall chain-link fence surrounding it. Bushes and trees grew along the length of the fence, and where they thinned, the backs of buildings could be seen.

They couldn't see any animal enclosures from where they stood, but they could hear the sounds of animals inside settling down for the night. Elephants were trumpeting, monkeys were calling, lions were roaring, donkeys were braying, and all these noises were mixed with the sounds of roosting birds.

"What kinds of monsters are making those loud calls?" Paelen asked. "They almost sound like Brue."

"I think those are elephants," Emily said. "They are big gray animals, not nearly as big as Brue, but almost as round. They've got a long trunk for a nose, huge ears, and tusks made of ivory. They are very beautiful. Sadly, some people on Earth hunt them for their ivory tusks and they've become endangered."

"Maybe we should bring Brue here one day to teach them not to."

Emily nodded. "That would be fantastic!"

They waited for cars to pass and then crossed the street. Paelen looked around. "It is too busy here. We must find somewhere safe to fly over the fence."

The zoo was much larger than they'd expected. They followed the fence past several streets before turning a corner and continuing past a few other streets.

"I think this is a good place," Paelen said as they neared a delivery gate. "I cannot hear or feel anyone around us."

Nerves knotted Emily's stomach. She had never felt more vulnerable. They were knowingly entering a CRU trap without her powers for protection. Emily looked around again. "Okay, get us over the fence."

Paelen lifted Emily in his arms and they flew over the fence. When they touched down, they ducked into bushes to get their bearings. Directly ahead of them was a paved trail. Across from the trail was a tall fenced enclosure. In the limited light, they couldn't see which animals it contained.

"Can you feel Pegasus strongly enough to tell us where he is?" Paelen asked.

"I don't know; I've never really had to before." Emily closed her eyes. She pushed aside her fear and focused fully on Pegasus. She could see his beautiful face in her mind. Taking a deep breath, she felt for him. The link was strong.

"I can feel him," she muttered softly. "He's still very angry."

"Which direction do you feel his anger from?"

Emily took another cleansing breath and reached out for Pegasus. She felt a light drawing sensation. It wasn't nearly as strong as the pull of the Flame shard, but it was there.

"I think he's there, down to the left along that trail."

Even though the zoo was closed, there were still a few zoo workers walking around. Emily froze when she saw a group of armed soldiers walking toward them on the paved trail.

She grabbed Paelen and they ducked into the bushes and kept low as the soldiers patrolled the area. Keeping off the trails and using the darkness to their advantage, they followed them around from the safety of the bushes that filled the area.

"If this is a zoo," Paelen commented, "there are not many animals here."

Emily agreed. "It does look more like a park, with all these trees. They must give the animals a lot of space."

They were grateful the Honolulu Zoo had so much greenery to hide in. They were able to zigzag their way through private areas where the public wasn't allowed.

As they approached a small building, they heard heavy footsteps on the paved trail. Once again they sought the shelter of bushes growing along the side wall of the squat building. They watched another group of armed soldiers on patrol.

"The place is crawling with them," Emily complained. "We'll never get the others out of here. Especially Chiron."

"You are right," Paelen agreed. "We cannot free

them. But if we find Fawn, she can get a message to Jupiter to meet us at Diamond Head. We can come back here once you have the shard."

"That's as good a plan as any, I suppose. But I still need to find Pegs. Maybe we can get him out. If not, I want him to know that we're here for him."

"He already knows that," Paelen said. "He can feel you here, just as you feel him; he knows—"

"No! This is insane! You can't do this to them. . . ."

A desperate voice blasted from an open window of the building, beside their hiding spot.

"Can't you see what an amazing opportunity this is? They come from another world! My God, that stallion has wings! What about that half-man, half-horse? He's impossible, but he exists *and* he's intelligent! What does it take to get you to see the wonder in that? We should be talking to them, learning from them, not locking them away for experimentation. It's barbaric and goes against everything this zoo stands for!"

Emily and Paelen looked at each other.

"Bingo!" Emily mouthed. They crept up to the open window to hear more.

"I don't care for your tone, Doctor," another voice said. "We have allowed you to stay to care for the animals, nothing more. If you can't do your job, I'll find someone who can! Your continued presence here is a courtesy. But my generosity will only extend so far. These prisoners are none of your concern—this is a national security issue, not Zoology 101!"

They heard footsteps and ducked deeper into the bushes as two soldiers ran into the building. "Agent R," one of them called, "the colonel has just received a call from Diamond Head. They've reported the capture of a girl."

"Emily?" Agent R demanded.

Emily flinched at the sound of her name. She really was standing right in the middle of the lion's den.

"No, sir. The colonel says she's called Lorin. Sergeant Walker is on the scene with her. She told him she's from Tartarus and is looking for Emily. When Agent G tried to talk to her, she attacked him and another agent. They're both in the infirmary. Walker says she has powers. She can fly and conjures fire with her hands."

Emily clapped her hand over her mouth to keep

from screaming. She looked at Paelen, and he was just as alarmed. Lorin was in Honolulu and she knew how to use her powers? This was the worst possible news.

"There's another girl like Emily?" Agent R said.

"Apparently so. Sergeant Walker is bringing her here."

"Excellent! With luck, we shall soon have two!" Agent R's voice changed. "Dr. Fleming, you have your orders. Just keep those prisoners alive until we capture Emily."

"But—"

"No buts. You will cooperate or we will shut down this zoo—permanently. Then what will happen to all of your conservation work?"

The threat hung in the air as the CRU agent stormed out of the building, followed by the soldiers.

Emily leaned back against the wall. "Lorin is in Hawaii."

"And they are bringing her here," Paelen said. "We must not be here when she arrives."

Emily stood up and peered through the open window. The room looked like a medical treatment area. Cages lined the side of the room. In two of them were sick animals. One contained a small monkey hooked up to an IV, and the other held a ring-tailed lemur. A tall, dark-haired man in his midthirties, wearing a white lab coat, was pacing the room. He had a kind face, but a concerned expression darkened it. They watched him pause and seem to come to some sort of decision. He stormed out of the building.

"C'mon," Emily said. "He knows where Pegasus and the others are being held. Let's try to get some information. I just hope he'll talk to us."

They followed the man closely into an area full of trees. With no one about, Paelen made his move. He lunged at the man and caught him across the shoulders. Wrenching him back, Paelen dragged him into the bushes. He clapped his hand over the man's mouth.

The doctor struggled in Paelen's grip, and even though he was strongly built and the larger of the two, he was powerless against Paelen's strength. Finally he gave up fighting.

"Please don't be afraid; we're not going to hurt you," Emily said softly. "I'm sorry we have to do this, but we can't risk being caught. I'm Emily, the girl the CRU are looking for. If you promise not to call those other men, we'll let you go. Do you promise?"

The man blinked his eyes and nodded.

Paelen removed his hand from his mouth. "Who are you?"

"Baird Fleming," he answered softly. "I'm the assistant director of the zoo and one of the veterinarians. I head up wildlife conservation."

"You're not with the CRU?" Emily asked.

Baird shook his head. "I'm with the zoo. You might say I'm the problem solver. And right now, I have a big problem with you two being here. This place is crawling with trigger-happy soldiers and those men in suits. I don't know who they are or what their agenda is, but they are *big* trouble for all of us!"

"They're the CRU—the Central Research Unit. They look for aliens and other unusual activity," Emily explained.

"You make it sound like they're the Men in Black."

"That's exactly what they are," Emily said. "Only they're much meaner and a lot more dangerous than the movie guys."

"I can't believe any of this," Baird said. "They've brought creatures here that defy nature!"

"They are not creatures," Paelen said sharply. "They are Olympians. Just like me. And they are our friends. If you have harmed them . . ."

"Whoa," Baird said. "Now hold on. I'm not doing anything to them. I think they're phenomenal. But Olympians—aren't they just myths?"

"Why does everyone keep saying that?" Paelen snapped.

"Olympians are very real," Emily said to the man. "So are Titans. And just as in the myths, they are fighting. Only soon, the fight is coming here. . . ."

Baird stared at her as though he didn't believe a word she'd just said. "Well, whatever they are, I don't want to see them harmed. I want to talk to them and understand how they can exist. I want to help them."

There was something about his warm brown eyes and strong determination to make a difference that reminded Emily of Joel. She felt a pang, but quickly shook it away.

"If you really want to help, you can," Emily said. "But we don't have a lot of time. You must take us to them. I have to see Pegasus before Lorin gets here!"

"Look, kids, I don't like these soldiers or those men in black any more than you do. And I especially don't like what they've done to your friends. But I've got a zoo to protect—I must think of the animals."

"If you don't help us, a lot of people are going to die and Earth will be enslaved."

"What are you talking about?"

"I told you, the Titans are attacking the Olympians and the fight will soon come here." Emily hated wasting precious time, but she told Baird everything she could as quickly as possible. "So you see, we've got to get a message back to Olympus to warn Jupiter to meet us at Diamond Head and not here."

"Can this really be true?" Baird whispered. "It sounds impossible."

"How much more proof do you need?" Emily cried. "You've seen Pegasus and the others. What does it take to convince you? Does Saturn have to come here before you believe Earth is in danger?"

Baird shook his head. "No—no, of course not. Look, they're holding the man-horse, vampire, and winged boar in the giraffe's night pens. The whole area is surrounded by heavily armed soldiers. I can barely get in there."

"What about Pegasus?" Emily asked. "Isn't he with them?"

Baird shook his head. "No. He's being kept in another part of the zoo."

"Why?" Paelen asked.

"Because he's too strong. He kept breaking the chains they put on him and tearing through the walls of the pen. We had to move him to a holding area that he can't get out of, or hurt himself in."

There was something very disturbing behind his words. He wouldn't face Emily and didn't look comfortable talking about Pegasus.

"Listen to me," Emily said. "If we can't get in to see them, you must get a message to Fawn."

"Fawn?"

"The pale girl," Emily said. "And she's not a vampire. She's an Olympian night dweller with very special gifts. She can communicate with her sister, who is still on Olympus. But she is also very delicate. If the sun touches her, she'll burn."

"I know," Baird said. "We found that out the hard

way. She was badly burned by the sun when they brought her in here, but we've kept her protected and she's recovering. But we have a problem. The soldiers weren't too gentle with the man-horse. . . ."

"His name is Chiron," Emily corrected him. "And he's a Centaur and an adviser to Jupiter. He's a very important Olympian."

"Well, Chiron is extremely angry about what's happening. The last time I went near him, he tried to kill me—so they bound him in chains. I can't get close enough to pass on a message."

"How far is he from here?"

Baird pointed down the trail to the left. "That way, a few hundred yards. But I told you, the giraffe pens are completely surrounded by soldiers. You'll never get into them."

Emily considered. "We don't have to get in, just near enough."

Baird seemed to be thinking this through. "I've got it. To the left of the pens is a row of tall bushes that you can hide behind. They can be seen from the pen doors."

"Good. Get us to them," Emily said. "You must

let Chiron know where we're hiding before he attacks you. I'll do the rest. It is imperative that Fawn gets the message to Jupiter."

"I can't go in there!" Baird said. "He'll kill me!"

"If you really care about animals, you'll try," Emily said. "Otherwise all your hard work will be for nothing. This zoo and everything in it will be gone."

Baird shook his head. "I must be completely crazy. That, or I'm dreaming . . ."

"Yes," Paelen agreed. "This is all a dream, so you can do this without fear of being killed."

"Why doesn't that make me feel any better?" Baird said. Then he paused. "Look, if I do this, will you two promise to get out of here? It's too dangerous for you. Those soldiers mean business."

"So do we," Emily said. "But we promise. If you get the message to Chiron, we'll go."

The veterinarian nodded and took the lead, pushing through the bushes. Where they ended, he, Emily, and Paelen darted across a path toward another building. Keeping low and close to the wall, they made their way around it. Baird put his fingers to his lips and whispered, "Soldiers are stationed inside."

At the back of the building, they crossed over a muddy trail and entered more bushes. "Okay, stay close," he whispered. "Just ahead is a set of smaller pens, and just past them are the giraffe pens."

After a few more yards, Baird stopped and crouched down. "There they are."

Emily peered through the leaves and saw a large, tall structure. It was made of thick bricks that rose over two yards in height. After that, a heavy metal mesh was welded to sturdy steel frames that climbed up to the roof. If Chiron was to see her, it would be through the door, which had the mesh starting at waist height. Soldiers stood around the pen. Weapons held high, they looked ready for war. Emily peered more closely and saw that one of the pens had a large hole kicked through the brick wall.

"What happened there?" she asked.

"That crazy stallion did it," Baird whispered. "I can't imagine his strength."

"He had to be really angry to do that," Paelen responded.

"He was," Baird said. "They hurt the vampire . . . I mean Fawn. And Pegasus went ballistic."

Emily caught Baird's arm. "What did you do to her?"

"Me? Nothing! But the soldiers were brutal. The only way they could keep Pegasus under control was to threaten the girl. That guy, Agent R, had his men drag her back into the sunlight to prove they'd hurt her."

Pain cut through Emily's heart as she imagined how terrified Fawn must have been as she was pulled into the sun. She had to suppress her anger toward the soldiers and the CRU. There was a bigger problem facing them.

"All right, stay here," Baird said. "He'll probably kill me before I get the message to him, but I'll try."

Just as he was about to move, Emily whispered, "Wait, I've got an idea! When you approach the door, quietly call Chiron's name. Tell him 'Emily and Paelen are here.' He will hear you, but the soldiers won't."

"Are you sure?"

Emily nodded. "Olympians have supersensitive hearing. They can hear a million times better than humans. Just let him know where we are. I'll do the rest."

Baird rose. "I can't say I understand everything that's happening here, but I don't want your friends to suffer. I'll do all I can. Now remember you promised. When Chiron gets the message, you leave!"

"We will," Emily said. "And thank you for all your help."

"Do you trust him?" Paelen asked when he was gone.

"We don't have much choice. Be ready to fly if anything goes wrong."

Emily closed her eyes and whispered, "Riza, please, you know what's at stake. Is there anything left? Can I use a bit of our power to convince Chiron?"

She lifted her hand, but it was Riza who let a tiny Flame flash. Even that small amount caused an intense pain in Emily's head that made her feel ill.

"Do not do it, Emily," Paelen warned. "We will find another way. You must not use your powers."

"I have to, but I'll be careful."

Baird walked confidently down the concrete trail. He approached the soldiers nearest the door. "I'm here to check on the prisoners."

The soldiers hesitated for a moment but then

allowed him to pass. When he reached for the door handle, Chiron charged, rearing and shouting threats. The sounds of chains rattled as the Centaur strained against his heavy restraints.

"C'mon, Chiron, hear him!" Emily muttered.

Just as quickly as it started, the attack stopped and Chiron went back down on all fours. His bare chest flared and his hands were flexing into fists, but he made no move against the veterinarian.

Baird cautiously opened the door and entered the pen. His hands were up in surrender and he was speaking softly.

Chiron pawed the ground with his sharp hoof and shouted threats at the soldiers, but his eyes shot to Emily and Paelen's hiding place.

"Now, Riza," Emily whispered. Once again, intense pain tore through her head as a small Flame flickered in her palm. It wasn't large and didn't last, but it was enough. The message was received. Chiron and the others knew they were there.

Emily panted through the pain. A moment later the Flame sputtered and went out, and she understood the terrible truth. Her powers were gone. All that was left was death if she tried to use them again.

"Now just calm down," they heard Baird saying, louder this time. "No one is going to harm you."

"What are these indignities?" Chiron shouted, playing to the soldiers. "Have you no idea who we are? What will happen if you do not release us?"

Baird took several steps closer. "Of course we do; we just want to understand . . ." Suddenly Chiron caught hold of the veterinarian and lifted him off the ground.

As the soldiers charged into the pen to help him, Emily saw Baird whispering in Chiron's ear. She breathed a sigh of relief. But then a twig snapped beside her and she froze. She turned and saw three soldiers pointing weapons at them.

"All right, both of you come out of there with your hands where we can see them!"

"Uh-oh," Paelen said.

Without thinking, Emily lunged. Moving instinctively, she knocked the gun barrel aside and punched the soldier in the midsection the way Diana had taught her. He went down with a grunt.

Paelen threw himself at the two others and had them down in an instant. But more soldiers were running at them.

"Go, Emily!" Chiron shouted through the cage.

Paelen slipped his arm around Emily's waist. "Fly!" he cried.

The sandals lifted them into the air. Before they could rise above the danger, a soldier caught hold of Paelen's left sandal and wrenched it off his foot. He and Emily crashed down to the ground in a heap.

Once again Emily tried to take on the soldier, but the exertion was proving too much for her. She was feeling too sick and weak to be effective. Her punch did little to stop him.

Gaining his feet, Paelen kicked the soldier away from Emily and sent him flying at the others, who were fast bearing down on them. Catching hold of Emily again, he lifted her up and started to run.

"Put me down," Emily cried. "Paelen, I can run on my own!"

"Not as fast as me!"

He was right. The distance between them and the

soldiers broadened with each step. Emily gazed back and saw the soldiers stop. She thought they'd given up. But then they raised their guns.

"Faster, Paelen!"

The sound of shots rang out, and Paelen grunted as he was struck in the back. He stumbled, but kept running.

"No!" Emily howled. "Paelen, stop—you've been hurt!"

"I am fine!" Paelen dashed off the trail and into a cluster of dark trees.

He'd said he was fine, but his breath was coming in short gulps as he made it to the chain-link fence surrounding the zoo.

"Emily," he gasped. "Get back to Diamond Head to wait for the Big Three. . . ."

"What about you?"

"I will keep them from following you. Remember, you are the Flame of Olympus: Your body is made of energy and cannot be harmed, even by a high fall."

"What fall?"

Without warning, Paelen caught Emily in both hands and threw her high over the top of the tall fence. She screamed and hit the ground hard, rolling onto her back and trying to catch her breath.

"You know you are not hurt. Now get up and run!" Paelen gasped, clinging to the fence. "Find Jupiter and get the shard!"

More shots rang out as the soldiers burst through the trees.

"Go!" Paelen ordered. He turned and roared as he charged at them.

Emily watched Paelen attacking the soldiers. Every instinct told her to stay and fight beside him. But she couldn't. She had no powers, and almost no strength left. Her only hope was to make it to Diamond Head to meet the Big Three.

Climbing shakily to her feet, she started to run.

The draw of the shard helped Emily find her way through Honolulu to the large volcano. After a few "dead-end" mishaps, she saw its dark peak rising out of the lights of the surrounding city.

Soldiers were everywhere, and military helicopters swooped and hovered over the crater as though they knew something big was coming. Keeping low and hidden, Emily continued around the volcano to the side facing the ocean.

"Lorin, what have you told them?" Emily mused aloud as she watched more military vehicles pouring into the area. Exhausted, feeling sick and as if her head was about to explode, Emily touched the side of the volcano, her hands shaking. "Pele, please hear me!" she called to the darkness. "Soldiers have shot Paelen. They've locked the Olympians in the zoo, and your sister has taken Joel. You put them under your protection. You must honor your word. Please save them!"

Emily raised her voice. "Please, Pele, hear me! They are hurting them! Baird won't tell me what they've done to Pegasus, but it's bad. I don't have the power to save them, but you do!"

She stopped and waited for a response. But there was nothing—only the gentle salt breeze coming off the ocean.

Emily sat down at the base of the volcano, feeling frightened and alone. With her powers exhausted, there was nothing to do but wait. The helplessness she felt was absolute. She knew Fawn would have received the message from Chiron, which meant Olympus had too. She just hoped that Jupiter and his brothers would arrive soon, or everything they'd fought for would be lost.

LORIN WAS FILLED WITH WONDER AS DAVID Walker drove them to the Honolulu Zoo. He had tried to get her to sit in the back of the truck, but she insisted on staying up front with him. She did not want to miss a single thing.

"Here we are," Sergeant Walker said as he pulled into the driveway of one of the delivery gates at the zoo. A gathering of soldiers was already there, waiting for them. As the truck came to a stop, they formed a large circle around it.

"Are they looking for more trespassers?" Lorin asked, eyeing the armed soldiers moving around the truck.

"No, they are here to protect you."

"From what?"

Sergeant Walker shrugged. "I don't know. But they are not going to hurt you, so don't be frightened." He helped her out of the truck and approached the gate.

Lorin followed him through the entrance and looked around. There was a single-story building to her left with the lights on. Up ahead was another set of gates, and beyond that she saw her first animal pen. "Pegasus is here?"

"That's what I've been told."

"Will you take me to him?"

"Sure, but first we have to check in. There are some people very anxious to meet you."

Lorin hesitated. "If they are like those other men, I do not want to meet them. I want to see Pegasus and then find Emily." She veered away from the building and walked toward the second set of gates.

"Lorin, wait!" the sergeant called, running after her.

"I have been waiting since I woke up in my prison cell. I want to see Pegasus, and I want to see him now!" Lorin waved her hand in the air and, with no one guarding the gates, they swung open and she breezed through.

The soldiers raised their weapons and were about to charge forward, but Sergeant Walker warned them off. "It's all right. I'll stay with her. Tell the colonel we're here and are going to find the stallion."

While half of the men ran into the building, the other half trailed behind them. "Tell them to go," Lorin said.

"I can't," Sergeant Walker said. "They are here to protect you."

"I can protect myself! I do not like them or their weapons. Make them go away, or I will!"

Fear rose in the sergeant. He turned and called to the men: "Stand down. We're fine. Return to your duties."

The men paused and then drifted away.

"They remind me of the warriors on Tartarus. All they want to do is fight, kill, and destroy."

As they moved deeper into the zoo, Lorin saw another group of soldiers leading two people down a trail. One had cuts on his face, and his right eye was swollen shut. The other was in heavy chains; his head down, he was being dragged by the men. There was something familiar about him.

As they came closer, Lorin inhaled. "Paelen, it is you!"

Paelen lifted his head slowly at the sound of his name. He frowned and asked weakly, "Do I know you?"

Lorin ran at him and threw her arms around him. His back felt very wet. When she released him, she saw fresh blood on her hands.

"You are bleeding!" she cried. "What have they done to you?"

"They shot me," Paelen responded.

Lorin turned on the sergeant. "Is this how you protect? Will you shoot me now?"

"No, of course not," the sergeant said. "I am sure there is a reason for this." He looked at the men. "Report."

"This one here is Baird Fleming, the zoo's assistant director. He's supposed to be looking after the animals, but we caught him passing on secret messages to the Centaur. He won't tell us what he told him, and he tried to fight back."

"And the other one?" Sergeant Walker demanded.

"He's an Olympian. He was with Emily when we were attacked. He put several of my men in the hospital. It took all of us to finally get him down. He's incredibly strong. The girl got away, but my men are searching for her. We'll have her shortly."

"You hurt him!" Lorin cried as she stroked Paelen's cut cheek. At her touch, his cuts began to close and fade and he was able to stand up straight as his strength returned. She inhaled in surprise. "Am I doing that?"

Paelen's eyes went wide. "You really are a Flame!"

Lorin blushed and nodded shyly.

"Just like Emily, you have the power to heal as well as harm."

"I will never harm you," Lorin promised. She looked down at the chains on Paelen's hands and used her powers to free him.

"Thank you, Lorin."

His voice was sweeter than she had imagined. She smiled at how he said her name. "I have been waiting to meet you. Have you seen Pegasus?"

Paelen shook his head. "I wanted to, but these men stopped me."

"That's enough, miss," one of the soldiers said, shoving Lorin back. "We're taking them to the colonel."

"No," Lorin said. "Paelen is with me. You cannot have him. He and I are going to see Pegasus."

"Lorin, please . . . ," Sergeant Walker said. "Let them do their job. We'll find Pegasus on our own."

Baird frowned and turned his bruised face to her. "Wait—you're the girl Emily was talking about. You're from Tartar . . . Teetar . . . ?"

"Tartarus," Lorin finished. "Yes, I am. What did Emily say about me?"

"She said you came here to kill her."

"I am not going to kill her!" Lorin cried. "She stole Riza from me and I want Riza back, but I will not kill Emily to get her. It is she who wants to kill me."

Paelen shook his head. "Emily did not take Riza from you. She was born with Riza in her. You both have the power of the Flame. It comes from the Xan. She does not want to fight, but she does need to speak with you."

"No," Lorin said. "She wants to hurt me and to keep you and Pegasus away from me. But I will not let her." She looked down at the shackles on Baird's wrists. They clicked and sprang free. "Now you can take us to Pegasus."

The soldiers escorting Baird came forward. "Back away, miss," they ordered.

"Stop!" Sergeant Walker warned. "She's dangerous—"

Before he had finished speaking, Lorin acted. She used her powers to rip the weapons from the soldiers' hands and fired two quick Flame blasts at the ground at their feet. "Leave us alone! Just leave us alone!"

She caught Paelen by the hand and faced Baird. "Now you will take us to Pegasus."

Lorin walked through the zoo, holding Paelen tightly. Occasionally she would stop to stare at an animal and Baird would explain what it was. While she allowed Sergeant Walker to walk with them, if any other soldier tried to confront them she sent a blast of Flame in his direction.

"If you continue to fire at them, they will get angry and hurt you," Paelen warned. "Trust me. We have fought their kind before."

Lorin smiled sweetly at him. "Do not fear, Paelen. I will protect you."

"I do not fear for myself," Paelen said. "I do not want to see you hurt."

Sergeant Walker was at her side. "Lorin, please, listen to him. You must calm down. If you keep this up, they will attack. I don't want to see you hurt either."

Lorin stopped and faced the sergeant. "You told those men I was dangerous, and you were right. Everyone keeps trying to control me. You, them, Saturn—but I will not be controlled. I will serve only myself, no others."

She turned to Baird. "Which way now?"

"This way," he said. "Just over there, in that building with the lights on. But you are not going to like what you see. I need you to understand that this was not what I intended. It was the only way to keep him from injuring himself."

Lorin frowned. "I do not understand."

"What have you done to him?" Paelen demanded. "I warn you, if you have hurt him, you will have more than Lorin to answer to. Pegasus is my friend. I will not see him harmed."

"We're just restraining him," Baird said quickly as they neared the building. "He's in an elephant squeeze. We use it when we have to do any kind of surgery or procedures on elephants. It's a special holding device so we can work on them without them moving. It simply immobilizes the patient so we don't have to use sedatives, which can be dangerous for larger animals."

There was something about the way he was speaking that caused alarm in Lorin. She looked at Paelen, and then back at the vet. "What have you done to him?"

"Nothing," Baird insisted. "I told you, we're using this medical device to hold him. It's not torture."

They rounded the corner. Up ahead was an extra-large metal gate leading into the area with the elephant squeeze. Lorin had her first glimpse of Pegasus and gasped.

The white winged stallion was trapped inside the squeeze. Two large pieces of metal formed a huge vise-like clamp that squeezed him tightly on both sides. The contraption was lifted off the ground and tilted so that Pegasus was suspended on his side, with his hooves dangling out of the base. His wings were forced open and held above his head. No matter how he struggled, he could not break free.

"Pegasus!" Paelen pulled away from Lorin and ran to the stallion. Pegasus whinnied at his approach.

"She is safe," Paelen explained to the winged horse. "But we have a problem. . . . This is Lorin of Tartarus."

Pegasus screamed and struggled in his restraints.

"Get back," Baird cried. "His kicks can kill!"

Lorin ignored the warning and approached the stallion's head. She gently brushed his mane from his eyes. "Do not be frightened, Pegasus. I want us to be friends."

Pegasus thrashed harder in the clamp as he struggled to free himself. The metal groaned under his immense strength.

Lorin caught Paelen's hand and stepped back. "Release him!" she said to Baird.

"No!" called a man dressed in black. He looked as old as Saturn, but had an angrier face. "Step away from the stallion."

"Who are you?" Lorin demanded. She noticed that both Sergeant Walker and Baird were frightened of him.

Paelen didn't need to be told; he already knew. "He is with the CRU."

"Very good, Paelen," the agent said. "If you know who I am, you know what I can do. Now I want both of you to step away from the stallion and tell me where Emily is."

"But you are hurting him," Lorin said.

"The animal is fine. Don't make me tell you again. Step away from the stallion!"

Lorin didn't like this man one bit. She especially didn't like the way he frightened Paelen. He tried not to show it, but his hand was quivering in hers. "No, he is not fine, and you are not going to tell me what to do!"

Agent R raised his hand and snapped his fingers. A large number of soldiers poured in from every direction and encircled them with their weapons raised. Among the soldiers were CRU agents dressed in black suits. "You make one move and I'll have my people open fire."

"Stop!" Paelen cried. "Agent R, if you know what Emily can do, I warn you, Lorin can do the same, perhaps even more. But she does not have Emily's restraint. You must stay back and let me speak with her before something terrible happens."

Lorin's heart fluttered with excitement. Paelen was defending her and wanted to speak with her!

"Yes," she warned the agent. "Stay back. I want to speak with Paelen. Then we are going to free Pegasus, find Emily, and take the shard."

"That shard is not yours!"

A woman's voice rose loud and clear. Everyone turned, and there stood an old woman with so many wrinkles her eyes could not be seen. Her long hair was white and she was hunched over, walking slowly with the aid of a large staff. Her red floral dress, several sizes too large, hung from her wizened frame. Standing directly behind her was a tall Centaur carrying a night dweller on his back. Beside them was a winged creature Lorin had never seen before.

The soldiers turned and aimed their weapons at the Olympians.

"Stand still!" Agent R ordered as he drew his weapon.

"Robert, put that silly thing down before you hurt yourself," the old woman commanded as she walked closer.

Agent R was taken aback. "Who are you? How

do you know my name? How did you free those prisoners?"

"'Those prisoners,' as you call them, are under my protection. I am not pleased by their treatment!"

"Pele, is that you?" Paelen called in surprise.

There was a sharp intake of breath from the Hawaiian soldiers around them as they recognized the name. They bowed their heads and knelt to the ground.

"Who is Pele?" Lorin asked Paelen.

"These are her Islands," Paelen said. "You would do well to show her some respect."

Agent R stormed forward to face his men. "Stand up and hold your positions!" he ordered.

The Hawaiian soldiers refused to move.

"Robert, don't be an idiot," Pele said. "I have watched you brutalizing my Islands long enough. You and your CRU people are no longer welcome here. You will leave immediately!"

The sound of her walking stick clicked on the ground as Pele sauntered past the men. She approached Baird and, with a wizened hand, stroked his bruised face.

"Baird, my handsome young man. It was brave of you to take them on, but very foolish. You could have been seriously hurt."

Baird stood there, wide-eyed and in awe. "I—I had to try to help them."

Pele smiled warmly. "I know you did, my sweet boy, and that is why I admire you so much and the work you do with the endangered animals of this world. But I can't let you endanger yourself." She pulled a red floral lei from her neck and reached up to place it over his head. She kissed his cheek. "You are now under my protection."

Pele looked at the Hawaiian soldiers. "Those who know me will understand what that means. No one here will harm him. In fact, I command you to protect him!"

"Look, lady, I don't know who you are . . . ," Agent R said.

"Yes you do, Robert," Pele said casually. "You and your men have been hunting me for years. But I am too clever for you. You will never take me from my Islands."

Realization dawned on his face. "You're the Hawaiian

Fire Goddess! What are you doing here? This matter has nothing to do with you."

"It has everything to do with me," Pele said. "I gave these Olympians my protection. I don't appreciate what you have done here. Now you will set Pegasus free and give him to me."

"No." Lorin released Paelen and stepped up to the old woman. "I came here for Pegasus. He is mine."

Pegasus struggled and whinnied in the elephant squeeze.

Lorin looked back at him and waved her hand. The machine groaned in response as the two metal plates shifted and Pegasus was placed back on his feet. Then the sound of groaning started as the vise-like clamp was forced open. Pegasus sprang free and moved toward Paelen. He flexed his wings and flapped them several times. Shaking his head, he nickered.

"See, he belongs to me!" Lorin cried.

Pele shook her head. "You are wrong, child. He belongs to no one. Pegasus is free to make his own choice, and he has chosen Emily."

"No!" Lorin cried. "Pegasus, you are mine, and

when I find Emily, I will tell her so! I will take back what she has stolen from me and get the shard. Then I will finally be complete!"

"Lorin, stop!" Paelen cried. He ran up to her and took her hand gently. His voice softened. "You do not need Pegasus when you have me. Just let him go—let them all go. We can leave here and be free. Just the two of us. We can go anywhere you want."

Lorin's heart fluttered. "Do you mean that?"

Paelen nodded. "We can leave right now. Forget the others—it is just us."

Lorin looked at everyone around her and hesitated. Her eyes settled on Pegasus. "But I want him too. . . ."

"Lorin." Chiron carefully approached. "We mean you no harm. But you cannot claim someone who is free. I beg you to leave us to do what we must. Emily needs that shard to survive. Without it, she will cease to exist. Riza, the last Xan, will be lost to all of us forever. Please, you cannot want that. Emily is just like you—you share the same powers. She is like a sister to you."

Lorin shook her head. Why couldn't they

understand? Without that shard and the power within Emily, she would never be whole. "Emily is not my sister! She is my enemy! I will have her power and I will have Paelen and Pegasus."

She lifted her hands and fired Flames at Chiron. Pele raised her staff and blocked the attack. The Flames were deflected into a tree, which exploded with the impact.

"Enough!" Pele slammed the base of her staff down on the ground. The earth rumbled as a large crack formed, shooting from the point of her staff straight at Lorin. Flames and lava rose from the split in the ground.

Paelen screamed as he was struck by a large glob of spitting lava and knocked down.

"Paelen, no!" Lorin cried. Furious, she raised her hands and fired blasts of Flames at Pele. The old woman shrieked and was driven off her feet, but recovered quickly. The image of the old woman shimmered and faded until in its place stood a powerful young woman. Her hair was blazing with fire and her eyes were red.

"Fool!" Pele screamed. She raised her staff and

pointed it at Lorin. Flames and lava shot out of the tip. The intensity of the heat blasted the humans and Olympians away from the area. When it struck Lorin, it sent her spiraling into the elephant squeeze.

"Go!" Pele shouted at the Olympians. "Emily awaits you at Diamond Head. Chiron, take Baird with you and keep him safe. I will deal with this foolish child and join you there!"

Lorin felt the heat from Pele's Flames, but they could not touch her. Around her, the steel squeeze melted into pools of liquid metal. She climbed free of the debris and stood amid the wreckage just in time to see Pegasus carrying the night dweller away. The other winged creature was with him, and the Centaur galloped in the same direction with Baird on his back and Paelen in his arms.

Lorin's eyes flew to Paelen, limp in the Centaur's arms. She turned her fury on Pele. "You hurt my Paelen!" Summoning her powers, she fired everything she had at the Hawaiian goddess. Flames, crushing force, commands to tear her apart—all flowed from Lorin.

Pele was struck. Her head flew back and she howled in pain as she felt the full fury of the Flame of Titus. The louder Pele screamed, the more power Lorin fired at her—until there was a sudden snap.

When the smoke cleared, Pele was gone.

34

EMILY SAT AT THE EDGE OF THE OCEAN-SIDE highway at the base of Diamond Head. Her eyes remained on the star-studded sky, searching for signs of Jupiter. She had heard nothing from Pele. So the Hawaiian wouldn't honor her pledge to protect the Olympians: They were on their own. Her only hope now was the Big Three.

Emily ducked down every time a car or truck passed by. Several military vans whooshed past her hiding place, but they didn't see her.

Her mind was consumed with worry for her friends. What had happened to Paelen? Where was Pegasus? And her thoughts constantly returned to Joel. She missed him so much and hoped fervently that he was all right. She needed him now more than ever. As more time passed, her fears increased, until she heard a sound that was pure music to her ears. Whinnies rang out of the darkness. "Pegasus!"

The stallion soared around the side of the volcano, a blazing white glow in the sky. He tilted his wings and touched down gracefully beside her. Emily ran to him and threw her arms around his powerful neck. She kissed his mane and wouldn't let him go.

"Emily!" Fawn cried from his back. "I think Lorin might have killed Pele."

"What?" Emily repeated. "When? How?"

Fawn slid off the stallion's back and embraced her. Her face was blistered from burns, and her arms were raw and weeping.

Emily was horrified. "I heard what they did to you. I'm so sorry!"

"I will heal," Fawn said. She explained what had happened at the zoo. "Paelen was ready to sacrifice himself for us. He offered to go away with Lorin if she would leave us alone. But he was hurt when Pele attacked Lorin. I do not know if he is all right."

Emily was stunned. "Paelen is hurt and Pele is dead?"

Pegasus nodded his head and nickered softly. "Pele has great power," Fawn translated. "But Lorin has more. Pegasus believes Lorin won. She knows that you are here. It will not be long before she comes to claim Riza and your powers!"

"But she'll kill Riza if she tries to take her from me."

"I do not think she cares. You were right. She looks your age, but inside she is just like a young, uncontrolled child. She wants what she wants without understanding what could happen. She has not been taught patience."

Emily looked up to the sky, praying that the Big Three would arrive before it was too late. "I don't have any powers left to fight her."

"None of us do," Fawn said. "She does not realize when people are trying to help her. Chiron tried to explain why you needed the shard, but instead of listening to him, she threw Flames at him. Pele saved him."

"I thought Pele had abandoned us," Emily said, feeling guilty. Especially since it was likely that the goddess had died to help them.

Fawn shook her head. "No, Pele defended us

when Lorin attacked. She gave her life for us."

Across the highway, past the Diamond Head light-house, the ocean started to stir. It swirled and rose. Bright rainbow colors flashed in the water, and a fig-ure appeared above the waterspout.

"It's Nā-maka-o-Kaha'i!" Emily cried. "We've got to go! Get on Pegasus!" When the night dweller was on the stallion's back, Emily climbed up behind her. "Fly, Pegasus. Get us out of here!"

"Child, wait!" Nā-maka-o-Kaha'i called. Suspended above the spout, she was even more beautiful than she was the last time Emily saw her. The brilliant col-ors rising from the waterspout gave her an extra glow that also sparkled on the fish swimming through her seaweed dress. "I mean you no harm. Pegasus, come, please—we need to speak."

"Don't, Pegs. It's a trick!" Emily called. "She's going to capture us like she did with Joel."

"You have my word this is no trick," the ocean goddess said. "Please, trust me. I have the boy with me; he is unharmed."

Pegasus whinnied and cantered across the highway to the edge of the flowering shrubs and manicured lawn that surrounded the lighthouse and overlooked the ocean.

The spinning waterspout swirled and moved closer to them. "My sister has been gravely wounded by that wild Titan."

"I thought you'd be happy about that," Emily called darkly.

Nā-maka-o-Kahaʻi shook her head. "I may not like my sister or always agree with her actions, but I would never wish her injured, especially by a Titan. I know what Pele did for the Olympians at the zoo, and Joel has told me why you are here. I have come to help. I will remove the water from Diamond Head, but I do not possess the power to open the crater to free the shard. Wounded or not, Pele must do that— or Jupiter, if he arrives in time."

Pegasus nickered and bowed his head to the ocean goddess.

"Go now to the top of the volcano. I will meet you up there and close the water springs Pegasus released."

When the ocean goddess started to move, Emily called, "Wait, what about Joel?"

"I will bring him with me." Just as quickly as it appeared, the waterspout subsided and the ocean calmed.

Pegasus stepped away from the flowering shrubs, flapped his wings, and launched into the air. He landed on the ridge path at the top of the volcano. Soldiers still stationed there started to run toward them. But before they reached Pegasus, the swirling waterspout rose out of the black waters within the crater.

"Hear me!" Nā-maka-o-Kaha'i called, her voice echoing loudly. "Human soldiers, leave here now. You have no part in this struggle. To stay is to forfeit your lives. You have one minute to leave or I shall cast you off the side of Diamond Head!"

Not far from Pegasus a soldier fell to his knees and raised his weapon on Nā-maka-o-Kaha'i.

"No, don't do it!" Emily warned.

A second soldier opened fire on the ocean goddess.

Nā-maka-o-Kaha'i said nothing. She turned on the men and raised her hand. A large blast of water struck the two soldiers with amazing precision. While they were knocked over the side of the volcano, the men around them remained untouched.

"Go!" Nā-maka-o-Kaha'i commanded. "Go, or you will meet the same fate!"

The soldiers didn't wait to be told twice and ran for the stairs leading down from the upper rim.

Nā-maka-o-Kaha'i raised her hands again. Soon the deep waters within Diamond Head started to swirl. As the crater drained, Emily was reminded of a toilet that had just been flushed. It didn't take long until the waters were gone, and Nā-maka-o-Kaha'i gone with them.

"Look down there—it is Joel!" Fawn cried.

Emily's heart lifted, but she could see nothing in the darkness below. Pegasus whinnied loudly and launched himself off the rim. He glided down into the crater and touched down on the sodden parking area.

"Joel!" Emily cried. Seeing him waiting for her was more thrilling than she could ever imagine. They were in such danger, but with Joel at her side, Emily knew she could face it. His hair was wet and brushed back and his clothing was dripping with salt water, but his face glowed.

Emily slid off Pegasus and ran to him.

Joel threw his arms around her. "I have missed you so much!"

"Are you all right?" Emily asked. She looked him up and down, checking for wounds. "Did she hurt you?"

"No, I'm fine. Em, that was the coolest thing! I was at the bottom of the ocean, but I could breathe! It was like I was a water nymph or something. I met humpback whales and all kinds of freaky creatures. But I was so worried about you. Are you all right?"

Emily nodded. "But Lorin is here and Paelen is hurt!"

"I know; Nā-maka has been filling me in on what's been going on," Joel said. He looked up. "The Big Three need to get here soon. Lorin is dangerous."

"They will not arrive in time."

They turned and saw Pele limping toward them. Her beautiful floral dress was in tatters, her hair was tangled and singed, and her right leg was badly burned.

"Pele," Emily called. She ran up to the goddess. "Are you all right?"

Pele shook her head. "That kid really packs a

punch! I come from Fire, yet somehow she was able to burn me all over, and I think she cracked a bone in my leg."

"She has the power of a Xan," Emily said.

"I don't know what that is," Pele said, "but her powers are unimaginable. Lorin intends to harm you."

"I know," Emily said.

"Emily is our only hope to defeat her. But only if Emily has her power back," Joel said. "The shard is here, beneath the surface. If you free it, Emily will have enough power to face her."

"I will do this if you promise to take your fight back to Olympus or Titus. I will not have my Islands endangered."

"I promise," Emily said. "We don't want to fight at all. It's Saturn who is causing all the trouble."

"I don't care who started it. I just want you off my Island. Now, Pegasus, take Joel and Fawn away from here. I do not wish them harmed. Emily, you will stay with me."

Joel bent down and kissed Emily. "Stay safe. I'll be right up there if you need me."

Emily put her arms around him and hugged him tightly. She stood on her toes so that she could whisper in his ear. "No matter what happens, Joel, please know how much I love you."

She kissed him again before walking toward Pegasus. "Keep them safe, Pegs. If things get out of hand, fly away from here. Don't risk yourself for me." She brushed his thick mane from his eyes. "I'll see you soon."

Pegasus nickered and pressed his head to her.

"Emily!" Pele snapped. "Lorin is coming. We don't have time to waste."

Emily watched as Pegasus carried Joel and Fawn onto the top ridge path of the volcano.

"Come," Pele commanded. "Show me where the shard is."

"This way." Emily walked Pele across the sodden parking area. The tarmac was cracked and broken from her first attempts to retrieve the shard. The whole area looked like a disaster zone: The flood had torn up trees and damaged the crater's buildings. She stopped on the spot where she felt the shard strongest. "It's here."

"Are you ready?"

"Yes," Emily said. "The moment you open the crater, stand back. I know the shard is big, but I don't know how big."

Pele raised her staff and slammed the tip down on the crater floor. At first all they heard was deep rumbling from within the ancient volcano. Then the sound of cracking as more of the tarmac surface of the parking area split open. Heat, smoke, and ash rose from the spreading crack.

The ground around them glowed orange as lava, long since hardened, melted into liquid again. Emily could feel the shard down there. As the heat blasted her face and blew back her hair, she held her hands over the opening and commanded the shard to rise.

"No!"

The ground beside Emily exploded and knocked her down as Lorin landed in the crater. Emily climbed to her feet and got her first look at the enraged Titan. She was nothing like what Emily had expected.

Lorin looked about her age. They were the same height, but Lorin had long blond hair in braids and blazing ice-blue eyes. Were it not for her tattered rags and the anger distorting her fine features, she would be nothing less than beautiful.

"That shard is mine!" Lorin cried.

"Lorin, please," Emily called. "We don't need to fight. But without that shard, Riza will die. All our powers came from her. They are not ours."

"You are lying! I have always had them!" Lorin stormed forward. "You will not take them from me." She lifted her hands and fired.

Pele darted in front of Emily and deflected the Flames. As she faced Lorin, she looked back over her shoulder. "Get that shard! I'll try to stop her."

Pele lifted her staff and pointed it at Lorin. A stream of Flames and lava shot from the staff and hit Lorin directly in the chest, but it was powerless to stop her.

Lorin raised her hands and fired back at Pele. The Hawaiian goddess was knocked off her feet. As she struck the ground several yards away, her staff fell beside her, still issuing fire and lava and causing the ground beneath them to shake and crack open.

Emily had only seconds to act. Without the shard, she had no power to fight Lorin. But she wasn't strong enough to summon it. There was only one thing left to do to keep Lorin from getting it. With the crack at her feet widening and lava spitting and bubbling to the surface, Emily looked up at Pegasus a final time. "I love you, Pegs. . . ."

It was as if Joel had read her mind, because as she turned back to the lava, his anguished cry cut through the distance between them. "Emily, no!"

Emily raised her hands above her head and, just as she had done from the diving board at the river outside Jupiter's palace, she dove into the molten pool of lava.

THE LAST THING EMILY HEARD BEFORE SHE
was swallowed by the lava was Joel's voice. He was in
pain, but she wasn't. It was almost like the first time
she sacrificed herself, in the Temple of the Flame on
Olympus. But then it had hurt. This time she felt
nothing.

"*Emily . . .*"

Emily recognized the voice and rejoiced. "Riza, I
have missed hearing from you!"

"*I have always been with you, but now is not the time
to linger. I have no strength left to keep us together. We are
fading. Please, join with me. Use the last of our powers to
summon the shard. It's our only hope.*"

Emily felt herself drifting away, as though floating

on a cloud. She knew Riza needed her, but the feelings she was experiencing were so peaceful, she didn't want them to end. Riza's voice started to ebb away. . . .

"Em, please hear me. . . ." A new and urgent voice rose around her, a voice filled with limitless love.

"Mom?"

"Yes, sweetheart, I'm here."

Her mother appeared, looking just as young and radiant as she had before the cancer had ravaged her body. Her curly brown hair and smiling hazel eyes were just as Emily remembered. "Mom, so much has happened. . . ."

"I know, my love, and I've been with you for all of it. Please, Emily, do as Riza asks. Call the shard into yourself. This is not the time to join me. You still have so much to do. Your father needs you, as do all the Olympians. Don't leave them. I promise we'll be together one day, but today is not that day."

"But I miss you. . . ."

"We'll be together again, I promise. Remember that I love you and couldn't be more proud of you. Now reach for the shard, Emily. Do it now!"

Her mother's voice and image faded. Emily cried after her, but she was gone.

"Emily," Riza called, her voice a weak, fading whisper. *"I'm sorry. I can't keep us together anymore."*

Her father's face flashed before her eyes, and then Joel's bright smile, and finally Pegasus. Emily couldn't leave them to face Saturn alone. Focusing all the strength she had left, Emily joined Riza in reaching for the shard.

In an instant, it was pulled from its prison in the depths of Diamond Head and straight into her. Emily's mind exploded with the full knowledge and power of the Xan. She heard Riza rejoicing. *"My memories!"* Riza cried. *"We have finally found all my missing memories. . . ."*

These were Riza's private memories, known only to her. Information that was never shared with Arious. Emily suddenly understood why she and Riza got along so well. Though they were thousands of years apart in age, they were the same: both strong-willed and independent and both yearning to do more. They were each filled with a spirit of profound curiosity about everything.

"I am Xan!" Riza cried joyously.

Emily shared in Riza's joy. "C'mon!" she cried. "Let's go save Pele and the Olympians!"

Now, with her powers restored and increased, Emily rose through the layers of molten lava. She marveled at the bright colors coming from the liquid rock. Suddenly everything she saw reminded her of a memory she received from Riza.

Bursting through the surface of the lava, Emily was stunned by what she saw. Lava was spewing from a gaping hole in the crater and shooting up hundreds of yards in the sky. Volcanic ash filled the air and billowing smoke from the eruption glowed red and orange. The side of the volcano was blown out, and lava was spilling down into Honolulu. The tsunami warning siren was screaming in the air, calling for the evacuation of the city.

Emily looked up. Pegasus wasn't on the upper rim.

"Pele!" Emily called. She felt Pele's presence and moved toward it. The Hawaiian goddess had collapsed on the ground, far from the burning hole in the crater.

"Emily," Riza called. *"I remember Pele and what she*

is. Get her into the lava. It is her element. She'll die if you don't!"

Emily levitated Pele's unconscious form and lowered her gently into the lava pool. Upon contact, Pele's eyes opened and she smiled as she descended deeper into the liquid rock.

"Emily!" Lorin cried.

The Titan landed on the surface of the crater, not far from where Emily was standing. They faced each other on the battlefield of the erupting volcano. Flames flashed all around them, and lava pooled at their feet. The ground rumbled in preparation for an even bigger eruption.

This was it, the final showdown—the Flame of Olympus versus the Flame of Titus.

36

"THE SHARD IS MINE, GIVE IT BACK!" LORIN cried.

Emily shook her head. "No, Lorin, it is Riza's. You will not have it—"

Before she could finish, Lorin fired a blast at Emily, but now the Flames had no effect on her.

Lorin looked like little more than an angry child, but Emily knew this belied her power. She couldn't let her do any more damage to Oahu. Emily fired back, but with only enough power to knock Lorin down.

"Lorin, stop," Emily called as she approached her. "We are both Xan, and they don't fight! All we will succeed in doing is destroying Hawaii."

"Then give me what I want and I will stop!" Lorin cried. "I need to be complete!"

Lorin fired again, but Emily easily deflected the flames and the power behind them. They struck the ocean-facing side of the volcano wall and blew a portion of it out over the water with an explosive blast.

"Complete?" Riza called. *"Emily, wait—I finally understand what she means!"* The ancient Xan started speaking through Emily's mouth. *"Lorin, you are right. you do need to be complete, and so do we. I know how to do it, but you must trust us."*

"No!" Lorin cried. "You just want to hurt me." Another blast of flame followed, but it was harmless to Emily. The volcano wall, however, was further damaged, and more of it tumbled into the ocean.

Emily understood what Riza meant and refrained from using her powers against the Titan. "Can't you understand that we don't want to hurt you?" she cried. "You are part of us, and we are part of you. Only by joining together will we ever be complete. You don't feel whole because you have Riza's powers, but not her heart or spirit. I have her heart and spirit and a lot of her powers, but not all of them. Every-thing deep within us yearns to be united again."

Lorin looked uncertain. "But . . ."

"We mean you no harm," Riza pressed. *"Please look around you at this devastation. This can't be what you want."*

"I want to be complete . . . ," Lorin called.

"So do I," Emily agreed. "If you join with me, we can be."

Lorin looked around as though seeing the damage and the erupting volcano for the first time. "What do we do?"

"We stop fighting and end this."

"What about Saturn?"

The words were no sooner out of her mouth when the skies above them burst open. The blazing lights of the Solar Stream illuminated three large chariots. One was surrounded by roaring flames; one was con-structed of screaming black skeletons; and one was being drawn by large sea stallions in a pool of water. The Big Three. Behind them followed a procession of Olympians.

A second Solar Stream portal opened beside the

first. Emily watched in horror as more chariots and flying creatures poured into the world, led by Saturn.

Blasts of power blazed across the night sky as the Olympians and the Titans brought their fight to Earth.

"Lorin, look!" Emily cried. She lifted the two of them in the air, away from the shooting lava. "Is this what you want? Their fight will destroy this beautiful island. Can't you see? No matter who wins, Earth will lose. Do you want all this destruction? Do you really want to fight me until one of us is dead?"

"I told you," Lorin cried. "I want to be complete!"

Jupiter's fiery chariot blazed across the dark sky. Jupiter fired lightning bolts at Saturn, who deflected them toward downtown Honolulu. They destroyed everything they touched. Buildings exploded and roads were instantly melted under the assault.

Sirens blared and car horns sounded as people tried to flee the battle.

Neptune, on his chariot of sea horses, waved his trident in the air and commanded the ocean to rise and knock the Titans out of the sky. They hit the ground with explosive blasts and grabbed anything they could get their hands on to throw at the Olympians. Cars, trees, even people—nothing was safe.

Emily had to act fast to save people flying through the air and lower them back down to the ground safely. Lorin watched Emily, and soon joined her doing the same.

Military jets arrived and opened fire on the Olympians and Titans, but they had no effect other than getting Saturn to fire back at them. Airships exploded in the sky and cast debris down to the ground.

Across Honolulu, the other extinct volcano, the Punchbowl Crater, started to erupt. Emily sensed Pele's presence. The Hawaiian goddess was using the eruption to fire streams of lava at the invading Titans.

Nā-maka-o-Kaha'i appeared on a massive waterspout, summoning the ocean to rise. Waves crashed over Waikiki Beach and flooded into the city center. Buildings were knocked down, and cars bobbed in the water like leaves.

"Please, Lorin," Emily cried. "If we work together, we can stop the destruction and end this battle before it's too late!"

Lorin gazed down on Honolulu. "My Paelen is

down there! So is Sergeant Walker. I do not want them hurt. Or all the animals at the zoo."

Emily flew closer to the Titan. "I don't want that either! But look around you—it's already happening."

"If I agree, will you kill me?" Lorin asked, sounding like a frightened little girl.

"Of course not! Don't you understand? We are the same. We can end this destruction—but only if we work together!"

Emily held out her hand to Lorin. "Help me stop this insanity."

Every moment the Titan hesitated, the battle intensified. More Hawaiian gods joined in the struggle to save their home. Some stood with Pele, others with Nā-maka-o-Kaha'i on the shore. There were even giant, birdlike gods with colorful plumage soaring across the night skies. Their screeches echoed throughout the island as they attacked the Titans.

Everywhere Emily looked there was fighting. The Island of Oahu was being torn apart.

Pele rose above the Punchbowl Crater in a blazing fireball and used her staff to knock both Olympian and Titan fighters out of the sky.

"Look," Emily said, pointing to the Hawaiians. "See how they fight to defend their home. We both know they can't win against the Titans or the Olympians, but they will die trying. Only together can we stop it!"

Lorin hesitated a moment longer.

Emily knew it was a big decision for her, the biggest of her short life, and it couldn't be rushed. But with each passing moment, more of Oahu was destroyed.

Finally Lorin nodded and reached for Emily's hand.

The moment they touched, their hands fused together and a great blazing light exploded from them, shooting out in all directions—though the biggest blast shot straight up into the stars.

Emily, Riza, and Lorin were finally complete.

"ENOUGH!" A VOICE LOUDER THAN THUNDER boomed across the sky. It seemed to carry across the whole island, if not all of Earth.

The volcano beneath Emily and Lorin instantly calmed and grew dark. The lava cooled and turned black. On the other side of Honolulu, the eruption at the Punchbowl Crater stopped and the lava flow hardened.

The waves crashing into the city were sent back into the ocean, and the waters calmed.

The sides of Diamond Head were restored, and beautiful, luminous beings appeared around the top rim. They were tall and slim and all holding hands as they circled the volcano many times over.

Their light robes billowed gently in the breeze caused by the cooling lava. They were singing, and the sound was so peaceful that everyone—Titan, Olympian, Hawaiian god, and human alike—paused to listen.

Riza started to weep. *"My people have finally found me. . . ."*

Their beauty stole Emily's breath as she and Lorin were lowered into the Diamond Head crater. When they touched the cooled surface, the other fighters were drawn in around them. The Titans and the Hawaiians stood staring up at the beautiful creatures. The Olympians fell to their knees and bowed their heads in respect. They alone recognized the Xan.

"THE FIGHTING ENDS, NOW!" a bodiless voice called.

Emily searched for Pegasus and her friends among the gathering, but they were missing. She saw Diana and Apollo dressed to fight. The Big Three, Hundred-handers, giants, Centaurs, and many other Olympians gathered on one side of the crater. Her eyes landed on the Sphinxes. Tom had a deep gash across his bare chest, and Alexis's wing looked broken.

Emily's father was absent, and she hoped he was safe in Olympus.

Chiron stood among their ranks with Baird Fleming still on his back. The vet looked terrified among the strange and powerful creatures gathered around him.

On the other side of the crater stood Saturn, his brothers, and countless other Titans of unimaginable shape and size. Emily noted a few Shadow Titans among the fighters.

Forming the third point in the triangle of fighters were the Hawaiian gods. Pele and Nā-maka—away from her ocean but safe on land—were easy to recognize, as were the birdlike gods Emily had seen in the sky. It was the others that she didn't know. She was surprised by just how many there were.

The Xan at the top of the volcano stopped singing. Their glow intensified, and Emily could feel their energy flowing out to heal the wounded Hawaiian island. It was only then that Emily realized she and Lorin were also glowing with the same intensity.

"Riza," the voice boomed.

A figure shimmered into view before them. It was

well over eight feet tall, with a bald head and calm, almond-shaped pearl eyes. Emily felt Riza's excitement as it became solid.

"Father!" she cried through Emily's lips.

"My child," the Xan said. *"We have been searching for you. Only now, when you came together, could we finally find you."*

"I have been in here, Father," Riza said. *"But I have been in fragments."*

The tall Xan raised a fine, long, almost transparent hand and lowered it onto Emily's and Lorin's heads. At his touch, Emily felt him enter her mind and scan through Riza's memories: from the moment she arrived on Xanadu, too late to join her people as they released themselves to the cosmos, to her trying to follow and accidentally fragmenting herself. Emily also saw the many human lives that Riza had lived after Vesta put the Heart of the Flame in a human girl. The memories went on to show Emily's life, starting in New York: the death of her mother and her first meeting of Pegasus on the roof through the struggles of the ancient war with the Titans. They ended at this moment on Diamond Head.

Emily realized that Lorin was seeing everything too. Then the perspective changed and they all saw Lorin's brief life—from the shard destroying her home on Titus to waking in Tartarus and all the things she had done since then.

When the Xan finished, he lowered his hand. A deep, sad sigh escaped his thin lips. He turned and summoned Jupiter.

"You have cared for my child well and we are grateful," he said with a voice as gentle as misty rain.

Jupiter bowed his head. "It has been our great honor to protect Riza, in all the forms she has taken. It is we, Olympians, who are grateful to Riza and all the Xan for the gifts you have bestowed upon us."

The Xan looked at the Titans and his pale, pearly-white face saddened further. *It grieves us to see how the powers of the Xan have been misused. But that ends now.*

The tall Xan raised his hand. The others above did the same. There was a sudden flash and all the Xan except for Riza's father shot up into the sky like beams of laser light. Then all the Titans, Olympians, and Hawaiians vanished, leaving only Jupiter.

Emily inhaled. "You didn't kill them, did you?"

Another soft sigh escaped the tall Xan. *"Have you learned nothing from Riza? We do not kill. We have sent the Hawaiians to the Big Island. The Titans have been returned to Titus and the Olympians sent back to Olympus. They are each banished to their own world until they can learn to live together."* He focused pale eyes on Jupiter. *"The Solar Stream will be denied to you until you can prove that you can use it wisely and without violence."*

Jupiter lowered his head in shame. "I understand."

"Return now to Olympus. . . ."

Before Jupiter could say another word, he vanished.

"Now, Riza, Emily, and Lorin," the Xan said. *"What to do with you?"* Once again he lifted his hand. Emily could feel his immense power—it was like the pressure she got in her ears when she traveled in an airplane, but much more intense.

In the blink of an eye, they were out of the Diamond Head crater and standing in the middle of the clearing on Xanadu.

"Pegasus!" Emily cried, seeing the winged stallion there. Joel, Paelen, Fawn, and Chrysaor were with him. Brue was standing behind Paelen, licking his back with her two tongues. Beside them stood a tall, calm female Xan.

"What happens now, Father?" Riza said.

"That, my child, is up to you. But you cannot remain as you are. Your powers are too immense to be shared between Emily and Lorin. They are too young and too inexperienced to deal with them." He focused on Emily. **"We saw what you did when you traveled back in time. Riza warned you not to kill Titans, but you defied her. Your actions have had consequences yet to be understood."**

"I am sorry," Emily said.

"I know you are," the Xan said. He looked at Lorin.

She was still holding Emily's hand, looking terrified. She stared at the Xan, but fear kept her speechless.

"It is unfortunate that you awoke with powers but without Riza beside you as a guide. No one has taught you wrong from right. You are wild, uncontrolled, and dangerous to everyone you encounter. You will cause us great worry if you are allowed to continue." With a wave of his hand, Lorin closed her eyes and collapsed to the ground.

"No!" Emily crouched down beside her and peered up at the Xan. "Please don't hurt her. She can be taught, I know she can. She doesn't have to die!"

"You beg for the life of one who threatened yours?" the Xan asked.

Emily nodded. "Please let her live. She didn't ask for this. Let us teach her. Riza and I can show her how to use her powers and control herself. She just needs time and people who care for her."

The Xan smiled, and Emily had the feeling that she had been put through some kind of test.

"Agreed," he said. *"It is your job to teach Lorin compassion and generosity."* He paused and tilted his head to the side. *"Now, as for you, young Emily, you also are a great concern. We have seen the good you have done with the Xans' power. But these powers have grown beyond your wisdom to use them. They must be contained."*

"How?" Riza asked.

"The time has come to separate you."

"What?" Riza cried. *"Father, you can't. Neither Emily nor I have a body. It is only our combined efforts that give us this illusion of a body. If you separate us, there will be nothing left of either of us."*

"We are aware of that," Riza's father said. *"We have a solution. But I must ask each of you a question. Riza, my daughter, long ago you tried to follow us when we released ourselves to the cosmos, but you failed. Tell me now, do you wish to join us on our journey, or do you want to remain here on Xanadu as companion to Arious and guardian of this Sanctuary? The choice is yours."*

Emily could feel the conflict within Riza. Part of her wanted to join her people, but another part of her knew she had lived among humans too long. She was filled with emotions the Xan had surrendered long ago. Riza loved to laugh, play, sing, and discover new things. She didn't want to give that up.

Emily desperately wanted to beg her to stay. She couldn't imagine her life without Riza in it. But she knew the decision wasn't hers to make.

I heard that, Riza said softly. *Thank you, Emily. I love you too.* Out loud she said to her father, *"I choose to stay. Xanadu needs a Xan, and the Olympians need to be guided if they are to earn the right to use the Solar Stream again."*

"Agreed," her father said. *"Now, Emily, your question. You have no body. The moment I pull Riza from you, you will cease to exist."*

Behind them, Pegasus reared, kicked out his hooves, and whinnied. Paelen shouted, and Joel cried, "Don't do it! Riza, don't let him kill Emily."

The tall Xan turned back to them. *"I have no intention of harming her. But Emily needs a body."* He focused on her again. *"You have a living father whom I can draw matter from, but no mother. What am I to do?"*

Emily recalled the beautiful face of her mother. Her warm, laughing eyes filled with love and her brilliant smile. At times Emily caught glimpses of her when she looked in the mirror. Now that was going to be taken away.

No one could ever replace her. But to survive, Emily needed a body. Finally she had a thought. "Maybe we could ask Diana. She has become my role model and has taught me so much."

"Then you must ask her. This must be given, not taken." Riza's father lifted his hand. A moment later Diana and Emily's father appeared in the jungle.

"What's happening?" her father cried in surprise. "Em?"

"Dad," Emily said. "This is Riza's father, a Xan.

He is going to give me a new body. But he needs matter from you."

"Of course. Anything, sweetheart."

"That's not all. . . ." Emily paused and looked at Diana. "It won't work unless we find a female donor for matter as well. Diana, you mean so much to me. You have taught me to be strong and face my fears. Will you help me?"

Diana, the fierce warrior of Olympus, faced the ancient Xan. Her expression softened a fraction as she looked back at Emily. "Take whatever you need from me."

"If you are certain," the Xan said, *"all I need is a strand of hair."*

They gave what was asked to the ancient Xan. "Do you need anything else?" her father asked.

"This will suffice," Riza's father said. He reached out his hand and laid it on Emily's head. She felt a brief instant of dizziness and then her world went dark.

EMILY'S EYES FLUTTERED OPEN. SHE WAS lying on a soft bed in the Chamber of Arious. The living computer hummed softly beside her and called, "Riza, she is awake."

Emily remembered the events right up to the moment she passed out. She sat up quickly and felt instantly dizzy.

"Take it easy, Emily," Riza said. "Let yourself adjust for a moment before you try to move. You need to get used to your new body."

The voice sounded so strange. It was soft and gentle, but filled with emotion. Most surprising of all, it wasn't in her head anymore. Emily looked around and saw a very tall Xan standing behind her bed.

She was bald, with beautiful, delicate features. Her wide almond-shaped eyes were as pale as pearls, and her iridescent skin changed color with the light. She laughed at Emily's stunned reaction.

The Xan came forward and pirouetted, and her light, silky robes flew around her. "So, what do you think? Father used a piece of the black glass to give me back my body. This is exactly how I used to look."

Emily frowned. "Riza, that's really you?"

"Of course it's me, silly! Who else would it be?"

Emily had seen Riza when she had been linked up to Arious, but there was something different, something more defined about this Riza.

Emily rose and embraced the tall Xan. Riza had to be eight feet tall and reed thin, but she was immensely strong. "I can't believe it's you!" Emily cried.

Riza laughed with the same, easy sound Emily had heard in her head a thousand times before. "If you think I've changed, you should see yourself!"

Riza led Emily over to one of the polished steel walls of the Arious computer. Looking at the reflections, Emily saw Riza towering above her, but she herself was completely unrecognizable. She was much taller than the old Emily had been. Her eyes were the deepest blue, but as Emily looked closer, she saw pearly white flecks in their depth. Her face was now more angular, and her lips fuller. Emily's dimples were gone, but her skin was alabaster smooth. She also marveled at the change in her hair. Instead of being brown, it was now much longer and raven black, just like Diana's.

Emily raised her hand and the reflection did the same. "Is that really me?"

Riza nodded. "You do have your father in you, but Olympian DNA is infinitely stronger, so you look a lot more like Diana. . . ." Riza paused and chuckled. "Oh, and you might have noticed those white flecks in your eyes. I slipped some of my own DNA in there for fun when my father wasn't looking."

Emily inhaled. "You didn't!"

"Of course I did," Riza said. "Now we are truly sisters and you are still part of the Xan. Besides, we are not so different, you and me. I don't care about following the rules either. This is why I was always in trouble."

Emily laughed and embraced her new "sister"

again. She turned back to her reflection. "So my real mother is gone from me?" Emily asked with a trace of sadness.

Riza shook her head and tapped Emily's heart. "She still lives right here, just as she always has. Now, though, you have two mothers."

"Are my powers gone?"

"Most, but not all of them," Riza said. "My father realized you'd had them too long and would not do well without them. Plus, with my DNA in you, you should have other powers. I'm just not sure what they are."

"You're not sure?" Emily asked. "But you're a Xan. You're supposed to know everything!"

Riza laughed again. "That's the price I pay for living with humans too long!" Before Riza opened the chamber door, she explained the changes that had occurred while Emily was growing in her new body. The Xan were gone, back on their infinite journey across the universe. And though she was saddened by their loss, Riza said she had a new family that she loved dearly.

She also explained that her father hadn't completely closed the Solar Stream to the Olympians. There were arches set up that could get them to Earth, the Nirad world, and Xanadu. All other travel was forbidden to everyone but Riza.

"What happened to Lorin?" Emily asked.

"My father removed most of my powers from her, but he couldn't get them all without destroying her. Lorin has been welcomed into Olympus and will be taught by you, me, and Vesta." Riza paused and grinned. "Oh, and I should warn you. Paelen seems quite taken by her."

"What?" Emily cried. "After everything she did?"

"She did save his life," Riza said. "And she is beautiful and adores him. She may have a child's inexperience, but she's a teen, just like you. They actually seem quite suited to each other."

Emily wasn't sure how she felt about that. She hadn't wanted the Xan to destroy Lorin, but she hadn't expected to have to see much of the Titan.

Riza started to laugh. "You're jealous! You always liked that both Paelen and Joel fell for you. Now you've got some competition."

"No way!" Emily said. "I just don't want her to hurt him."

Riza laughed harder. It seemed so strange to see the beautiful, normally calm Xan having a belly laugh.

Riza reached for the button that opened the door. Behind it stood Pegasus and her family. Pegasus whinnied and rushed forward.

"Pegs!" Emily cried. "I'm so glad to see you!" She threw her arms around the stallion's neck. "Look, I have a real body!"

Emily inhaled the sweet, warm aroma of the stallion. Only now did she realize that she hadn't been able to smell him since she had entered the Temple of the Flame. It was wonderful.

"Em?" Joel gasped from behind Pegasus. He looked her up and down. "Is that really you?"

Emily released Pegasus and looked at Joel shyly. "Yes. I'm a little changed."

"You're a lot changed!" Joel cried. "You don't look like you anymore. You look just like . . . Diana."

"And what is wrong with that?" Diana challenged. She was standing with Emily's father and smiling.

"Nothing," Joel said. "It's just that . . ."

"I'm still me, here inside," Emily said cautiously.

Joel nodded hesitantly. "I know, but it's going to take some time to get used to." He dropped his head and stepped back.

Emily wanted to rush into his arms, but his uncertainty stopped her. "Joel, it is me—"

"Forget him! I like the new you just fine. Not that I did not like you before," Paelen said. "It is just good to have you back in any form!" He embraced her tightly and whispered in her ear, "Do not worry about Joel. He still feels the same. But he is only human. It will take him time to get to know you again."

Emily hugged him back and whispered, "Thank you."

"Hey, what about me?" her father said. He pulled her away from Paelen, put his arms around her, and kissed her cheek. "No matter how tall you are now, you're still my little girl!"

The old-model Emily barely came up to his shoulder and he always kissed her on the top of her head. Now she was as tall as him and he couldn't stretch that far.

"Whoa," he cried. "Em, Em, stop—you're squeezing too tightly—I can't breathe!"

Emily released him and saw that his face was bright red.

"That is my fault," Diana said. "I forgot to warn you that you now have an Olympian body. You are as strong as me." She gave Emily a light peck on the cheek, but her eyes shone with pride and warmth. "I will have to change your training to address this. You now have to learn to control your strength."

Emily looked back at Riza and smiled. "I've got to learn to do a lot of things again—like living without you in my head or the fact that I have a body that can get hurt."

Pegasus nickered.

"And getting used to your reduced powers," Paelen translated for him. "Pegasus says he will help you with everything. Plus, you now need to eat ambrosia to stay healthy and strong."

Emily gazed at the stunning stallion and smiled. "Thanks, Pegs. I need you now more than ever." Her eyes trailed to everyone around her and she felt . . . complete.

The Xan may have removed most of her powers, but as Emily stood among those she cared for best, she felt the familiar stirrings of power rising from her core. Riza was truly the last Xan. But deep inside, Emily knew she would always be the Flame of Olympus.

ACKNOWLEDGMENTS

You, the reader, will never know just how many people have touched the book that is now resting in your gentle hands. From my agents, Veronique Baxter and Laura West, to my wonderful editors: Naomi Greenwood and Fiona Simpson, right down to the proofreaders, designers, and everyone else who works their magic to bring you this book.

So I think it's only fair that I should also thank some very special people who helped me make this the best book it could be.

First, I would like to give a very special thanks to Baird Fleming of the Honolulu Zoo. This wonderful man, filled with passion for the conservation of the environment and all the species that live in it, took time from his busy schedule to give me a private tour of the zoo, so that when I wrote about it in the book, you would see what I did—including the elephant squeeze! Thank you from the bottom of my heart, Baird, and all the staff of the Honolulu Zoo.

I would like to thank Stanley and the staff of the Outrigger Reef on the Beach Hotel, for letting me explore the super-private rooftop suites—so that our beloved Pegs would have somewhere to land and a safe place for the gang to stay.

In fact, during my visit to Hawaii (for research purposes only; I promise I didn't have any fun at all while I was there, or visit the beaches . . . Okay, I did have fun!) I met so many wonderful people who helped bring this book to life. Including Yara Lamadrid-Rose, who gave me loads of information on Diamond Head, the amazing, ancient volcano. And Dave, you know who you are . . . who introduced me to Pele!

And then, my dear reader, I thank YOU. Thank you for reading this, and going on another wild adventure with me, Pegasus, Emily, and all the Olympians.

Finally, you know it wouldn't be me if I didn't make a special plea to you, the future caretakers of this wonderful world we call Earth . . .

Please do a better job of protecting the environment and the different species of this world than we, the current generation, have done—though some are trying very hard to make a difference.

While I have been trying to write this book, I have been suffering with grief for what is happening in the "Cove" Japan, and in the Faroe Islands—where people are senselessly slaughtering intelligent and sensitive whales and dolphins. It really hurts me to read about it each day. It would be easier if I didn't read about it, but I can't turn away. None of us should.

We've got to stop it so that you, my beloved readers, will have the opportunity to enjoy these amazing animals where they belong, in the wild. Not on dinner plates or in a museum once they are extinct.

I will leave you with some lines from "Whales Weep Not!" by D.H. Lawrence, which is one of my favorite poems about whales . . .

> *They say the sea is cold, but the sea contains*
> *the hottest blood of all, and the wildest, the most*
> * urgent.*
> *All the whales in the wider deeps, hot are they,*
> * as they urge*
> *on and on, and dive beneath the icebergs.*

The right whales, the sperm-whales, the hammer-
    heads, the killers
there they blow, there they blow, hot wild white
    breath out of the sea!

And they rock, and they rock, through the sen-
    sual ageless ages
on the depths of the seven seas,
and through the salt they reel with drunk delight
and in the tropics tremble they with love
and roll with massive, strong desire, like gods . . .